Praise for the novels of Brenda Jackson

"The only flaw of this first-rate, satisfyingly sexy tale is that it ends."
—*Publishers Weekly*, starred review, on *Forged in Desire*

"Jackson was the first African-American author to make both the *New York Times* and *USA TODAY* romance bestsellers list. And after twenty years in the business, books like *Love in Catalina Cove* prove that she's still a prevailing force in romance."
—*BookPage*

"[A] heartwarming romance."
—*Library Journal* on *Love in Catalina Cove*

"Jackson's winning formula of heat and heart will draw readers in."
—*Publishers Weekly* on *The Wife He Needs*

"[Jackson's] signature is to create full-sensory romances that deliver on the heat, and she duly delivers.... Sure to make any reader swoon."
—*RT Book Reviews* on *Forged in Desire*

"Brenda Jackson is the queen of newly discovered love... If there's one thing Jackson knows how to do, it's how to pluck those heartstrings."
—*BookPage* on *Inseparable*

T0130804

**Also available from Brenda Jackson
and Canary Street Press**

Catalina Cove

LOVE IN CATALINA COVE
FORGET ME NOT
FINDING HOME AGAIN
FOLLOW YOUR HEART
ONE CHRISTMAS WISH
THE HOUSE ON BLUEBERRY LANE

The Protectors

FORGED IN DESIRE
SEIZED BY SEDUCTION
LOCKED IN TEMPTATION

The Grangers

A BROTHER'S HONOR
A MAN'S PROMISE
A LOVER'S VOW

For additional books by *New York Times* bestselling author
Brenda Jackson, visit her website, www.brendajackson.net.

BRENDA JACKSON

The Cottage on Pelican Bay

CANARY STREET PRESS

If you purchased this book without a cover you should be aware that this book is stolen property. It was reported as "unsold and destroyed" to the publisher, and neither the author nor the publisher has received any payment for this "stripped book."

CANARY
STREET
PRESS™

PLEASE RECYCLE · THIS PRODUCT IS RECYCLABLE

Recycling programs
for this product may
not exist in your area.

ISBN-13: 978-1-335-47497-1

The Cottage on Pelican Bay

Copyright © 2024 by Brenda Streater Jackson

All rights reserved. No part of this book may be used or reproduced in any manner whatsoever without written permission.

Without limiting the author's and publisher's exclusive rights, any unauthorized use of this publication to train generative artificial intelligence (AI) technologies is expressly prohibited.

This is a work of fiction. Names, characters, places and incidents are either the product of the author's imagination or are used fictitiously. Any resemblance to actual persons, living or dead, businesses, companies, events or locales is entirely coincidental.

For questions and comments about the quality of this book, please contact us at CustomerService@Harlequin.com.

TM is a trademark of Harlequin Enterprises ULC.

Canary Street Press
22 Adelaide St. West, 41st Floor
Toronto, Ontario M5H 4E3, Canada
CanaryStPress.com

Printed in U.S.A.

To my husband, Gerald Jackson, Sr.
All of me will forever love all of you.

To my readers who fell in love with my Catalina Cove series,
this one is for you.

Brethren, I count not myself to have apprehended:
but this one thing I do, forgetting those things which are behind,
and reaching forth unto those things which are before.
—*Philippians* 3:13

1

Two years and nine months ago

"Vaughn, my flight made it to New Orleans," Zara said into the phone as the sound of thunder grew louder. "But with the weather the way it is, I won't try driving to Catalina Cove tonight. I'll take a shuttle to one of the hotels at the airport and stay until morning." Another clap of thunder was almost deafening.

"That's the best thing," Vaughn Miller said to his sister. "Although the hurricane isn't headed this way, it's causing enough wind and rain to make you think it is. I understand several trees are down on the main road from New Orleans to here anyway," he added. Catalina Cove was an hour drive from New Orleans.

"My goodness. I just heard that the airport is closing and won't reopen until tomorrow sometime. I feel sorry for all those people who'd come to New Orleans for the summer music festival and can't get a flight to return home," she said.

"Well, hopefully, they won't be stranded for long. Things are supposed to be better tomorrow, Zara."

"Let's hope so," she replied.

For Zara, this was an unplanned trip. She was coming home to lick her wounds and Vaughn was the one person capable of cheering her up. When she'd called to let him know she was flying in, he hadn't asked why. He'd just said he would be there when she arrived. More than anything she needed her big brother's hug.

Home…

She hadn't thought of Catalina Cove as *home* since she'd left for college over ten years ago. "I'm hoping to see you tomorrow, Vaughn."

"Same here."

A short while later, after Zara had checked in to her hotel room, she was ready to go to the hotel's bar for a drink to calm her stressed nerves. Although her flight had landed safely, the turbulence had been almost unbearable.

When Zara entered the bar, not surprisingly it was crowded with people, mostly stranded travelers who probably needed a drink to unwind as much as she did. She was about to turn and go back to her room and order room service when her gaze connected with a man sitting across the bar.

And he was staring at her.

She'd been the object of men's interest before; however, usually they weren't the object of hers. At least not with this intensity. He was absolutely gorgeous, and the way he was staring at her had certain parts of her inwardly quivering, while warm blood rushed through every vein in her body. Strong sensual vibes were radiating between them even from across the room.

And he was sitting alone…

Zara drew in a deep breath. Should she? Umm…why not? She'd always let the guy make the first move, but doing that hadn't gotten her anything but a man who'd cheated on her. As far as she was concerned, there was no time to play coy. She was a single woman and thanks to an unfaithful boyfriend, she was no longer in a committed relationship.

But then what about that *legs closed, options open* rule she'd implemented after her breakup with Maurice four months ago? She had kept her legs closed. So why did she view this guy as a viable option? For the first time in her life, she felt like a woman on the prowl and that man who was sending out all these deep, sexual vibes to her was her intended target. Her legs began moving as she scooted around tables and chairs, making a beeline in his direction.

What if he was married? Gay? Or just didn't want to be bothered? But the way he was looking at her could eliminate all three possibilities. The handsome man stood as she approached his table. The way his gaze was roaming over her, he was taking in everything about her. From that smile on his face, he liked what he saw. His expression wasn't lecherous by any means. It was warm yet appraising.

Her eyes were just as assessing, and she thought he looked pretty darn good in those jeans and pullover shirt. Her gaze shifted to his hands. Specifically, the third finger of the left one. He wasn't wearing a ring and there wasn't an indication one had been there. She figured his age to be thirty-five or -six. He had cocoa-colored skin, brown bedroom eyes, a nose that added a perfect symmetry with his features, and a pair of sensual-looking lips.

When she reached him, he extended his hand. "Hello, I'm Saint. Would you like to join me?"

Suddenly, she wasn't sure if she wanted to join him or not.

It was bad enough his eyes were dazzling her, but the deep huskiness of his voice was making her stomach somersault. Then there was his touch when she took the hand he offered. A rush of desire clawed her insides. Never had she felt such primal attraction to a man before. What in the world was wrong with her? He even smelled good. His masculine scent filled her nostrils as she inhaled.

"Hello, Saint. I'm Angel, and I'd love to join you." From the twinkle that appeared in his eyes, she knew he didn't for one minute believe her name was Angel, just like she didn't believe his name was Saint.

When Zara sat down, she decided not to beat around the bush, and asked, "Are you married, Saint?"

"No," he said, reclaiming his chair.

"What about engaged or in an exclusive relationship?"

"No to both. What about you, Angel? Are you married, engaged or in an exclusive relationship?"

Fair question. "Not anymore."

He lifted a brow. "To which of the three?"

"I'm no longer in an exclusive relationship," she said.

"Oh, I see."

If the way he was looking at her was anything to go by, he really did see. More than she liked or preferred. At that moment a waitress came up to take her order and he told the woman to put it on his tab.

"You don't have to do that, Saint."

"I want to," was his response.

She flashed him a grin. "Okay. I'll never argue with a man who's a Saint."

The sound of his chuckle made every hormone in her body sizzle. "The storm has you stranded as well," she said.

"Yes. I take it you're in the same predicament?"

"That's right," she answered. There was no reason to correct his assumption that she was stranded due to the airport being closed. Her plane had landed. She just couldn't drive where she needed to go.

"Do I detect a French accent?" he asked.

An amused twinkle appeared in her eyes. "Yes. And do I detect a Northwestern one for you?"

"Guilty as charged."

"No need to feel guilty." She leaned closer. "I like it."

He angled over the table and said, "And I like yours."

She knew the exact moment he'd realized he had dipped his head closer than he'd probably intended, and their lips were within inches of touching. Instead of pulling back, their gazes locked. She noticed when his smile faded, and his look became as intense as hers.

Suddenly a deep sexual hunger flared to life within her. She was driven to lick her tongue across the fullness of his lips. So she did so, with shameless fortitude. Zara wasn't sure what she'd expected...other than the glint of surprise that appeared in his dark eyes at her bold move.

Playing it cool, she said, "I like your taste." Licking her lips, she settled back in her chair.

"Do you?" Looking like he was gathering his wits, he sat back in his chair as well—as if for the time being he needed to be a safe distance from her. She wasn't bothered by the thought of that. She also liked the fact his lips were still wet.

"Yes, Saint, I do." At that moment the waitress returned with the drink she'd ordered, a piña colada. She felt his eyes watching her as she tried her drink. He was probably wondering if she was usually this daring. He would be shocked to know she wasn't. But there was something about this man, who'd introduced himself as Saint, that brought out a naughtiness in her she didn't know existed. That said a lot for a twenty-eight-year-old woman who'd only slept with two men in her lifetime.

When the waitress left and they were alone again, he said, "I believe I would like your taste as well, Angel. So, when can I sample it?" The sound of his husky voice spiked arousal in her, sending images of him doing that very thing—tasting her, but in a different way—flitting through her mind. Heat curled inside her at the look he was giving her.

She eyed him back while thinking that she knew nothing about him other than he was handsome as sin and had the ability to generate desire in her very core. It didn't help matters that since her breakup with Maurice, she hadn't been interested in sharing a bed with a man…until now.

She sipped her drink again. Going for broke, as well as for bold, she said, "I know of a way for you to do that, Saint."

"And what way is that?" he asked, as a jolt of sexual energy bombarded Saint's senses. He thought this gorgeous creature sitting across from him was definitely no angel.

Yet, he liked it. Hell, he liked everything about her.

When she had entered the bar, she'd done so with the sexiest walk he'd ever seen by a woman in all his thirty-four years. His heart had pounded with every step she took in a sexy sundress that showcased a pair of beautiful shoulders. When she'd come to a stop in front of him, he'd gazed into the most captivating pair of hazel eyes. They were perfect for her almond-colored skin. As far as he was concerned, everything about her was perfect. Even the way her hair was pulled back from her face and held hostage by a clip complemented her features. She had a plump pair of sexy lips, and he liked the size of her breasts and the pair of shapely legs in sandals.

He knew Angel wasn't her real name and figured she'd said that because she didn't believe Saint was his. Although he was born Evans Toussaint, those who knew him called him Saint. A part of him thought maybe he should correct her, but decided that if he did, she might feel compelled to come clean with her real name as well. If she felt more comfortable using an alias, he didn't want to put her on the spot. As far as he was concerned, she could think—or do—whatever she wanted. If this angel wanted to be naughty, he had no problem letting her. Just like he had no problem letting her discover he was no saint.

And to think, after what his ex-girlfriend had put him through, he'd been convinced his body had lost any desire for a woman. He certainly hadn't been interested in anyone since he'd broken up with Mia almost a year ago. Now, not only did he like Angel's naughtiness and boldness, but damn, a strange abundance of heated lust—strong, thick and unrelenting—had taken over his body. Intense heat flowed between them. This woman had him floating on a cloud of sensations the likes of which he'd never experienced before. Was she an angel or a witch? She had to be one or the other because this thing between them defied logic. At least in this universe it did.

"Give me your room number and expect me in half an hour," she broke into his thoughts to say.

He honestly didn't think she was serious and decided to call her bluff. "I'm in room 954."

She nodded and then, without another word, she finished her drink, stood and walked out of the bar, and not once did she look back.

2

Saint moved away from the window in his hotel room when huge bolts of lightning flashing across the sky made standing in front of it unwise. He was not surprised the airport had closed. There had been reports of a tornado in Baton Rouge and as far as he was concerned, that was too close for comfort. He felt bad for all the stranded travelers who had attended the summer music festival that was held every year in August in New Orleans.

He thought of one such traveler and checked his watch. The woman who called herself Angel had less than ten minutes, but he honestly didn't expect her to come. Even if she had intended to do so in the beginning, chances were when she'd left the bar she had changed her mind. Why wouldn't she? She knew no more about him than he knew about her.

But then…wasn't that how a hookup was supposed to work? Even with her boldness, he suspected she didn't have casual sex on a regular basis. He had seen the look in her eyes when she'd said she was no longer in an exclusive relationship. There had been pain in their hazel depths, and he had a feeling it was not only deep but was also rather recent.

He didn't know Angel's story but guessed it was pretty much like his. She said that she was no longer involved with anyone, and neither was he. He wondered how long ago it had been for her. It had been close to a year for him. But there were times when it felt less than that.

He was told that time eventually mended broken hearts. He hoped like hell that was true. Eleven months ago, his girl-friend, Mia Givens, had turned down his marriage proposal for the second time in four years saying she could see no reason for them to move past being an exclusive couple.

He'd seen plenty of reasons. They were getting older, and he felt they should want more. He wanted them to settle down permanently and, more than anything, he wanted a family. Then there was the issue of her getting a big promotion at work that would require her to move to Florida. She'd wanted him to quit his job and pack up and move with her—without any type of marital commitment.

Mia had told him she wasn't ready to get married. Her ca-reer came first and at the moment neither marriage nor chil-dren were on her radar—and she wasn't sure they would ever be. He'd been smart enough to know when to cut his losses and move on. In the end, she'd moved from Seattle to Flor-ida without him.

Mia had taught him a lesson he would never forget. Never give your heart, body and soul to any woman. Okay, he would delete the thought of not giving a woman his body, since he had no problem sharing that part of himself with the woman he'd met tonight. She would be the first one he'd thought about sleeping with since Mia.

Checking his watch again, he saw Angel had five minutes. He drew in a deep breath, reaffirming his suspicions that she was a novice at this. The same thing held true for him, since he'd never indulged in a one-night stand before, either. However, some of his friends had. According to them, the exchanging of information was a no-no. There was no need when the affair would only last the night and chances were the couple involved would never see each other again. Their hookup was about appeasing a sexual hunger, which undoubtedly was something they both had.

That much had been obvious with all the heat and sexual energy radiating between them. He could only speculate about the reasons for what might or might not happen tonight. He honestly didn't think it had anything to do with his exgirlfriend. Saint was convinced his only reason for wanting to lose his mind in lust for a few hours with a woman he didn't know was due to the personal stress he'd been under lately.

Being an only child wasn't easy, especially when you had parents who wouldn't accept that with an older age came limitations. The trip he'd made into Catalina Cove this time had been to check on his father, who had gotten injured while, of all things, parasailing behind a boat. A man in his sixties had no business doing such a stunt, and Saint was glad the injuries weren't as bad as they could have been.

It was just six months ago when his mother had nearly cut her finger off with a knife she'd purchased from one of those cooking shows she liked watching on television. She'd been convinced she could chop the vegetables with the same skill and speed as she'd seen the chef on the show do. Not only was she proved wrong, but she'd needed several stitches as well. He'd rushed home after his father called saying his mother was a difficult patient. Not surprisingly, his mother had called last week claiming the same thing about his father.

More than once he had discussed the possibility of their moving to live with him in Seattle. They refused to even consider the idea. Catalina Cove was where they were born, and it was where they wanted to die. That meant he would eventually have to move back home to a town he felt he'd outgrown. He had built a life in Seattle. He liked it there, rainy days and all. He would admit things had been hard after his breakup with Mia, but once she'd moved away and he didn't have to worry about chance encounters, he'd been adjusting to their breakup.

Saint moved toward the bed and was about to sit on it to remove his shoes, certain the woman wasn't coming, when suddenly there was a knock. With his heart pounding in his chest, he walked to the door and opened it.

The sensuousness of her scent caught him immediately. There she stood, looking more beautiful than before. Without the clip holding her hair back, a mass of curls flowed freely around her shoulders, making her look younger and more carefree. She had changed out of her sundress into a form-fitting minidress and wore a pair of stilettos. Both shoes and dress were blue, and at that moment he would describe them as shocking blue. Then there was that low dip in her neckline that brazenly revealed there wasn't a bra covering her breasts. Not that he was complaining. And he didn't miss the bottle of wine and wineglasses she had cuddled to her chest.

"Hi," she said, flashing him a grin that made him even more aroused.

"Hi, yourself. Come on in, Angel," he said, taking a step back.

"I think I will, Saint."

And she did.

Zara placed the bottle of wine and glasses on the table before turning around to Saint. Lord knows she'd tried talking herself out of coming here but it hadn't done any good.

She couldn't stop thinking about the vibes she'd felt between them when they'd met. Everything about him made her body tingle. Then there had been the unexpected wildness in his taste when she'd boldly glided her tongue across his lips. That hadn't been enough and now she wanted the whole shebang. And his masculine scent was just as arousing as the rest of him.

He was leaning back against the closed door as if trying to figure out what to make of her. Did he assume this was common behavior for her? Should she explain spending the night in a stranger's room wasn't the norm for her? Especially when she knew what would be taking place in that bed? Little did he know, due to her recent experience with what was supposed to be a love connection—one she'd assumed would last forever—she'd placed getting involved in a serious relationship on her *Never To Do Again* list.

When he shoved his hands into the pockets of his jeans, her breath stuttered when she saw how aroused he was. There were some things a man couldn't hide and from all appearances, he wasn't trying to. Drawing in a deep breath, she said, "I told you I would come."

He held her gaze and said, "And I'm glad you did."

The rich huskiness of his voice had desire warming her to the core. She needed to break eye contact with him, so she looked around and noticed his room was identical to hers. When she returned her gaze to him, she felt the need to say, "Just for the record, I've never done anything like this before."

"Neither have I, Angel."

Did he expect her to believe that when he seemed so accepting of what was happening between them? But then, wasn't she? "Then why do you think we're doing it now?" she asked.

She watched as he slowly moved away from the door to come stand before her. That masculine scent, which had affected her before, was tantalizing her again now. It was filling her nostrils and making her feel somewhat lightheaded. "I think the foremost reason is that we're hot for each other, Angel. I felt your heat the moment I saw you, and there's no doubt in my mind that you felt mine."

He was right. She had felt his—but still. "I haven't slept with a guy for seven months, and he was my steady boyfriend." There was no need to tell him that although she and Maurice hadn't been intimate for that period of time, she'd only discovered his betrayal four months ago. She hadn't suspected a thing because he'd taken more business trips and so had she.

"We'd dated exclusively for two years," she added.

"It's been twelve days short of a year for me, and I was in an exclusive relationship as well. We were together for four years."

Four years was a long time, Zara thought, and figured he had to still be hurting. Maybe not to the same extent as she was since his wasn't as recent. Since she didn't know the details of why he and his ex-girlfriend had broken up, she might be all wrong in assuming he was still going through pain. He may have very well managed to get on with his life.

It didn't really matter and Zara pushed all thoughts of his ex and hers from her mind. His closeness was causing sexual hunger to stir in her midsection, and a need to be close to him was hammering away at her senses. Taking a step closer, she reached up and wrapped her arms around his neck. "You know what I think?"

His penetrating gaze held hers, making her pulse flicker and leap. "No, what do you think?" he asked.

"Their loss is our gain."

The spread of a smile across his lips was just as arousing as the rest of him. Regardless of what he called himself, she had a feeling this man was no saint. But then, she was no angel.

"I totally agree," he said in that husky voice she loved. "Now, will you tell me the remedy to not tasting you, Angel?"

Her body grew heated. "Yes."

"Okay then, what is it?"

"This." Leaning up on tiptoes, she pressed her mouth to his.

Saint couldn't remember ever feeling this consumed with desire while kissing a woman, or more precisely when a woman kissed him. He was letting her take the lead for now and thought she was doing a pretty good job of it. It was as if she was putting all she had into it, and every single cell in his body was responding in kind.

He liked her taste, and the sensuous movement of her tongue was driving him toward the edge. Never had he engaged in a kiss so energetic, so vibrant and so damn erotic. When she released his mouth and he gazed down at her, the depths of her hazel eyes basically told him everything he needed to know. She'd enjoyed the kiss as much as he had.

"So, what do you think, Saint?"

Her arms were still wrapped around his neck and his were around her waist. It didn't take any time for him to reply. "I think that your taste is as stirring and electrifying as you are. Had it lasted any longer I wouldn't have been able to hold myself back." He wondered if she thought he wasn't holding back now, if the hard erection pressed against her middle was anything to go by.

"I don't want you to hold back anything tonight. I don't want you to act like a saint because I have no intention of behaving like an angel. Understood?"

Yes, he understood. For whatever reason, they were both dealing with their own personal disappointments that included broken hearts, life burdens and overall stress. Tonight they would kick back, erase everything from their minds and concentrate solely on pleasuring each other.

Saint definitely didn't have a problem with doing that. He needed it. She would be the first woman he would make love to since his breakup with Mia. Although he felt he had moved on, there were some days when he truly wondered if he had. "Yes, I understand."

He lowered his mouth to hers. The moment their lips locked again his tongue went into action. The last time she had dominated the kiss. Now it was his turn. Desire was sweeping through his body, and he channeled every ounce of passion stirring inside him into their kiss.

Saint drew her closer, needing the contact. He convinced himself that was the reason his hands had moved from her waist and were resting firmly on that ass he'd liked looking at when she'd left the bar. He'd sat there a full ten minutes after she had walked out just thinking about all the things he wanted to do with her—naked and in the flesh.

When he deepened the kiss, the erotic moans she began making stirred a need within him. To him, nothing was headier than a woman's response to a kiss. When breathing became a necessity, he broke off and her last moan was in protest. That was when he swept her into his arms and moved toward the bed.

When he reached it, he placed her in the middle of it. Then his hands were all over her. The way she'd returned his kiss had fired up his blood, and molten heat had begun escalating all through his body. He needed to touch her and was glad she was just as anxious as he was to satisfy this sexual need between them.

Quickly pulling back, he reached out and gently cupped her face in his palms and stared into the depths of her eyes.

The last thing he wanted was to come across as pushy. Leaning closer, he asked, "Are you sure about tonight?"

"Yes, I'm sure."

He took note of her kissed swollen lips and flushed cheeks, the way she was breathing, which was erratic like his. Lowering his arms, he took her hand in his and whispered, "I believe there's a reason we met tonight, Angel. Two strangers with broken hearts. We have healing to do and tonight could be a start."

Her hazel eyes smoldered back at him. "I think you're right, Saint."

To prove that, he again captured her mouth with an intensity that hopefully gave her a preview of what was to come. He loved her taste and had no problem ravishing her mouth to let her know it. This time she was the one who broke off the kiss to whisper, "Make love to me."

He pulled back and in a frenzy began removing his clothes while watching Angel remove hers. Within moments their clothes were in a pile on the floor. He then sheathed himself with a condom and had gotten even more aroused seeing the look on her face as she watched him. When he joined her on the bed, his tongue went into action and after kissing her again, he began a journey to lick every inch of her skin, starting at her neck.

By the time he'd reached her breasts he was convinced he had located at least two of her hot spots. Namely, her neck and the center of her chest. Her moans were a dead giveaway. When he reached her breasts and slipped a nipple between his lips, he knew he'd found a third. He'd never known a more passionate woman in the bedroom. The thought of that was consuming him, making him feel a yearning that was causing his entire body to ache.

Finally finished with her breasts, he leaned back on his haunches to stare down at her. She was beautiful. Stunning. From the top of her head, past her breasts to her stomach with a colorful tattoo of a pelican taking flight right above her navel. Then his gaze drifted to the area between her legs. The gorgeous sight made his erection throb and his tongue feel thick in his mouth for wanting to taste her there. He released a deep, guttural groan at that very thought. Easing toward her, he kissed her all over her body again, starting with her mouth but bypassing her breasts as his concentration was on moving south.

He licked her pelican and loved how the texture of the tattoo felt against his tongue. Her moans continued. Glancing up, he saw she'd closed her eyes. Spreading her thighs apart, he slipped them to his shoulders and buried his head between her legs. The moment his tongue tasted her there, he growled low in his throat; her scent and taste were rocking him to the bone.

Zara nearly shot off the bed the moment Saint's tongue contacted her flesh. When he deepened the invasion and claimed her clit, like he had every right to do so, her hands grabbed hold of the bedcovers. She couldn't stop the moans flowing from her lips. The way he was kissing her down there set off sensations that were bound to overtake her mind and senses. He was gobbling her up like she was a meal he'd gone without and was intent on getting his fill—the more he tasted, the more he wanted.

When he lifted her hips for his tongue to go deeper, she felt herself losing control. Unable to help herself, she pushed her body against his mouth. Suddenly, something within her exploded and she screamed out his name.

Wow. She'd never had an orgasm of such magnitude. Her

ex hadn't been into oral sex when it came to her, but didn't have an issue when it was performed on him. She'd thought that was outright selfish of him, and when they couldn't reach an agreement on it, they'd decided to omit it as part of their lovemaking. But now she saw what she'd been missing. Saint definitely knew how to use his tongue and had no qualms about doing so. In fact, he seemed to downright enjoy it, and she was glad she was reaping the benefits. She felt as if she'd had an out-of-body experience that had claimed her very existence.

Before pulling his mouth away, he gave her womanly core one last long, deep lick. Zara knew when he lowered her legs from his shoulders, but she didn't have the strength to open her eyes.

She heard shuffling sounds and felt movement. "Angel?"

It was at that moment she forced her eyes open to stare up at him. The dark eyes looking down showed concern. "You're alright?"

Unable to speak, she nodded.

"Now I'm going to give you a stormy August night that I hope you'll always remember. Allow yourself to let go for me."

She thought if she was to let go any more than she just had, she would probably die from pleasure. She could feel sexual energy flowing between them, hot, raw and carnal. Gazing up at him made her aware of the male power and strength of him, and she saw deep, sexual need stirring in the dark depths of his eyes.

Feeling and seeing all of that sexual hunger was making her ache with desire. She needed him to take the ache away. As if he understood, he slid inside her, stretching her wide, and going deep and then deeper. When he'd gone to the hilt, he paused and leaned down and took her mouth.

Then it was on.

Saint made love to her in a way she needed. Thrusting hard into her over and over again, while his mouth made love to hers. She was aware of how deep his shaft was going inside her, almost reaching her womb. No man had made love to her this way, without any inhibitions. Each thrust rubbed her clitoris, sending a riot of sensations escalating through her.

Digging her nails into his shoulders she moved her body, determined to share in this mating, and he began riding her harder and harder. Suddenly, something snapped inside her, and she screamed his name. Seconds later she felt his shoulder muscles tighten beneath her fingers and he hollered the name Angel.

At that moment she knew he'd done just what he'd said he would do, give her a stormy August night to always remember.

3

Three more rounds of lovemaking and several orgasms later, Saint was awakened when Angel eased from his arms. He figured she was leaving but already regretted she would be doing so. Opening his eyes, he watched her naked body leave the bed. Instead of getting dressed, she went over to the table and grabbed the bottle of wine and the glasses she'd brought with her.

Pulling himself up in bed, he asked, "What are you doing?"

She turned around and beamed at him. "Pouring our wine."

When given such a cheerful reaction like that, she could be pouring cyanide and he would gladly drink down whatever she gave him. Damn. He was definitely under the spell of an angel right now. He had made love to her all through the night. *Correction.* They had made love to each other. The only time their bodies had separated was when one of them needed to use the bathroom. Of course, for him, it was the frequent changing of the condoms. He was glad he had stopped by the hotel's gift shop to pick up a pack since the only one he'd had was that one kept in his wallet. Already they'd gone through a half dozen.

"Here you are."

She handed him his glass of wine, and to keep her from spilling any, he took hers as she slipped back in bed beside him. "Thanks," she said, settling against the pillow to sit up next to him before taking her wineglass from him. "I propose a toast."

"What's the occasion?"

"A pathway forward. Until tonight I wasn't sure it was possible for me," she said.

"And now you think it is?"

"Thanks to you, yes. You're an awesome guy, Saint."

"And I believe you're an awesome woman. With you, I was able to channel my feelings into something else. Namely, someone else. You're the first woman I've been attracted to since my breakup. You gave me the strength to do something I've never done before. In the past I put everyone else before myself. Tonight I focused on self-love and the sharing of pleasure with you."

The wide grin she gave him at that moment pulled at his insides. "Sounds like you've found a pathway forward as well."

He thought about what she'd said. "Yes, I think that I have."

"Then let's toast to our awesomeness."

They tapped their glasses and took sips. He stared at her over the rim of his glass. Lowering it, he said, "About our real names…"

She reached up and pressed a finger to his lips. "Real names don't matter to us. You're Saint and I'm Angel. Please, let's leave it at that."

Although a part of him preferred not doing what she requested, he would abide by her wishes. The last thing he needed or wanted was to get back into a serious involvement of any kind with a woman. However, after a night spent with Angel he could believe when the time was right that he would be able to. He still had a lot of healing to do, and it might be a process that would take years. He was okay with that and believed that one day someone would come into his life, and she would be the one meant for him. He could now accept that woman had not been Mia.

"I should leave now and go to my room," she said, cutting into his thoughts.

Looking at the clock, he saw it was four in the morning. "You're welcome to stay here with me for as long as you want. Checkout is at eleven, but my flight won't leave until one. That is, if the airport reopens. It's still storming pretty bad outside."

After taking another sip of his wine, he asked, "What about you? What time does your flight take off?"

It was imperative to Zara that Saint didn't know any more about her than he already did…which wasn't much. That was why she'd dismissed his suggestion of revealing their real names. The fake identities they were using were good enough, especially when their paths would never cross again. At least she hoped not. Last night, not only had she acted footloose and fancy-free, but she had also been his for the taking and in positions she'd never known existed. She had behaved in a way with him that she'd never done with any man, and a part of her knew she would never play out the role of Angel in her lifetime with anyone else.

"What time does your flight take off?" he asked again.

He obviously assumed she hadn't heard his question. She didn't want to outright lie so she said, "Not sure." Their glasses were empty, and after taking his wineglass she placed both on the nightstand.

"Is there any reason you can't stay with me for the rest of the night, Angel?"

She could think of a number of reasons, but at the moment none of them mattered. Tonight she wasn't being her logical self and she didn't want to be. "No reason at all, Saint."

When his features displayed his delight, she immediately felt a crackle of sexual energy pass between them. She still wasn't sure what it was about Saint that could arouse her so effortlessly. All she knew was there was this carnal attraction that had desire clawing inside her that didn't want to be denied.

"I'm glad to hear that," he whispered, before pulling her into his arms.

4

Present day

Zara Miller smiled when she heard that special ringtone that belonged to her brother, Vaughn. She picked up her cell phone from her desk, wondering why he was calling so early on a Monday morning.

"Good morning, Vaughn. How are things going?"

"Everything's going great, and the two ladies in my life are as wonderful as ever."

The two ladies he was referring to were his wife, Sierra, whom he had married a couple of months ago, and her seven-year-old goddaughter, Teryn. Sierra had become Teryn's legal guardian when Teryn's mother, Rhonda, who'd been Sierra's best friend from childhood, had died of cancer.

"You're still coming home at the end of the month to attend Jaye and Velvet's engagement party, right?" Vaughn then asked.

"Yes, I'm still coming. Why?"

"You might want to add additional weeks here to start packing," Vaughn said. "I heard from the Historical Society and they are eager to take inventory of the contents of Zara's Haven. That means you'll need to pack up anything you want to keep."

Zara's Haven was the stately estate of their family home. It had been named for the first Zara, her great-great-great-grandmother, who'd been the wife of the town's founder, the notorious pirate Jean LaFitte. Vaughn decided not to move into Zara's Haven after his marriage. Zara, who owned several dress boutiques in New England and New York, had made Boston her home for years. That meant the twelve-bedroom stately mansion that sat on the Gulf of Mexico would be vacant the majority of the time. For that reason, she and Vaughn had decided to list it with the New Orleans Historical Society to make Zara's Haven a historical landmark.

Jaye and Velvet were friends of theirs. She had prepared herself for the return to Catalina Cove for a weekend visit to attend the couple's engagement party.

"Will you be staying at Zara's Haven or the cottage while you're here?" Vaughn asked, intruding into her thoughts.

"I'll be staying at the cottage." The cottage on Pelican Bay had been a wedding gift to their mother from their father. When their parents were killed in a boating accident years ago, their will gave Zara and Vaughn joint ownership of Zara's Haven, but the cottage on Pelican Bay was left only to Zara.

She recalled going to the cottage on Pelican Bay with her mother regularly while growing up. She would spend hours on the island playing with her dolls while her mother, who'd once been a gifted artist in Paris, would spend her days in front of an easel, painting. It was the time she and her mother had spent together that she would cherish always.

"I'll let you know when my flight arrangements have been made," she then said.

"Sounds good. I'll let you get back to work now."

"Give Sierra and Teryn my love, and I'll talk to you later, Vaughn."

"Alright, Zara. Goodbye."

After hanging up the phone, she continued sitting at her desk and thinking that although she had prepared herself for the return to Catalina Cove for a weekend visit to attend Jaye and Velvet's engagement party, staying any longer than that had not been part of the plan. All because of that shocker she'd gotten when she'd gone home a few months ago to attend a celebration cookout given for her brother and Sierra.

She leaned back in her chair as she remembered what had caused her such shock...

Three months earlier

Zara walked back into the party from the patio to join her soon-to-be sister-in-law, Sierra. Both Vaughn and Sierra had been totally caught unawares. Vaughn had known about the surprise bridal shower today for Sierra, but what he hadn't known was that the guys—namely, husbands and significant others of the ladies'—would be there as well. What was supposed to have been a surprise bridal shower had turned into a celebration cookout for the couple. Her brother hadn't even known she had come to town for the occasion. It wasn't easy pulling anything over on Vaughn and she'd been all for it.

Suddenly, she felt as if someone was staring at her. She scoped the room and went so still her punch cup almost slipped from her hand. She blinked, not believing whom she was seeing. It couldn't be him. No way the man who'd just arrived, and who was staring at her with the same shocked expression she knew was on her own face, was the same man she'd had a one-night affair with a little over two years ago. Two and a half years to be exact. What was the guy she knew only as Saint doing here?

"Zara, are you okay?" Sierra leaned over to ask.

No, she wasn't okay. How did he get invited to the party? He was standing beside Jaye Colfax, the new banker in town. Were the two related? Best friends? Was that why he was here in Catalina Cove?

"That guy who arrived with Jaye Colfax. Do you know him?" she asked, unable to break eye contact with him.

Following her gaze, Sierra said, "Sure. I'm surprised that you don't. Probably because he graduated from high school six years before us and a year before Vaughn. His real name is Evans Toussaint, but most people living in the cove have always called him Saint."

"Saint?"

"Yes."

Zara's head began spinning. So the man who'd had some sinfully erotic movements in the bedroom was known as Saint? He hadn't been someone that had attended that summer music festival like she'd assumed. And he'd given her his real name or the name he usually went by. "Is he here visiting?"

"Like the rest of us, when he left for college he didn't return, other than to visit with his parents. However, since they are getting up in age, he decided to move back to the cove a couple of months ago." Sierra tilted her head to study Zara, who'd finally broken eye contact with Saint. "You've met him before, haven't you?" she asked softly.

Zara drew in a deep breath. "Yes. It was two and a half years ago. A stormy night in August. Due to the weather, the airport in New Orleans had closed down. I had flown in to visit Vaughn, but the drive into Catalina Cove was hazardous so I checked in to a hotel at the airport for the night. That's when I met Saint, at the hotel bar."

She paused a moment. "He said his name was Saint and that his flight out of New Orleans had been canceled. Of course, I thought he was pulling my leg with his name, so I told him my name was Angel."

Sierra grinned, which was a good indication her future sister-in-law knew what had happened that night. "I honestly thought I would never see him again, Sierra."

Sierra leaned in closer and said, "Well, it seems that fate has decided otherwise. And just so you know, the sexual vibes emitting between the two of you are strong. People couldn't help but notice your reaction to each other."

That was the last thing Zara wanted.

"And another thing you might want to know, Zara."

"What?"

"Vaughn is Saint's boss."

Bringing her thoughts back to the present, Zara stood from her chair and walked over to the window. Sierra had been right. A number of people at the cookout that day had witnessed her and Saint's surprised reaction to seeing each other. Including her brother. Since nothing got past Vaughn, she was certain he'd figured out how she and Saint had first met. To this day, he hadn't asked her anything about it.

What Zara appreciated more than anything was that her brother treated her as an adult, one that he knew was fiercely independent. He felt that she was mature enough to handle her business and make her own decisions. If she made mistakes along the way, they were her own to learn from. The only time Vaughn gave her advice was when she asked for it.

The blowing of a horn made her focus on the traffic outside

the window. Very few shoppers were out today. So far it had rained every day this week, and the weather was a lot colder than it had been. It was a good thing she'd had the boutique store sale last week and not this one.

Zara detested cold weather and she would be the first to admit Catalina Cove had pretty good temperatures all year round, and their winters were not like Boston's. She also knew the cove was one of the best places to live and raise a family... if you were interested in that sort of thing. She wasn't now, although at one time she had been. Her ex-boyfriend, Maurice Calvino, had destroyed her dreams of marriage and family.

Refusing to think about Maurice, she moved back to her desk to sit down. She would meet with her boutique assistant, Sherri LaBlanc, to let her know she would be returning yet again to Catalina Cove. It would be the fourth time in less than six months. First, there had been the luncheon Sierra had hosted for members of her bridal party; the second time had been for Vaughn and Sierra's celebration cookout; and then for their wedding in March. Now she would be returning to attend Jaye and Velvet's engagement party and to pack up Zara's Haven.

Her insides were tingling at the thought of seeing Saint again. She just hoped her willpower at resisting him was better than the last two times.

5

Evans Toussaint arrived at work later than usual due to a dentist appointment. As he strolled through the wide hallway that led to several offices on the executive floor, he was thankful that once he'd made the decision to move back to Catalina Cove, he'd landed a job and a pretty good one. In fact, he was earning more now than he had while working as manager of that bank in Seattle.

He believed that timing was everything, and it had certainly worked in his favor when he'd been hired by Lacroix Industries. Under the parent company's umbrella was the Lacroix Blueberry Plant, Lacroix Tool and Die Maker and their most recent venture, the Lacroix Housing Development.

Although Saint was involved with the management of all three subsidiary companies, he'd been hired to specifically spearhead a particular project Reid Lacroix had instituted a few years ago. In memory of the man's late son, Reid, the wealthiest man in Catalina Cove, had created the Julius Lacroix Loan Program, which offered low-interest loans as an incentive to get people to consider moving back to Catalina

Cove and opening a business. To maintain the integrity of the town, it had to be a Reid Lacroix–approved business.

Reid was well-liked and respected by everyone and employed half of the people living in the cove at at least one of his businesses. Everybody knew that if Reid liked you then the entire town loved you. Very few people went against him on anything. Last year he had chosen Vaughn to take over as CEO when Reid retired in a few months.

Saint knew one of the reasons Reid had chosen Vaughn as successor, rather than choosing one of the men who'd worked for the company a lot longer, was because Reid trusted Vaughn to not only take the company to the next level, but also to preserve its legacy for Reid's twin granddaughters. Vaughn had been Reid's deceased son's best friend and was godfather to the twins.

"Good morning, Saint," a feminine voice said as he rounded the corner.

He glanced over at the older woman sitting behind the huge administrative assistant desk and gave her a cheerful response. "Good morning, Mrs. Dorsett."

The woman shook her head. "Will you ever feel comfortable enough to call me Kate like everyone else around here?"

"No," he answered truthfully. Kate Dorsett's son Brody, who'd graduated from high school the year before Saint, had been one of his playmates while growing up in Catalina Cove. To Saint, the attractive older woman sitting behind the desk had always been known as Brody's mom or Mrs. Dorsett. Old habits were hard to break.

The Toussaints and Dorsetts—who were part French, African and Spanish—had been born and raised in the bayou, and the two families still resided there. Their ancestors had been known as Bayou Creoles. When Saint moved back to the cove, he had purchased a four-bedroom home on five acres that was located on mossy property connected to a bayou. It was close enough to his parents, and within a mile of the major roadway that took you to the business district of Catalina Cove where he worked.

"Well, you still have five months to get on the bandwagon before I'm out of here," she said.

Mrs. Dorsett had begun working for the company as Reid Lacroix's father's secretary. Then when Reid took things over when his father passed away, she'd become his administrative assistant and had held that position for close to thirty years. Now that Reid was retiring, he had convinced Mrs. Dorsett to do the same.

Her husband had passed away a few years ago, and she'd wanted to keep working to stay busy. "How's Brody?" he asked.

"He's still single, and I'm still not a grandmother, so what does that tell you?"

"Now you sound like my mom," Saint said, amused.

He just hoped Mrs. Dorsett hadn't taken to playing matchmaker like his mother was doing. He had threatened to change his cell phone number if she gave it to one more eligible prospect from her church. He was getting at least three to four calls a week from women inviting him over to dinner.

"If I do it's because Irene and I pray constantly that there's hope for you and Brody yet," Mrs. Dorsett said, breaking into his thoughts.

"If it had been left up to me, I would have been married years ago." He knew he could say that to her since Mrs. Dorsett and his mother were childhood friends and talked all the time. There was no doubt in his mind that she knew about his two marriage proposals Mia had turned down.

"Well, some people don't know what they got until they lose it. It was her loss and I believe one day she will see that. Now, with Brody it's another story. No woman has ever gotten a marriage proposal out of him. He's not getting any younger."

"Well, that's something you can't rush these days. No matter how old you are."

"What?"

"Love."

"Umm, maybe I need to put a fire under Brody's behind."

He laughed. "I wouldn't do that if I were you. Need I remind you that Brody is Catalina Cove's fire marshal? You put fire anywhere near him and he'll put it out."

She waved off his words. "Whatever. By the way, Vaughn wants to see you. I almost forgot to tell you."

He doubted that was true. Mrs. Dorsett never forgot anything. Like the time he fell out of that tree in her yard at the age of ten and ended up with a broken arm, which she reminded him of on occasion. Professionally, she was as sharp and efficient as they came. He knew she would be missed when she retired along with Reid. She had the ability to make the lives of every one of Reid's executive team members much easier.

"Thanks for letting me know," he said, pivoting to head toward Vaughn's office. He knocked when he reached the door.

"Come in." Vaughn tossed the papers he was looking at aside when he saw him. "I take it you survived the dentist," he said as if amused.

Saint took the chair Vaughn offered to him. "Yes, but I wish Reid would have that same talk with Dr. Wilcox that he had with Mrs. Dorsett. It's time for him to retire. I recall going to him as a kid."

Vaughn barely held back a laugh. "We all did. He claims

he'll retire as soon as someone comes along to take over his dental practice."

"That's what I heard as well. So far none of the applications I've gotten for low-interest loans have been for dentists. However, I am keeping my fingers crossed."

Vaughn leaned back in his chair. "I heard that a lot of people are applying for teaching positions."

"Are you surprised after the school board voted to give all teachers a huge pay raise? They can thank Reid for maneuvering that," Saint said, amused. "Now Catalina Cove pays their teachers more than any city in Louisiana. Anyone applying, who was born and raised here, and returning to the cove to live, is a shoo-in if they have the right credentials."

Vaughn grinned. "When Reid speaks everybody listens. That will teach the school board members a lesson for going along with Webb Crawford's foolishness regarding Velvet. That put them on Reid's shit list, and at his recommendation, every last one of them retired except Marcie Connors, the lone woman on the board. Since she hadn't been told by the other school board members what the meeting was about, she wasn't asked to retire," he said.

Webb Crawford, a wealthy businessman in town, pressured the Catalina Cove school board to fire Velvet Spencer, a teacher at one of the high schools, after she chose to have an affair with the new banker in town, Jaye Colfax, instead of with Webb. When she was brought before the board on cooked-up allegations, a number of people were shocked to discover Reid had been a friend of Velvet's parents' and had personally invited her to Catalina Cove. On top of that, Velvet didn't need her teacher's salary because she was an heiress. Needless to say, Webb and all those school board members who supported his craziness had left the meeting with egg on their faces.

Vaughn leaned back in his chair and said, "I wanted to meet with you for a couple of reasons. First, to let you know Reid has reached a decision on the bids he received for the housing project. There were several good companies, and he's decided to go with Colfax Construction Company that's run by Franklin Colfax."

"Jaye Colfax's brother, right?"

"Yes. We'll announce our decision at the next town hall meeting."

At that moment the buzzer on Vaughn's desk went off. "Excuse me while I get this," he said to Saint. He clicked on the intercom. "Yes, Kate?"

"Your sister, Zara, called and wanted me to let you know she'd booked her flight and will be arriving in town on Thursday morning."

"Thanks, Kate."

Saint's stomach muscles tightened as desire warmed his spine at the mention of Zara's name. She was coming back to Catalina Cove? Would she stay at the cottage?

"Saint?"

He looked up at Vaughn. "Yes?"

"Are you okay?"

There was no way Saint could answer that truthfully. Although he'd always considered Vaughn a friend, he was also his boss. Saint wasn't sure just how much he knew about his and Zara's history.

"Yes, I'm fine." Since he'd overheard what Mrs. Dorsett had said, he really didn't have to ask, but did so anyway. "Zara's coming to town?"

"Yes. Sounds like she'll get here Thursday morning."

"I see." He was certain the ever-observant Vaughn saw as well. In fact, anyone who'd attended the cookout given for Vaughn and Sierra had seen. It had been a surprise encounter between him and the woman he'd met two and a half years earlier who'd called herself Angel. At the time she'd been twenty-eight and he'd been thirty-four.

Their surprise hadn't been able to lessen the over-the-top case of the hots they still had for each other. And he was certain that a slew of people, including Vaughn, had known when they'd left that party together.

Saint met Vaughn's gaze as he sat leaning back in his chair, eyeing him speculatively. Zara was Vaughn's sister. Yet, to this day, Vaughn had never brought it up. Since Vaughn hadn't, maybe it was time that Saint did. Clearing his throat, he said, "About me and Zara…"

Vaughn held up his hand to stop whatever Saint was about to say. "No discussion is necessary. Zara is thirty. I respect her as the adult she is and believe she knows how to handle her business. I trust you the same way." Then Vaughn chuckled. "Nonetheless, I have a feeling Jaye and Velvet's engagement party next weekend will be rather interesting."

Yes, it would be, Saint thought. The prospect of seeing Zara again had him heating up. So far each and every time their paths crossed, sexual chemistry between them would reach its peak to the point they would give in to temptation. He hoped this time they did a better job of controlling it.

Zara opened the door to the cottage on Pelican Bay and was immediately rushed with memories of the last time she'd been there. It had been the night of Vaughn and Sierra's wedding in March, two months ago. She loved the cottage and appreciated her mother for bequeathing it to her.

Rolling her luggage to the main bedroom, she preferred to stay here in the cottage instead of the family mansion. She would be all alone in that monstrosity of a house since Vaughn had married and moved out. She liked it here just fine, she thought, moving around the two-bedroom cottage that had a living room, dining room, eat-in kitchen and two and a half bathrooms on the ground floor.

Upstairs was a spacious loft where her mother would set up her easel to paint. Zara always considered that space as her mother's artist's nook, which was surrounded by floor-to-ceiling windows. Tucked in the corner was the table where Zara would sit with her coloring books, crayons and baby dolls.

Nearby was a huge bookcase that contained a lot of her mother's favorite books. Sometimes, after Vivian Miller had concluded her painting for the day, she would read Zara a story. Her mother's favorite had been *The Three Musketeers*.

On those days when her mother needed her full concentration to work on painting, Zara would focus her time and attention on her dolls by designing outfits for them. That was when she'd discovered that although she'd inherited the gift to paint from her mother, she much preferred designing fashions.

A lot of her mother's work was on display in the Catalina Cove Art Gallery. Most were paintings her mother had donated to the gallery when her parents had moved to Paris. The rest had been donated by Zara and Vaughn after their parents' deaths. Vivian Miller had been specific in the will as to which of the paintings were to be given away and to whom. She'd even specified which were meant for Zara and for Vaughn.

The paintings she'd left for Zara were those her mother had known were Zara's favorites. One hung on the wall in her boutique in Boston and the others were hanging here in the cottage. Her mother's favorite subjects to paint were the pelicans that flocked to the bay, attracted by the warmer waters from the Gulf.

As far as Zara was concerned, no one could capture the beauty of a pelican on canvas like her mother. Back then, her mother would place her easel on the deck to paint the pelicans in their habitat. Zara loved the pelicans as much as her mother did, which was why she had one tattooed above her navel.

In the master suite, Zara placed her luggage on the bed and looked out the huge window that faced Pelican Bay. She'd had an early flight from Boston, so it wasn't even ten in the morning yet. Already, she could see through the trees the sun beating down on the shimmering blue ocean. It was definitely a nice spring day in May.

Everyone living in the cove knew the parcel of land Catalina Cove sat on had been a gift to her great-great-great-grandfather, the notorious pirate Jean LaFitte. It had been given to him by the United States government for his help in protecting New Orleans during the War of 1812. At the time New Orleans was one of the most important ports in the United States. Because Pelican Bay had been LaFitte's private domain and the first stretch of land that he and his band of marauding smugglers reached upon returning from the seas for downtime, they'd made sure the bay was kept well hidden. The numerous trees that grew from the ocean waters instead of on land made it an ideal island for privacy since no boats, large or small, could pass through.

The only way to the bay was from land adjacent to Zara's Haven. To retain its privacy, her father had installed a security gate that surrounded the entire perimeter of the property. Years ago, the only access to the bay was by boat from the secured property. For her mother's convenience, her father had built a covered, mile-long pier from the estate to Pelican Bay.

Zara loved the pier and recalled the walks she and her mother would take across it to the cottage. Vaughn told her that while living in the mansion, occasionally he would jog back and forth across the pier in the mornings. At night the pier would light up, thanks to timers that came on at dusk and went off at daybreak.

When she had reached the Catalina Cove city limits, she had contacted Vaughn to let him know she'd arrived in town. She had contacted her sister-in-law, Sierra, as well, who invited her to lunch at the restaurant she owned, the Green Fig. She said that she'd prepared Zara's favorite soup as the "soup of the day"—black bean with crab meat and andouille sausage. That was Vaughn's favorite as well. He'd raved about it so much that she'd tried it and was glad that she had. It was totally delicious.

An hour later she had finished unpacking and was headed to the shower, looking forward to meeting Sierra for lunch.

Zara entered the Green Fig soup café and was greeted by Levi Canady, Sierra's assistant manager. Levi, an ex-cop who'd retired early from the police force due to an injury, was a childhood friend of Sierra's father's. "Hello, Levi."

"Hello, Zara. Sierra and the ladies are waiting for you. Right this way."

The ladies? Following Levi toward the back, she beamed in happiness when she saw the women seated at the table. They were friends of Sierra's that Zara had gotten to know and considered friends as well. First, there was Velvet, who'd recently gotten engaged to the town's banker. The huge diamond ring on her finger was blinding. Then there was Ashley—a very pregnant Ashley—who was married to Ray Sullivan. Ray owned a boat tour company as well as the water-taxi service in town. Their baby was due this summer.

Also seated at the table was Vashti Grisham, who owned Shelby by the Sea, the local bed-and-breakfast inn, and was married to Sheriff Sawyer Grisham; Bryce Witherspoon-Chambray, who was the daughter of the Witherspoons, who owned a popular café; and last but not least was Donna El-loran, who like everyone other than Ashley, was born and raised in Catalina Cove.

"Welcome home, Zara!" The women cheered and then stood to give her welcoming hugs. Although she'd lived in Boston for the past few years, the one thing she liked about returning to the cove was the people who would be there to welcome her back.

When everyone had returned to their seats and she'd taken hers, Zara grinned at a beaming Velvet. "Congratulations, Velvet, and that ring is gorgeous. Sierra told me about the school board meeting. I'm dying to know what happened when everyone found out you're an heiress, and when you returned to school the next day with that rock on your finger."

Velvet laughed. "Most people were shocked, believe me. But it didn't matter. I knew who my true friends were and couldn't care less for anyone who wanted to befriend me after the fact."

"And just to let you know..." Bryce barely held back a laugh and said, "Once word got out that Jaye and Velvet hadn't been strangers like the townspeople assumed, but they had been involved in an affair that had lasted three years, and that Jaye's sole purpose for being in Catalina Cove was to get back the woman he loved, and going so far as to orchestrate the buying of a bank and becoming her neighbor to do so, Webb Crawford is still walking around town with egg on his face. He definitely made an ass of himself for even thinking he had a chance with Velvet."

"Same thing for his sister Laura," Donna added. "I heard she left Catalina Cove to travel abroad and hasn't returned yet. She's probably too embarrassed to show her face after all those outbursts she made at the meeting while trying to make Velvet look bad."

Zara laughed, knowing there was never a dull moment in Catalina Cove, and appreciated her friends giving her an update. "So, tell me about the wedding, Velvet," she said.

Total happiness spread across Velvet's lips. "The wedding will take place the first week in August in Phoenix. Reid Lacroix will be giving me away. Jaye and I will live here until after the wedding and then we're moving to Phoenix."

"So you won't be teaching in Catalina Cove after this school year?" Zara asked.

"No. I've already gotten hired at the high school where I taught when I lived in Phoenix before. Jaye and I plan on building a summer home on the ocean property he purchased for me in Reid's new development. We'll return to spend every summer in the cove."

"What about that guy you were tutoring after school?" Donna asked. "Allen Bordeaux's son."

Velvet showed her happiness and excitement when she patted her hands together. "Lenny finished all the classwork he needed to do and passed all the exams. That means he will be attending high school in the fall and has already been accepted to play on their varsity baseball team."

"That's wonderful."

Zara then turned her attention to Ashley Sullivan. "Do you know what you're having yet? Boy? Girl? Or another set of twins?"

Ashley threw her head back and laughed. She already had an adorable set of three-year-old twins. A boy and a girl. "Don't you dare suggest more twins. According to my doctor, Ray and I are having another son."

"That's great and congratulations to you and Ray."

At that moment the waitress came to take their orders. After the waitress left, Donna announced that she and Isaac were expecting another baby. Right in time for Thanksgiving. They were hoping for a girl this time but would be grateful for any healthy baby they got. Phones were passed around to show recent photos of everyone's kids, and Zara provided information about what the fashion trend this fall would be like.

"Okay, Zara, you know what we're all dying to ask," Vashti said, grinning from ear to ear. "We were all at Sierra and Vaughn's celebration cookout and saw your reaction to Saint and his reaction to you. It was obvious the two of you were shocked at seeing each other."

"Things were so hot between you two that for a while we all felt like we were in a heated furnace," Donna added.

"That's what I heard," Zara said, shaking her head.

"And I happened to notice how he kept his eyes on you at Vaughn and Sierra's wedding," Bryce said, cocking a curious eye.

After taking a sip of her water, Zara tilted her head at Bryce, snickered and said, "Umm, you don't say."

"We do say, and just so you know," Vashti interjected, "in school Saint was a very well-liked and popular guy. He was captain of the football, basketball, track and swim teams. A real hottie. He graduated the year before me, Bryce and Vaughn did."

Bryce piped in with a grin, "And unlike a lot of guys he was always kind, and his popularity didn't give him an ego. He was handsome and had a great-looking physique even back then."

"Of course, we noticed the two of you leaving the cookout together early," Ashley said with a grin that was even larger than Bryce's. "If you want to tell us it's none of our business we will understand."

Zara rolled her eyes, grinned and said, "No, you won't."

That got everyone laughing. Vashti then said, "Yes, we will, but be forewarned that we'll only draw our own conclusions, and they might be hotter and more erotic than the real thing."

Zara grinned, shaking her head. Leaning closer to the table and in a low, conspiratorial voice said, "I seriously doubt anything could be hotter and more erotic than the real thing, ladies, trust me. And with that said, my lips are sealed."

6

"Good morning, Saint."

Saint looked up from his breakfast and tried keeping the frown from his face. Kristen Hunt. He understood she was someone his mother felt he should get to know better because she was single and an attractive churchgoing woman. She seemed to be a nice person, but deliberate or otherwise, she seemed to pop up almost everywhere. At first, he figured it was a coincidence but now he was beginning to wonder. And those suspicions were annoying the hell out of him.

"Hello, Kristen."

"Surprise seeing you again this morning."

Was it? Since moving back to the cove he'd made sure he checked in with his mother periodically. During those calls he would mention any stops he planned to make before and after work. Had it been a chance meeting yesterday evening when he'd run into Kristen at the grocery store? And the day before at the dry cleaners? He would have a talk with his mother and explain there was such a thing as stalking, and it was something that did not turn him on.

And speaking of turning him on…

Kristen didn't. There was no chemistry between them. Zilch. Irene Toussaint had no way of knowing that. Maybe he should explain it to her. Then again, maybe he shouldn't.

"I'm on my way to work and decided to drop in and grab a cup of coffee. I saw you sitting over here and wanted to speak and to let you know that my invitation to dinner is still out there."

She had reminded him of that yesterday, the day before and a time before that. "Thanks, I'll keep that in mind," he said, although he knew that he wouldn't. The last thing he wanted was to pursue a serious relationship with anyone—especially not any of the women his mother was throwing in his way.

"Okay, I'll be seeing you," she said.

No time soon, he hoped. "Have a nice day, Kristen."

"You do the same, Saint."

He watched her leave and was glad she hadn't invited herself to join him like Robin Dyer had done last week. Robin, a single teacher in town, had cornered him in the Ribs Shack. Even when he'd told her that he had an important call to make, she had slid into the booth across from him anyway. Had she not assumed he'd wanted to make the call in private? He'd put an end to that nonsense when he told her he'd suddenly remembered something he had to do and asked the waitress to pack up his meal for him to take out.

He took another sip of his coffee and then bit into his blueberry muffin while noticing how busy the Witherspoon Café was. He was glad he'd come early and had gotten a table when he had.

"Hi, Saint."

He waved to the woman who'd called out to him as she rushed out the door. At least she hadn't stopped to chitchat.

As he took another sip of coffee, he thought about the woman he'd been thinking about a lot lately, ever since he'd heard she was coming to town. By his calculations she would have arrived yesterday. Namely, Zara Miller. He still thought of her as Angel during the wee hours of the night while remembering the time he'd spent with her.

It was during those times when he would lie in bed and recall the night they had spent together in his hotel room. The next morning, he hadn't awakened to an empty bed like he'd assumed he would. She was still tucked close to him, asleep. Either she was a sound sleeper, or he'd worn her out the night before. By the time she had finally awakened, he had showered, repacked and ordered room service to deliver breakfast.

The moment she'd seen him she'd smiled at him. That expression signified she hadn't regretted anything about the night before. That had made him cross the room and give her one hell of a good-morning kiss. He had been tempted to undress and crawl back into bed with her, but time would not allow it. He'd had a plane to catch.

After kissing her, he had stood back and watched her slide into the T-shirt he'd worn the day before to go into the bathroom. She had used his hotel-room toiletries to freshen up before joining him for breakfast. They talked about how the weather had improved and the state of the economy. Neither mentioned anything about the night before. Nor had they shared personal information about each other.

After they'd finished eating, she had gone into the bathroom to change clothes. Before leaving she'd tried returning his T-shirt, but he'd told her to keep it. For some reason he wanted her to have something to remember him by. Then they kissed goodbye, and it had been long and deep. Afterward, he was convinced the taste of her had remained on his tongue for a long time.

"Hello, Saint."

A feminine voice cut into his thoughts of the past and in a way he was annoyed by it. He didn't recognize the woman standing in front of his table but returned her greeting anyway. "Hello."

He must have given her a strange look because she then asked, "You don't remember me, do you?"

He had no reason not to be honest with her. "No, I don't."

"That's understandable since it's been years. You had a crush on me in the sixth grade."

Did he? He didn't remember but then he had to have only been around eleven at the time. "What's your name?"

"Samantha Groover."

That name didn't ring a bell, which meant she obviously hadn't left a lasting impression on him. "It's been a while, Samantha."

"Yes, it has. I just moved back to town. I was working at the Colfax Bank in Tulsa, Oklahoma, as a credit analyst agent and jumped at the chance to transfer to the branch that opened here in the cove. My folks were glad about that."

"I'm sure they were." He hoped she saw they were running out of things to say and would move on. However, no such luck when she said, "Your mom came into the bank the other day. I hadn't seen her in years."

He nodded, certain there was more. "She did?"

"Yes. And of all things she remembered that crush you used to have on me. She said you had moved back to town and were still single and hadn't gotten married yet."

He took a sip of coffee while thinking that he definitely needed to have a talk with his mother, and soon. On a given day at least one or two women would approach him saying they'd run into his mother. "And?"

A wide grin spread across her face. "And I couldn't believe it. You were the most sought-after guy in our junior and senior class. It doesn't seem right that you're still single. All the girls wanted you. I would have rekindled your interest in me then if I hadn't been going steady with Oscar Belkins."

He wasn't sure what made her so certain she could have *rekindled* anything. Instead of making a comment, Saint took a quick look at his watch and was glad she took the hint.

"Well, you need to go, and I do, too. Which way are you headed?" she asked.

To douse the thought that they would be leaving together, he said, "Nowhere. I need to check my phone app to see how the stock market is doing." He pulled his phone from his jacket.

"Oh. Okay," she said, disappointedly. "While you have your phone out, let me give you my number."

He didn't recall asking for it and knew if she gave him hers then she would expect his, and he just wasn't feeling it. Lucky for him at that moment his phone rang. Thank goodness, he'd been saved by the bell, although it was one of those annoying telemarketing calls that he hated getting. "Sorry, I need to take this."

"Sure. You know where I work."

And then she walked out, and he had a feeling she was deliberately swaying her hips as she did so. Releasing a deep breath, he leaned back in his chair and stopped his phone from ringing. All three women who had spoken to him this morning were nice-looking, but not one had pressed his buttons, set a spark or caused anything like a pang of longing to shoot through him.

The waitress came up to his table and asked, "Would you like more blueberry muffins?"

"Yes, thanks."

When she walked off, Saint allowed his thoughts to drift back to the one woman who had the ability to make his breath catch on a surge of yearning every time he thought about her. Some of those thoughts had stirred his libido in all kinds of forbidden ways. He recalled how in the days, nights, weeks and months that followed that night with her, he had thought about her often. Nearly constantly.

He was glad he'd told her to keep his T-shirt. More times than not, he wished he would have kept something of hers to remember her by. However, in a way he had kept something of hers, although it was intangible. It had been the sanctity of his memory of her.

Two and a half years after that night with her, when he'd returned to Catalina Cove to live, he had attended his boss Vaughn Miller's surprise celebration cookout party. That was when he'd seen Angel again. She had been just as shocked to see him.

"Here you are," the waitress said, placing a plate of hot blueberry muffins in front of him and refilling his coffee. "Will there be anything else?"

"No, thanks. You can bring me my check."

Back at the office, Saint was busy most of the day. After a meeting with the new bank manager in town, he grabbed lunch at Spencer's, then was back at the office for a two o'clock meeting.

After joining his parents for dinner after work, he walked into his home close to six that evening. After removing his suit and throwing on a T-shirt and jeans, he grabbed a beer from the refrigerator and went to sit on his screened-in patio.

As Saint gazed out at his land, he couldn't stop his mind from going back to that day three months ago in February when he had discovered Angel's true identity. Once they'd gotten over the shock of seeing each other, he had waited for an opportune time to talk with her privately. The party was in full swing when he'd finally found that moment to approach her. They knew they needed to talk and agreed the party wasn't the place and should go elsewhere.

As he sat alone sipping his beer, Saint's mind was filled with memories of that night when he and Zara left the cookout together.

7

Three months earlier

Saint was fighting hard to keep his eyes focused on the road with Zara seated beside him in the car. He knew her real name now. It wasn't Angel but Zara. He'd finally gotten around to asking someone he figured would know. Saint also knew something else.

He took a quick look over at her and said, "You're Vaughn's sister." It wasn't a question but a statement, and he knew she took it as such.

"Yes, and as you probably know by now my name is Zara Miller." She paused a moment and said, "And you're Evans Toussaint. I understand Saint is what most people call you."

"Yes, it is."

"That night when you introduced yourself to me as Saint, I figured it was a name you'd made up. That's why I told you my name was Angel."

"I figured as much," he said. Although the bayou was dark

and there was little light on the streets, he knew his way since he'd lived here his entire life, until he left for college.

"Why didn't you correct me on my assumption?" she asked.

"I tried to. If you recall, I suggested we share our real names. You didn't want to do that," he reminded her.

She did recall that at the time, she hadn't. "You're right, I didn't. That night, sharing our real names wasn't all that important. I honestly thought you were someone who'd attended the summer music festival in New Orleans that weekend in August. Someone I would never see again."

"That was a logical assumption to make since a number of the stranded travelers were. I'd come to Catalina Cove that week to check on my parents. My father had had an accident the week before."

"I hope he was okay," she said.

He heard genuine concern in her voice. "He was fine and was just being an ornery patient to Mom. But then I guess he figured it was payback since she wasn't the best patient to him months earlier when she'd cut her finger and had to get stitches." He suppressed a laugh, then said, "They like to get on each other's nerves every once in a while."

"You're amused by it?" she asked.

"Can't help but be. My parents were high school sweethearts. I guess after over forty years of marriage it was bound to happen. But trust me, it doesn't often. They love each other very much and are thicker than glue."

When the interior of the car got quiet, she said, "That night when you were leaving Catalina Cove, I was arriving to visit Vaughn. However, due to the storm it wasn't safe to make the hour drive from New Orleans."

No wonder she'd given him a vague answer when he'd

asked about her flight out of New Orleans. "Just so you know, Zara. I don't regret that night."

"Neither do I, Saint. And I was telling the truth when I said being with you enabled me to make a pathway forward."

He recalled her saying that, but at the time she hadn't gone into any details. Would she now? There was no harm in asking. "Will you tell me why you felt you needed one?"

She didn't say anything for a long moment, and he honestly wouldn't be surprised if she told him that it was none of his business. Instead, she said, "Four months before we met, I had broken up with my boyfriend."

"The one you had dated exclusively for two years?"

"Yes. That's the one." She got quiet again and then added, "He was cheating on me."

"He cheated on you?" he asked to make sure he'd heard her correctly. Saint couldn't imagine any man in his right mind doing such a thing. Especially to her.

"Yes. I caught him."

A frown settled in his features. "In the act?"

"Close enough. He and the woman had been seeing each other for around six months. I guess he started getting a guilty conscience and ended things with her. He purchased her a parting gift, a diamond tennis bracelet. Somehow, there was a mix-up with the order since he'd bought me something from that same jeweler before. In error, I got the gift instead. I knew the moment I thanked him for it, by the shocked look on his face, that it hadn't been meant for me. I called him out on it, and he admitted everything."

Saint shook his head. Not only had the guy cheated on her, but he had purchased the other woman a parting gift? An expensive parting gift at that. Finding out what an ass her boyfriend was had to have been hard for her.

"Maurice felt he should be forgiven since his affair with the woman meant nothing," she then said. "He claimed she was someone he'd recently met, and it was just sex and no emotions were involved." She chuckled scoffingly. "Like just the sex part wasn't bad enough. He tried making me feel guilty by saying it happened during the time I was traveling extensively while checking on my boutiques, and we weren't spending a lot of quality time together."

She paused before continuing. "He felt I should give him credit for coming to his senses and ending things with her. He thought I was being unfair to him for throwing away two years of what he saw as a good relationship without trying to work things out between us."

He needed to know, so he asked, "Did you take him back?"

"I almost did until I discovered through a mutual friend that his affair with the woman hadn't been the first time. The two of them had been a couple in college and were known to hook up every so often over the years. Evidently, he'd had no problem continuing to do so after meeting me. When I confronted him about it, he admitted they had a history but said he was finally over her. I felt he should have told me the truth about them being involved other times before, and not make it seem like he hadn't known her until the affair."

After glimpsing out the window, she looked back at him and said, "At that point, working anything out wasn't an option with me. He even thought he was being a nice guy by telling me I could keep the bracelet he'd purchased for the other woman. Can you believe that, Saint?"

He liked the sound of his name off her lips. He'd liked it that night and he liked hearing it now. "I would say that he had a lot of nerve."

"Yes, he did. Once I knew I couldn't trust him that was it

for me. He was trying to wear me down, trying to get me to change my mind about getting back with him. I felt the need to get away and make decisions. Thanks to you, I did. That night with you I found a pathway forward like I told you. Now I am the consequential independent woman minus the rose-colored glasses."

"What were you before?" he asked.

"A woman who believed in happy endings. One who also assumed she had to depend on a man for her happiness. Now I know there aren't any happy endings, and I'll never depend on a man for anything again. I've taken control of my life and will do whatever I want and whenever I want. I control my own destiny, make my own decisions and will only take advice if and when I ask for it."

Saint was proud of her for making those decisions and from the sound of it, she was proud of herself as well. That night they'd spent together, he'd still been stinging from his breakup with Mia. Asking her to marry him twice and being rejected had prompted him to make a number of decisions himself.

Some things weren't meant to be, and he could accept that marriage was not for him. That made him feel sad in a way because he knew how much his parents wanted him to one day marry to give them grandchildren.

"I don't believe in happy endings, either," he said. "So, I guess that's something we have in common."

"Yes, I guess we do."

It only now occurred to him that although she'd wanted to leave the party she hadn't said where she wanted to go. "Where am I taking you, Zara?"

They had left the bayou and this section of roadway wasn't as dark. Peeking over at her, he could see her face in the moonlight. She was beautiful. He'd thought that the first time he'd seen her, and he thought so now.

"I should tell you to take me home, Saint."

He loved her French accent. It was as deep as Vaughn's. "I'll take you wherever you want to go." He wasn't ready for them to part ways.

The shock of seeing her again had worn off. What hadn't worn off was the chemistry that flowed between them so effortlessly. He hadn't fully understood the intensity of it that night and honestly, he couldn't understand it now.

That night in his hotel room was to have been one and done. It hadn't. At least not for him. Whether she knew it or not, he hadn't been involved with anyone since her because he'd been convinced no other woman would measure up. No other woman had stirred to life the degree of desire like she had.

As far as he was concerned, Zara was the epitome of feminine temptation. Even now in the confines of the car the sexual energy between them was all-consuming. He felt it and had a feeling she did, too. Sharing conversation with her had alleviated it some but not completely. Even now, a deep hunger for her was stirring to life in his midsection and he knew why. Memories of their night, together with seeing her again, had pleasurable sensations racing up his spine.

He came to a stop at a traffic light, and he knew the moment she'd turned in her seat toward him. When he looked over at her, he saw a fanciful look in her eyes. Just seeing that look made his nerves dance and his brain race.

"More than anything, I'd like to go dancing tonight. This was to be a quick trip for me just to attend Vaughn and Sierra's celebration cookout. Tomorrow evening I'm flying out to return home."

"Where is home for you?" he asked, realizing just how little he knew about her.

"Boston."

"How long have you lived there?"

"Close to eight years. I never returned to the cove to live after leaving for college. I resided in Paris for a while when my parents moved there," she said. "So, what about it, Saint? Will you take me dancing? There's this nightclub in New Orleans that has the best music and dance floor. I try to go there whenever I come back to Catalina Cove."

He didn't have to think twice about his answer. "Yes, I'd love to take you dancing. If that place in New Orleans is where you want to go, then that's where we're going."

Zara knew she should have told Saint to take her home. Instead, she'd asked him to take her dancing in New Orleans. That was an hour drive for them to share space in this car. Sexual energy was crackling between them. The hot, raw and carnal kind. That ball of fire that had burst into flames in the pit of her stomach when she'd seen him hadn't gone out. It was still burning brightly.

So why was she playing with fire? Why was she listening to that voice inside her head reminding her that she hadn't been in a man's bed since his? The bigger question was why she was tempted to yield to the primitive force inside her. Namely, that sexual hunger that had begun raging the moment she'd seen him again.

Knowing silence between them was only increasing the heat, the need and the desire, she decided to generate conversation between them by asking him something that she wanted to know. "You said you don't have any regrets about our night together. Why not?"

When the car came to a stop at a traffic light, he turned to face her. The look in the depths of his dark eyes sent more desire pulsating through her. His gaze returned to the road, as he began talking. "That night I told you that I had broken up with my ex-girlfriend almost a year before. Up until then I'd felt I had gotten over her and moved on. Spending time with you made me realize what I had been doing was breathing but not living."

"Meaning what exactly?"

"I was going through the motions of living but hadn't fully been doing so. I had thrown myself into my work. Suddenly, that had become the only thing that mattered to me. Then there was the issue of my parents."

She lifted a brow. "And?"

"And…like I told you that night, my ex-girlfriend and I had dated for over four years. She had become close to my parents, and I was close to hers. Naturally, both sets of parents assumed we would eventually marry. Needless to say, our breakup wasn't easy on anyone. They couldn't understand it and didn't want to accept it. They got it in their heads that we just needed a little time apart to get our shit together. As far as I was concerned, there wasn't anything to get together. The woman I loved didn't want a future with me. I'd gotten that and wanted to move on."

When he came to another traffic light, he looked over at her. "When time passed and I thought my folks were finally accepting what I was telling them, that's when they began doing crazy stuff. Stuff they'd never done before."

"Like what?"

"Earlier I mentioned the reason I had gone to Catalina Cove that night was due to my father's accident. What I didn't tell you was that he'd decided to join a parasailing team. He got injured while parasailing. Mom, on the other hand, decided to become a chef."

She shrugged. "I don't see where there's a problem with your mom becoming a chef. That would mean more tasty meals for your dad, right? However, your dad joining a para-sailing team…umm? How old is he?"

"He'll turn sixty-four his next birthday. And as far as Mom becoming a chef and learning to cook a lot of different meals, might seem harmless until she almost lost a finger with one of those high-powered knives she'd ordered off the television."

"Ouch."

"Yes, and her accident occurred just six months before Dad's."

She recalled him saying his mother had almost cut her finger off and had to get stitches. "Your parents waited awhile to have you?"

"They married straight out of high school. They wanted kids right away, but it took them almost ten years of trying before they succeeded. I was their one and only."

He got quiet for moment and said, "There were a few more minor accidents with them after that night we met, and I knew it would only be a matter of time when I would have to make decisions where they were concerned. When I broached the subject of them moving to Seattle, they—"

"Seattle?" she interrupted to ask. "You were living in Se-attle before moving back here?"

"Yes. I played professional football there for a while, and after leaving the team I decided to stay there."

"I recall picking up on your Northwestern accent that night we met."

"Yes, you did. Anyway, when I suggested to my parents that they move to Seattle, they let me know that not under any circumstances would they leave Catalina Cove. For me, that meant at some point in time, I'd have to move back home."

"The thought of that bothered you?"

"Let's just say it wasn't anything I had figured on. When we are kids, we think our parents are going to be around forever."

She would have to agree with him. Neither she nor Vaughn had been surprised when their parents had decided to move to Paris. What she and Vaughn hadn't counted on was two years after the move, they would be killed in a boating accident.

"When it seemed the older they got, the more mishaps they were getting into, I decided to move back home. I love my parents and owe them everything," he said.

She digested his words before saying, "That night we met, you said you were not involved with anyone, Saint. Are you seriously involved with someone now?"

"No."

"So, what's your story? Why aren't you?"

8

Saint's hands tightened on the steering wheel. She was asking him something he'd rather not talk about. But then he figured she probably hadn't wanted to share anything about what a prick her boyfriend had been, but she had. At least his story, as she'd put it, wasn't that bad. There hadn't been any betrayal. What there had been was no desire for a commitment, which basically meant no love.

He said, "To fully explain why I'm not involved with anyone now, I'll have to explain my prior relationship with my ex-girlfriend."

"Okay."

He slowed the car at another traffic light and said, "Mia and I met at a wedding. She was one of the bridesmaids and I was one of the groomsmen. We hit it off and after a few dates we became an exclusive couple. We enjoyed our relationship and after a year and a half I felt we were both ready for more. I asked her to marry me. She turned me down, saying it was too soon, and that we should live together for a while to see if we were compatible. So, we did."

"Were you compatible?"

"I thought so. We got along great. Everyone said we complemented each other. We rarely had an argument and we liked being together. Like I told you, my parents thought the world of her, and her parents said I was the son they always wanted. Our parents even struck up a close relationship and began doing things together. Everything seemed perfect."

"But?"

"Two years after my first proposal, I assumed the time was right. We'd been together four years and weren't getting any younger. I thought we should settle down, make everything legitimate and consider starting a family. I asked her to marry me for a second time."

"So, what happened?"

"Mia threw a tantrum. Literally. She accused me of being selfish by wanting to mess up a good thing. She told me that she still wasn't ready for marriage and doubted that she would be anytime soon. Nor was she ready to have children and wasn't sure if she ever would be. In other words, she didn't want a husband, children or wedding vows. She wanted us to continue as we were."

"Living together in an exclusive relationship?"

"Yes." Saint paused a moment and then said, "There was no way that I could do that. I wanted more. Namely, a committed future with her that involved marriage. After she turned down my second proposal, I knew there would never be a time I'd do a third and figured it was time to cut my losses and move on."

She remained silent; however, he knew there was another question coming and had a feeling what it would be. "Are you hoping that the two of you will get back together one day?" she asked.

"No." If she thought his response had been quick it was because he felt strongly about it. "Mia has moved on with her life and so have I. Soon after she turned down my proposal, she took a job in Florida. It's been three years, and I haven't heard from her and doubt that I ever will. We've both moved on."

There was no need to tell her that although he hadn't heard from her, his mother had. She had been close to his parents and still called them on occasion to see how they were doing. Likewise, he'd done the same for her parents. At least he had in the beginning. He stopped calling them when he discovered the couple was holding on to hope that he and Mia would get back together.

Saint had been disappointed when both sets of parents thought he should have put his foot down with Mia. To do what? Force her into marriage? He knew now that he'd done the right thing by breaking things off and not going to Florida with her.

Moving back to Catalina Cove had been the best thing he could have done. Initially, it had been for his parents' benefit, but now he would be the first to say it had benefited him as well. He loved his job and liked the house he'd purchased. Both kept him busy. Too busy for a serious involvement with a woman.

"So, I guess at one time you had to do your own pathway-forward thing, too," Zara said, breaking into his thoughts.

"Yes, I did. However, at the time I thought of it as surviving a heartbreak. For me that meant not setting myself up for another. Mia proved that forever, and happy-ever-after, aren't for everybody. Giving a woman I loved four years of my life, only to have her turn down my marriage proposals, was a kick to my heart that is hard to recover from. I doubt that I ever will."

He'd never been a man who routinely indulged in casual relationships. Those type of affairs weren't for him. He figured that he would meet a girl, date her and concentrate solely on her. He never understood why some men felt the need to have a different woman in their bed every night of the week if they could. His mom had been the only girl for his dad and vice versa for his mom. He'd honestly believed it would be the same way for him.

"I'm not into casual relationships." Had he just said that when the one he'd participated in that night with her had been as casual as any connection could be? "At least typically, I'm not. That night I spent with you was an exception."

"You do date, though, right?"

"On occasion, yes, although I haven't done so since returning to Catalina Cove. I've been too busy with my new job." No need for her to know the dates he'd had while living in Seattle had been blind dates his friends had set up.

"I see."

He doubted she did see. "But that hasn't stopped my mom from trying to fix me up with every single woman in the cove since I've moved back. She wants grandbabies."

"Your mom is actually trying to hook you up with women?"

"Yes," he said in an annoyed tone. "However, my mother wants something far more serious than a hookup, trust me. She wants me to meet a woman who, unlike Mia, has marriage on her mind. But a part of her is still hoping that Mia comes to her senses, and we'll get back together. Although I've told Mom that won't be happening."

When he saw the bright lights of the French Quarter, he asked, "So where is this place in New Orleans that we're going to for a night of dancing?"

"You're a good dancer, Zara."

She looked across the table at Saint, taking in his kissable lips, chiseled jaw and those penetrating dark eyes that could wet your panties if you stared into them too long.

"And so are you," she said, being totally honest. When she'd told him of her desire to go dancing, she figured he would just dance to the slow songs with her like Maurice used to do whenever he took her dancing. But not Saint. He had danced with her every single time, even the line dancing. Not only was he a good-looking man but his well-defined masculinity was on full display with that open-button shirt and what she thought of as pulse-tripping jeans. His pectorals and biceps were in fluid motion with his dance moves, and she wasn't the only woman noticing.

There wasn't anything about Saint that wouldn't grab a woman's attention. She liked the slow dances with him the best. That was when she would breathe in his scent and revel in the hard body pressed against hers. When he tightened his arms around her, a restless throb of desire invaded her senses.

Sharing a car ride with him to New Orleans had been sexual torture at its best. Whenever she'd felt his eyes on her and looked over at him, she would see the dark intensity in their depths. And when he spoke, his deep, husky voice would set off vibrations deep in the core of her body.

"Where did you learn to dance?" she asked after a waitress had brought them each another beer.

He leaned back in his chair and smiled. It was that same sexy smile that had had her stripping off her clothes that night at the hotel faster than he'd stripped off his. That same smile that crinkled the corners of his eyes while tipping up the corners of his mouth.

"I learned to dance in college. I got a football scholarship to Louisiana State University and my defensive line coach had this thing about movement. He figured the best way to increase our speed and agility was through dancing. It was important for us to be quick on our feet. A dance instructor attended our practice sessions at least two to three times a week, and a number of us were even enrolled in ballet."

"I bet that was fun."

He barely held back a laugh. "We didn't think so at first, but we eventually did. During the offseason some of the guys and I would keep up the practice by going dancing a lot."

"At night clubs?"

"Night clubs weren't allowed."

"Not even during offseason?" she asked.

"For a college player on scholarship, offseason only meant there weren't any scheduled games. We still had practice sessions without coaches and trainers. Then there is mandatory study time. However, there were a lot of parties on campus that we could attend."

Zara found what he'd said interesting. "I took dancing while growing up and I loved it. That prepared me for cheerleading in high school."

"I heard you were very popular in high school and in your senior year you were Miss Catalina Cove High."

She wondered who'd told him that, so she asked.

"Vaughn. He is a proud brother who would mention you on occasion. Of course at the time I hadn't known his sister Zara was my Angel."

His Angel. The way he'd said it made her feel things she didn't want to feel. Made her remember things she didn't want to remember. At least not now. But then how could she not remember that night when the man she'd shared it with was here with her? And she was just as attracted to him now as she had been then. Not wanting to think such thoughts, she surveyed the room. Several people were still on the dance floor enjoying the live band.

"What college did you attend?" he asked, breaking into her thoughts.

"Boston College. Then I moved to Paris to attend a fashion design school for my graduate degree."

He took another sip of beer, and she watched as he placed the beer bottle to his mouth. She recalled just how delicious his lips had been that night and how much pleasure she'd gotten from his kisses. And she couldn't help but recall the number of times that night they had kissed.

"Did you always know you wanted to be a fashion designer, Zara?"

"Not until high school. I assumed I would be an artist like my mom since I did a few paintings that even she thought were good."

"When did you decide being an artist wasn't your calling?"

Zara thought about that time. "The summer before my senior year of high school, and I'd made captain of the cheerleading squad. I designed our uniforms. I would have made them as well, but my parents considered a seamstress job beneath me and hired one. They figured that would be their contribution to what they considered my interest at the time."

Her features lit up in a mischievous grin. "Little did they know that Ms. Juanita and I had worked out a plan. She let me help her sew the uniforms. On a lot of days when my parents thought I had stayed after school for study hall, I was at Ms. Juanita's house helping her with the uniforms. That was our secret."

"Mrs. Juanita Beckett?"

"Yes." Zara wasn't surprised he knew who she was talking about. The older woman had been Catalina Cove's seamstress for years.

Saint placed his beer bottle on the table and extended his hand to her. "Ready to hit the dance floor again?"

It was a slow number, and she recalled the last one they'd danced to had left her entire body tingling with desire. When she placed her hand in his, she instantly felt her stomach curl in sexual excitement. From the look in his eyes, she knew he'd felt it, too.

Standing, she said jokingly, "I'm glad it's a slow song. Not sure I have the energy to shake my booty right now."

He laughed and the sound awakened every single nerve in her body. When they reached the dance floor, he placed his arms around her waist and swayed her into the dance. Body to body. She felt his hands' languid, swirling strokes up and down her back. He was doing so with such tenderness she almost groaned. The muscular power of him surrounded her, and all kinds of sensations were swamping her.

During all the other slow dances, she had rested her face against his chest. For this one, she hooked her arms around his neck, which meant looking up into his face. She was drowning in him. It was a vivid repeat of the last time they'd shared space, heat and each other.

There was something about Saint that made her think that he actually was a saint. Or possibly from another world or period in time. All she did know was that two years ago on a night she would never forget, he had brought calmness to her turbulent and troubled world. Tonight he was indulging her by doing something she loved. Dancing.

It hadn't taken her long to decide she liked dancing with him. She loved the way he held her body close to his. She was literally being consumed by the scent and feel of him. She wanted to break eye contact with him but couldn't. At that moment need began overtaking her. Although she wished otherwise, that same need was tearing away at her common sense.

To save her sanity she shifted her gaze from his, determined to look anywhere but at him. All kinds of thoughts were going through her head and all of them were way too naughty. She'd never engaged in what she considered casual sex until him. Now their paths had unexpectedly crossed a second time and she wanted to share a bed with him again. She *needed* to share a bed with him. What was there about him that would make her want to indulge in a hookup? It was so unlike her.

But then, what was like her? She had believed in forever-after only to fall in love with a man who had betrayed her. So why bother? There was no way she would risk giving her heart to another man again.

At least she knew her intuition hadn't been wrong about Saint that night. He was someone who was kind, thoughtful and considerate. That hadn't changed. For him to bring her here showed what a terrific guy he was. Too bad his ex-girlfriend hadn't appreciated that about him.

Another thing she noticed was, just like before, he was easy to talk to and they still connected on a number of levels. Because he'd gone through his own heartbreak, he was able to relate to hers. Not only that, he understood how it was to love someone deeply and then for that person to show you that they truly didn't love you back.

She shifted her gaze back to Saint to find him staring at her. The look in his eyes, as well as the particular song being played, seemed to have them in a seductive trance. Her entire body throbbed just by him looking at her. Shifting her arms from his shoulders she slid them around his back. His magnificent, muscled back.

At that moment she felt the need for her chest to be pressed against his. Her breasts were beginning to feel achy and needed the contact. She wondered if he realized sexual vibes were pouring off him. Off them. Then, as if their lips were magnets drawn to each other, she leaned up and met his lips in a kiss.

She immediately thought that just like that night in his hotel room, this kiss was meant to be. Here. Now. And she honestly didn't care who was watching them. Maybe she should, but she didn't. It was as if this moment in time was theirs to take and they were taking it.

They ended the kiss and she knew she couldn't fight the need any longer. For two years she had thought about him, remembered that night, remembered him. She had thought their meeting had been a chance encounter and she would never see him again. However, tonight she was proved wrong. He was here, and tonight they were back in New Orleans of all places. And dancing.

When the song finally ended, they slowly parted, and she looked up at him knowing if a bed would have been close by, he would have swept her off her feet and carried her to it. And she would have been glad about it.

"I'm glad our paths crossed again, Zara," he said in a deep, throaty voice that she found so sinfully erotic.

Her lips curved in a smile. "So am I, Saint, and I don't regret that kiss." And she truly meant it.

"Neither do I. Do you want to dance some more?" he asked as another slow song began playing.

She shook her head. "No. I'm ready to leave."

He took her hand. "Where to now?"

Zara met his gaze and said, "My cottage."

"And where is your cottage, Zara?"

"On Pelican Bay."

9

"Nice place," Saint said, surveying the cottage as he followed Zara into the kitchen. But then he should not have expected anything less. He recalled how wealthy her family was when he'd been a kid. That was during a time when the "haves and the have-nots" didn't mingle. Times had definitely changed. Vaughn's marrying Sierra was proof of that. He recalled her father used to work for Vaughn's.

During the drive from New Orleans, Zara had told him all about this cottage and the fond memories she had spending time there as a little girl with her mother while she painted. It was their little refuge, and her mother had often described it as a little bit of heaven. A peaceful and picturesque paradise. Her mother had bequeathed it to her upon her death.

Since it was dark, he hadn't seen much of it on the walk across the lighted pier. He'd taken hold of her hand on that stroll and doing so had felt right. Just like one part of him was saying it was right for him to be here, another part of him was asking: What the hell was he doing here? She was his boss's sister for Pete's sake.

"When I became a teenager, this used to be my retreat," she said, breaking into his thoughts. "By then Mom's hands had begun bothering her and she couldn't paint like she used to." Reaching into the cabinet to grab a bottle of wine, she added, "That's when she stopped coming over here."

He tried not to notice the tautness of her jeans on her backside. "Is this where you stay whenever you return to the cove?" he asked.

She poured two glasses of wine and crossed the room to him. "No. This is the first time I've stayed here since my parents' deaths ten years ago."

Ten years? He could only assume that meant she'd never spent time with her ex-boyfriend here. "Thanks," he said, taking the glass she offered him. "I know you said after you left for college you never returned to the cove to live, but did you come back to visit? Even after your parents moved to Paris?"

"No," she said after taking a sip. "Not long after I left for college my parents moved permanently to Paris. I spent my summers and holidays with them there. Although they moved abroad, the reason they didn't sell Zara's Haven and this cottage was because they'd planned to return on occasion to visit."

She paused a moment. "They never did," she said sadly.

Saint knew why. He'd heard from Vaughn how his parents had been killed in a boating accident two years after moving to Paris.

"I didn't come back to the cove until Vaughn moved back here," Zara was saying. "Then it was only during the holidays. Whenever I did return, I'd stay at Zara's Haven with him."

"But not this time?"

"No. My trip home this time was a surprise. Vaughn mentioned since Teryn is doing a sleepover with a friend, he's staying overnight with Sierra at her place. I'm staying at the cottage tonight because I didn't want to stay in the huge mansion alone."

He took a sip of wine then said, "Yet, you'll stay here alone? On a secluded island?"

She took another sip of wine. "It's secure here," she said. "You had to drive on a private road and then go through that security gate. You wouldn't have entered if I hadn't given you the access code. But then," she said, viewing him over the rim of her glass, "I'm not alone, am I?"

He met her gaze and felt the heat. That same heat he'd felt the moment their shocked gazes had connected at the party. Even now a rush of desire was clawing at his insides. Goose bumps were forming on his skin just from looking at her. Standing in front of him, she sipped her wine and stared into his eyes. It felt like a pulse-kicking moment. Especially when his mind was filled with all the things that he wanted to do to her.

"Why am I here, Zara?" He had to ask her that, since he was filled with a desire to consume her the same way a flame from a candle sucked up oxygen.

"I wanted you here with me, Saint."

Although he knew the reason, he wanted her to tell him anyway. "Why?"

She took a step closer as if doing so would garner all his attention. If only she knew just how much of his attention she already had.

She said, "Earlier tonight you alluded to the fact that typically you aren't into casual relationships. But…"

He lifted a brow. "But what?"

"You and I shared one such night two years ago, didn't we?"

Yes, they had and for months after it happened, he'd tried to understand what had driven him to do it—although he didn't regret the experience at all. "Yes, we did. Like I said, you were an exception. I enjoyed being with you and I'll even go so far to say I needed it."

"I enjoyed being with you and needed it, too," she admitted. "However, I don't want you to think I'm a promiscuous woman, Saint, because I'm not. In fact, I haven't made love to anyone since that night I spent with you."

Her admission surprised him. "Why?"

Zara shrugged. "I haven't had any desire to do so. And, like you, I've been busy." She paused and then said, "Besides, I haven't met another guy who I was sexually attracted to the way I was with you that night."

Since she was being forthright with him, he saw no reason not to do so with her. "I totally understand since I haven't shared a woman's bed since you, either."

Now that surprised Zara. Why would a virile man deny himself that way? "Why not?"

"Earlier tonight I told you the reason I'm not seriously involved with anyone. Another reason is similar to yours. I haven't met a woman who I was sexually attracted to the way I was with you that night. So far, no other woman can push my buttons the way you do. All you have to do is look at me and I get hot. I see you and I want you. I touch you and I want you. I smell you and I want you."

His words had sexual excitement curling her stomach. "You are a very passionate being, Saint."

He took a sip of wine. "So are you."

She appreciated his compliment. "Thanks. So, what are we going to do about all this passion that's going to waste?" she asked, deliberately easing closer to him. Although the intensity of her desire and attraction for him mystified her, in no way did it bother her. He also didn't seem bothered by the intensity of the heat they were generating.

"Do you have any suggestions?" he asked, holding her gaze.

"Yes, I have a few," she said, inching closer to him. "I suggest we work it out of our systems."

"Out of our systems? Is such a thing possible?" he asked, amused.

She knew why he was asking. If a full night of lovemaking two and a half years ago hadn't eradicated their desire for each other, what hope was there that a repeat performance would render a different result? "Not sure, but we can definitely try. And as far as your hang-up on indulging in casual relationships, think of this time differently."

"How so?" he asked, placing his wineglass on the table.

"Nothing we do will be considered casual in normal terms. It will be a hookup of a purely sexual kind. No emotional attachment. No commitment. No expectation of anything other than the moment." She had offered him the type of relationship most men would jump at. "That's the arrangement. You game, Saint?"

"Yes, I'm game. There's no way I couldn't be," he said, holding her gaze.

He continued to stare at her for a long moment before reaching for her wineglass. He placed it on the table beside his. Then swept her into his arms and headed in the direction of where he'd seen a bedroom earlier.

10

Present day

It was a warm, sunny day as Zara strolled toward the Wither-spoon Café, a restaurant known for serving a wonderful break-fast, a delicious lunch and a mouthwatering dinner. She had awakened that morning for the taste of their blueberry muf-fins. Nobody in Catalina Cove made them better than the Witherspoons.

Parking near the shipping district she decided to take the leisurely walk to the café. She loved this part of Catalina Cove. The downtown area was a replica of New Orleans's French Quarter. That had been a deliberate move on the part of the cove's founder, her great-great-great-grandfather, the pirate Jean LaFitte, after the US government turned down his re-quest to be given New Orleans.

Zara greeted those she passed. Some she knew and others she didn't. Over the years, a number of people had moved to Catalina Cove. A lot of them, thanks to the low-interest loan plan Reid had established, were people who'd grown up in the cove and were moving back home.

On Saturday night Vaughn, Sierra and Teryn had treated her to dinner at the Lighthouse Restaurant. Sierra had asked if she'd ever considered moving back here and the answer had been a resounding no. She had outgrown Catalina Cove even before she'd left for college. Returning on occasion to visit was enough for her.

She continued walking on the wide sidewalk, passing the historic buildings that were now various shops and cafés. Sierra's café, the Green Fig, was one of them. A short while later, she stopped when she came to a vacant building and stood facing the huge glass front. The Catalina Cove zoning board had strict laws against architectural changes, especially to this section of town. The buildings had been preserved and looked as they had when they'd originally been built. She liked it.

Her mind drifted to thoughts of how this place could be transformed into one of her boutiques. The four she presently owned were scattered around the New England area and there was one in New York. They had become so popular and successful that they were often featured in fashion magazines. She'd never considered having a boutique in the southeastern part of the country.

She began walking again and inhaled the scent of the sea. With the shipping district just blocks away there was no way she could not. She'd also noted the vacant building was a two-story structure like Sierra's café. She found herself imagining a second floor that would display her fashions as well.

Stop it! she mentally ordered herself. *Forget about that For Sale sign you saw in the window. The last thing you should want is to have any reason to stay connected to Catalina Cove.* However, she knew she had that connection whether she wanted it or not.

Vaughn, Sierra and Teryn lived here. They were her family. Besides that, she knew Vaughn wanted a big family and she could see them starting one soon. That meant several nieces and nephews for her to love on and spoil.

There was one reason for her not to have too many ties to the cove and that was due to Saint. She hadn't seen or talked to him since Vaughn and Sierra's wedding. They had hooked up the night of Vaughn and Sierra's celebration cookout in February, after Saint had taken her dancing. They'd hooked up again the night of the wedding in March, after Vaughn and Sierra had left for their honeymoon. That was a double dose of Saint within a thirty-day period, but she'd had no complaints, just memories of two nights of pleasure in his arms that were still emblazoned in her mind.

The one thing Zara liked about their hookups was that they were never planned. They just happened, and so far, they'd occurred whenever she came to town. She'd been back a few days now, and so far, they hadn't run into each other. She wasn't sure Saint even knew she was in the cove, unless Vaughn had mentioned it to him. By mutual agreement she and Saint hadn't exchanged contact information. Keeping in touch wasn't part of the arrangement.

She entered the Witherspoon Café and the first thing she noticed was that it was crowded. The second was an awareness that suddenly began stirring to life in her midsection. She carefully studied the room and saw Saint. He was staring at her with that same hot, powerful intensity.

And as usual, her intense attraction propelled her legs to move toward him.

Saint, who'd been sipping coffee and eating blueberry muffins, felt his heart skip a beat, then start to race, when his eyes collided with Zara's. Her features conveyed her surprise at seeing him.

He was surprised as well. As she headed toward him, he stood and watched her weave her way around tables and customers— just as she'd done the night they'd first met. She looked just as stunning as she had then. Today she was wearing a pretty printed sundress that showed off her beautiful shoulders and gorgeous legs. Usually, when other women approached him vying for his time and attention, he would quickly find an excuse not to be bothered. No such excuse would be given to Zara.

Saint still hadn't figured out why he'd broken a couple of rules for her, and as he stood watching her move toward him, he knew if push came to shove, he would break a few more. Hell, push didn't have to come to shove. All she had to do was give him an indication that her thoughts were aligned with his, and he was all in. Literally.

As she drew closer, he began feeling overwhelmed. Zara Miller would and could have that effect on any man. The woman was striking and stunning, all rolled into one and sprinkled with a large amount of gorgeousness. When her lips curved into a smile, he knew he was a goner.

"Hello, Saint."

As usual, her voice was distinct, soft and breathy—that was, until she was in the throes of passion. Then it would become raspy, impeccably sexy and unequivocally arousing. "Hello, Zara. Would you like to join me?" he asked, gesturing to the empty chair at his table.

"Weren't you about to leave?"

If he was before, he sure as hell wasn't about to now. "What gave you that idea?"

"Your bill is on the table."

Saint looked down and saw that it was. "I still have time," he said, without checking his watch.

"In that case, yes, I'll join you."

Not only did she look good, Saint noticed that she smelled good, too. But then she always did. He leaned in as he pulled out the chair for her and asked, "How have you been, Zara?"

"Fine and what about you, Saint?"

"The same."

At that moment the waitress came to take her order of coffee, a side of bacon and blueberry muffins. He asked for a refill on his coffee. Before she walked away, he asked the woman to add everything to his bill.

"You don't have to do that, Saint."

"I want to."

He felt sexual energy passing between them. In a way he was glad she was still just as affected by him as he was by her. "Vaughn mentioned you were in town," he then said.

"Yes, I arrived a few days ago."

"For Jaye and Velvet's engagement party?"

"Yes, and to pack. Vaughn and I have decided to list Zara's Haven as a historical landmark and open it to the public for tours. That means it's time for me to do something I've avoided doing for years. Namely, pack up the stuff in my parents' room and my room that I want to keep. Neither Vaughn nor I will be living in the house."

The waitress returned with Zara's coffee and to refill his. Saint was well aware that Vaughn was planning to build on a tract of oceanfront property he'd purchased from Reid. In the meantime, he and Sierra were living in the spacious apartment above her restaurant. There was no need to ask where Zara was staying while in town. It would be the cottage.

Just thinking about the cottage and the two times he'd

spent the night with her there made sexual need jolt his insides. She was still the only woman he'd shared a bed with since his breakup with Mia. The intimate times he'd spent with Zara—their hookups—would just happen, without any preplanning. They weren't friends with benefits. Nor were they lovers. They were just two people who couldn't control the degree of lust that would consume them whenever they saw each other.

The arrangement to combat their dilemma was…no emotional attachment. No commitment. No expectation of anything other than the moment. So far, it worked for them.

"How is the fashion business going?" he asked. He took a sip of his coffee and watched her sip hers. He liked the way her mouth was positioned on her coffee cup and recalled one night when it had been positioned on a certain part of him the same way.

"Business is going great. My assistant is handling things in my absence for the next six weeks, and I have all the confidence in the world she'll do a good job."

"You'll be in Catalina Cove for six weeks?"

"Yes, unless I finish packing earlier."

At that moment the waitress returned with her bacon and blueberry muffins. Even though he'd just had his own, his mouth watered at their wonderful smell.

"It's sad when one of the main things on my list whenever I return to the cove is to come here for the Witherspoons' blueberry muffins."

He suppressed a laugh. "You mean Ms. Debbie's blueberry muffins. Everybody knows she's the one who bakes them."

Zara's lips curved in an amused expression. "Okay, Saint, I stand corrected. Ms. Debbie's blueberry muffins." She paused a moment and asked, "How are your parents doing?"

One thing he liked about their hookups was, when the lovemaking was over, they relished their cuddle time. That was when he would hold her in his arms, and they would talk about anything and everything. She'd even told him about her *legs closed, options open* rule she'd implemented after her breakup with her ex-boyfriend, and that she'd tossed the rule to the wind the moment she'd met him. None of their cuddle time was meant to build any emotional attachment. It was merely time they enjoyed together.

Saint figured one of the reasons was because neither would be ready for their time together to end. He would tell her about his parents or the changes he was making to his house, and she would talk about her fashion boutiques.

"Mom and Dad are fine. Moving back home has definitely made life easier for them and for me. Now I don't go to bed worrying about them doing stuff they aren't supposed to do." He chuckled. "That doesn't mean they don't test my patience at times. They still like to flex their independence, and I've learned to step back and let them. They need to feel useful and not dependent."

"Any new activities for them?"

"Dad did hint about getting a motorcycle last week, but I squashed the idea pretty fast. And Mom wouldn't be Mom if she didn't remind me every chance she gets how much she wants grandkids before she gets too old to enjoy them."

"They didn't have a problem with you moving back home, did they?" she asked, amused at what he was sharing about his parents.

"Not as long as I don't cramp their style, as they put it. However, there is an issue I need to talk to my mom about before it gets out of hand."

"Oh, what?" She bit into one of her muffins. When a

crumb got caught on her top lip, his stomach clenched when she swiped it off with the tip of her tongue.

Saint shifted in his chair before saying, "She still thinks I need a steady woman in my life. She still won't accept that I'm fine with the woman-less life I'm living now."

"I understand how you feel. As much as I miss my parents, what I don't miss is their belief that an arranged marriage is the best way. My parents believed a couple should marry for wealth and not love."

He leaned back in his chair. "They honestly thought that?"

"Yes. Vaughn and I always suspected although they respected each other, their marriage was one of convenience. Our suspicions were confirmed when we found a marriage agreement among their important papers after they died."

Saint lifted a brow. "A marriage agreement?"

"Yes. At the time my parents met, Mom was the daughter of a wealthy French industrialist. Dad, of course, was a wealthy American business magnate and philanthropist. He wanted a French wife and saw Mom as the perfect woman for the job."

"Why did he want a French wife?" Saint asked.

"For the bloodline. He felt if he didn't, the French blood in his offspring would be diluted."

Evidently, Saint had an I-don't-believe-it look on his face. That made her grin and say, "I know it sounds crazy that anyone would think that way, but it's true. That's why I know Dad would have loved Maurice. He's French and comes from a wealthy family."

Although the last thing he wanted to hear was anything about her ex-boyfriend, he asked, "Is that why, while growing up, French was the main language spoken in your household?"

"You heard about that, huh?"

"Yes, Vaughn mentioned it to me. He knew since I was a

Bayou Creole that I probably spoke either French or Spanish as a second language. My parents are fluent in both. However, I'm fluent in just French. I figured whenever the folks would speak Spanish around me it was because they were discussing something they didn't want me to know about," he said, grinning.

She laughed softly. "I hate to say it but you're probably right."

Saint looked at his watch. "Unfortunately, I need to leave for a meeting at the office."

"Alright and thanks for breakfast. I enjoyed sharing it with you, Saint."

"And I with you, Zara."

He held her gaze for a moment and then he leaned in close. His voice was low when he asked, "Will I be able to see you while you're here, Zara?"

Her voice was just as low when she answered, "I was hoping you'd want to, Saint. You know where I'm staying."

"The cottage?"

"Yes."

"And the access code to the security gate's the same?" Saint remembered it from the last two times.

"Yes."

Saint straightened in his chair. Just the thought of spending time with her again sent a rush of adrenaline, as well as contentment, all through him. He motioned for the waitress to bring him a new check. There was no need for him and Zara to discuss their plans for later any further. Instead, they talked about the possibility of rain over the next few days as well as the Blueberry Festival that would be held in a few weeks.

He placed enough cash on the table for both their meals

and a generous tip. As he stood to leave, he said, "Enjoy the rest of your stay in the cove, Zara."

She met his gaze over her coffee cup. He saw the heat in her eyes and figured it probably mirrored his own. Lowering the cup, she said, "I'm sure that I will, Saint."

11

Zara sat at the easel in the loft and painted. She'd gotten the idea after leaving the Witherspoon Café that morning and walking to the shipping district to watch the boats come and go.

She'd always enjoyed walking along the pier and when she saw the arts-and-crafts store, the only one in the cove, she decided to do something she hadn't done in a long time. That meant she would need paints and brushes. She was glad to see Ms. Fanny, who'd owned the place for years. The older woman said she could recall when Zara would come in as a little girl with her mother to get her art supplies. Zara remembered those days as well.

When she returned to the cottage, she'd taken a leisurely swim in the bay. Once she began painting, she hadn't known where her creative thoughts would lead her, until her paintbrush began moving across the canvas. A short while later she wondered what had possessed her to paint the vacant storefront she'd seen earlier that day. She hadn't reproduced just an empty building; she had worked with different colors and painted what she visualized as another one of her boutiques.

She paused to study the image and saw how this one was different. The storefront was classier than the others, chic while still maintaining that classic Catalina Cove look. It had a French flair with flower planters, triple awnings and a huge sign that read, Zara la Vogue, the French translation of Zara Fashions—which was different from the other stores she owned, all named Zara's Fashion Boutique.

She decided there wasn't anything wrong with a little day-dreaming and over-the-top thinking. That was what it would be for her to even consider opening one of her boutiques in this town. The space was way larger than all her other shops, which meant she would consider it as the main store. But she didn't want to move back to the cove. It had been easy for Vaughn to come back here to live, but it wasn't that easy for her, especially after living in Boston.

It wasn't that she absolutely loved Boston, because she didn't. She detested the cold winter, and then there was the traffic that seemed to be more horrendous each day. So was the cost of living. Although she and Vaughn would be considered wealthy by most people's standards—considering the proceeds from the oil business her parents sold when her father retired, the trust funds, as well as extensive properties she and Vaughn jointly owned in Paris—they'd decided to work and not to live extravagantly just because they could afford to. Between the two of them, they had established several foundations for their charitable work.

That was one of the things she and Maurice had disagreed on. He was the grandson of a wealthy businessman and could be just as snobbish as her parents had been when it came to social classes. Now that she could reflect on her two years of exclusiveness with him, she could see the old Zara had toler-ated a lot of things that the new Zara wouldn't.

That included her bedroom experience, which she'd assumed was okay and acceptable. Not anymore. The three hookups with Saint had satisfied her more than her sexual encounters with Maurice. That night spent in Saint's hotel room had been the hottest sexual experience of her life. She had been left thinking nothing could be better than that.

She was proved wrong when she'd seen him at Vaughn and Sierra's celebration cookout, and then again on the night of their wedding. Each time was better than the last. That was probably why she was feeling antsy now, and the reason a spike of heat had settled right between her legs.

Since she didn't have Saint's cell number and he didn't have hers, there was no way to know if the hookup would be tonight or even if it would happen this week. She'd basically let him know at breakfast that he was welcome at any time.

Since meeting him, other men had tried capturing her interest. So far, none had done so. She hadn't met another guy with such a deep and strong attraction like she felt with Saint. Her attraction to him was even stronger than what she'd felt for Maurice. And in the bedroom…well, although she tried not to compare, in all honesty there was no comparison. It was Team Saint hands down, or bodies down. Each and every time.

She also enjoyed the times they spent just talking, over wine or cuddling in bed. Like Vaughn, Saint had a strong background in finance. She'd also discovered he was good when it came to problem-solving. The last time they were together she told him about the issue she was having with the landlord of one of her shops. The man was refusing to make necessary changes to the building that he had agreed to do.

Saint suggested since the landlord was being difficult to call his bluff and tell him she would not be renewing her lease. If that didn't work, and if she really liked the location of that shop, she should buy it. Owning the property would be a better deal since it would be a valuable long-term investment.

She had followed Saint's suggestion and called the landlord's bluff. It worked. However, the idea of owning the buildings of all four of her shops was appealing. Already her attorney was looking into making that happen. More than anything she would love to own her shop in Boston on Newberry Street, a popular shopping, dining and entertainment district. She'd made offers to buy it twice and had been turned down both times.

She could have easily gone to Vaughn for his advice, but she knew her brother. Whereas Saint was a problem solver, Vaughn was a fixer. He would have wanted to handle it for her instead of letting her handle it for herself. For the most part, Vaughn accepted her as the independent woman that she was. However, he clung to this belief that when it came to the women he loved, a man had to handle business for them even if they were capable of handling it for themselves.

Three hours later, Zara stood and stretched her body. She decided to stop painting for a while. Sierra had dropped by earlier with her favorite soup and turkey sandwich. It had been too much to eat for lunch and she'd saved the rest for dinner. Moving over to the window she looked out at the bay. It was such a spectacular sight. Simply awe-inspiring. Peaceful. Now more than ever she understood why her mother found it easy to paint here. It was the perfect getaway. And… she thought as a feeling of intense longing flowed through her, it was also the best lovers' hideaway.

She'd been with Saint two other times at this cottage and was definitely looking forward to a third.

Saint parked his car beside Zara's rental and got out. While having dinner with his parents he had spoken with his mother about staying out of his love life—or trying to remedy his lack of one.

She had again expressed to him how much she wanted grandkids. However, as he'd already told her, he wouldn't get into a loveless marriage to have them. There had to be love, and presently, he had no intention of falling in love again.

Saint looked around and took note on how secured the property was. He figured Mr. Miller had made doubly sure of it since his wife and daughter had spent so much time on Pelican Bay. The property was resplendently landscaped and the brick walkway that led to the pier was adorned with all kinds of impressive rosebushes that were native to the area. He immediately recognized the noisette roses, tea roses and Bourbon roses, mainly because his mother grew the same kind in her rose garden.

The pier was wide enough for two couples to walk side by side. The floor was made of redwood cedar, which was the best type of wood to prevent decaying due to moisture. Decorative ornamental iron railings lined both sides, which gave the pier a very distinctive look. Zara had told him the first night he'd visited the cottage that the pier was a mile long and you could barely see the roofline of the cottage at the halfway mark. And speaking of the halfway mark, that was where the main pier jutted out to narrower piers on both sides. Wooden chairs were in place so you could sit and enjoy a spectacular view of the bay.

He paused when he saw that one of the chairs had a blue towel draped across it. That made him wonder if Zara had gone swimming from the pier earlier that day. He'd never seen her in a swimsuit and the thought of her in one had sexual energy pulsing through his body. He resumed walking, knowing every step he took brought him closer to the cottage and to her.

Saint didn't have to figure out what was going on between him and Zara. They both were satisfied with the arrangement they'd agreed on. He didn't worry about who she was with when they weren't together and vice versa with her regarding him. They didn't have an exclusive relationship. They'd each had that before and it hadn't worked out.

Why was he constantly reminding himself of that lately?

He pushed that question to the back of his mind when he saw the cottage. Although she'd said her father had had it built for her mother as a wedding gift, Saint thought it was a perfect reflection of Zara. It was impressive, stylish and captivating, with its pitched roof, wraparound porch, adilynn arch windows and landscaped yard. A varied mixture of flowers surrounded the cottage and made it look like the perfect retreat.

Or as it was sometimes being used…a lovers' hideaway.

Once his feet touched the brick walkway leading to the porch, he recalled the last time he'd come here, the night of Vaughn and Sierra's wedding. Zara had given him the key to let himself inside, and he'd arrived before her. Within minutes of her opening the door and walking in, he had her naked, sprawled across the bed and that gorgeous mane of brown hair spread across the pillow.

He wasn't sure if she was expecting him tonight or not. No plans had been made. However, she had made it pretty clear he was welcome, and he felt damn good about that. Since he didn't have her phone number there was no way to let her know he was coming. He would talk to her about that. He felt it was time for them to at least exchange numbers.

When he reached her door, he could hear music from inside—namely, the soulful sound of Aretha. He lifted his hand to knock. Once. Then again. The door opened and there she stood, wearing an oversize T-shirt, shoeless with her toes painted a bright coral that matched her fingernails. Her hair was tied back from her face, and he was tempted to reach out and set it free to see it flow around her shoulders.

Standing before him was the epitome of his fantasy woman. He suddenly felt a surge of emotions that made his entire body ache. But then he quickly recalled their agreement.

No emotional attachment. No commitment. No expectation of anything other than the moment.

"You came."

Did she think he wouldn't? "Yes, I came," he said, as his gaze raked over her.

His strong desire for her should be unnerving. However, it was the only thing that did make sense right now. The sexual chemistry between them seemed stronger than ever. They failed miserably each time they tried working each other out of their systems.

His chest expanded when he recognized the T-shirt she was wearing. His. The New Orleans Saints shirt he'd given her that first night in the hotel room. It hit her midthigh and she looked so damn sexy in it. He could clearly see the outlines of her nipples and they were hard, pressing against the cotton fabric. And he had a feeling her bra wasn't the only thing missing underneath that T-shirt. Not that he had any complaints.

She stood aside for him to enter and he got a whiff of her scent. When she closed the door, he turned to her, opened his arms, and she walked right into them.

12

Zara didn't understand why she was so intensely delighted that Saint had come. She was no longer dependent on any man for her happiness. She had worked hard since her breakup with Maurice to assure that. However, she didn't feel her independence was threatened by the fierce need she felt when it came to Saint. As strange as it might seem, being with him only enhanced it. Mainly because with him she could be the woman she was. She could be herself with no limitations.

Since her breakup with Maurice, she'd become strong-willed, determined, and didn't play nice when she didn't want to. She didn't put up with anyone's crap and had no problem going after what she wanted and turning her back on what she didn't. And today, right now at this very minute, she wanted Saint.

From the huge, hard bulge pressed against her midsection, she could feel he wanted her, too. She leaned into him and when he whispered in her ear just what he wanted to do to her, his words were like an arousing melody that caused a throbbing in her core.

"Saint…"

Instead of answering her, he pulled her even tighter against him. It was as if he needed to hold her. That was all good because she needed to hold him as well. Maybe she should seriously question why but she couldn't. The only thing she could do was enjoy being held by him. With his arms wrapped around her, she felt emboldened by his strength and closeness. And as if he knew what she needed, he leaned down and kissed her. Had it been nearly two months since she'd last shared this type of intimacy with him? Two months since being kissed by him, touched and made love to?

He released her mouth and then, taking her hand firmly in his, he escorted her out of the living room to her bedroom. "I like seeing you in my shirt, Zara. In it you look like an angel. My Angel."

His Angel.

Hadn't she convinced herself weeks ago that no man would ever consider her his again? However, for some reason she knew Saint didn't mean it that way. This handsome and sensual man didn't want her to belong to him any more than she wanted him to belong to her. He was merely caught in the moment. It was understandable with this degree of passion between them.

She looked up at him, marveling at how he stood towering over her as he removed the T-shirt from her body. He didn't seem surprised to see she was totally naked underneath it. How had he known?

When she asked him, he said, "There are some things a man can tell. I take it you knew I was on your property."

"Yes. I knew the moment you put in the access code. There's a buzzer and a camera that alerted me. I guess I never mentioned that to you before."

"No, you've never mentioned it," he said, unbuttoning his shirt.

She watched the slow movement of his hands. There was just something arousing watching a man remove his clothes. Especially this man. Her body was aching for him. Did he know it? And why did he have to look so damn sexy? "Now you know."

"Yes. Now I know." He tossed his shirt aside.

His shoulders were massive and masculine, and his abs were tight and impressive. She was tempted to rub her hands over his chest. Just thinking about doing such a thing sent an intense sexual greed through her. He must have seen the deep longing in her face and removed his pants and briefs rather quickly. Or it could have been seeing her naked had made him want to speed up. Whatever the reason, she was totally appreciative. They reached for each other at the same time and ended up tumbling onto the bed in each other's arms.

Their mouths joined in a kiss that made her head reel. It was as if he needed her as much as she needed him. The wildness and hunger of his kiss revealed as much, and bone-melting heat began spreading throughout her body. If the manner in which he was making love to her mouth was indicative of the way he intended to make love to her body, she wasn't sure she would survive the experience. It was a good thing she'd eaten well today. She had a feeling she would need her strength.

When he ended the kiss, he stared down into her eyes a second before whispering, "You're beautiful and you taste delicious."

She had news for him. She thought he was handsome and just as delicious. In her mind, beauty wasn't just in one's looks but in the way a person carried themselves. The times she'd spent with Saint had always been special, which was why she always wanted more.

He leaned closer and his warm lips moved across her cheek-bones, her chin, and nuzzled her ear before returning to her lips.

Then Saint's mouth was on the move again. With toe-curling determination, his lips moved toward her chest and captured one nipple in his mouth. She moaned at the sucking sensation—gentle and then strong—as he began to devour it.

"Saint…"

He paid homage to the other breast as his hands traveled down her body to comb his fingers through the damp curls between her legs. She wasn't sure how long she could last and when he inserted a finger inside her and wiggled it around a few times, she came, climaxing hard against his hand. He quieted her scream with a kiss.

Releasing her mouth, he moved away from the bed to get a condom packet from his slacks. After sheathing himself, he returned and placed his body over hers. He leaned down and kissed her again. When he broke off the kiss he stared into her eyes as he joined their bodies. She was certain that she felt him all the way to her womb.

His skin was hot against hers. He was just as hot for her as she was for him. When he lifted her hips, she clasped her legs around his waist. That was when he began thrusting hard in a rhythm that had her purring while at the same time her thighs began to quiver.

How was he able to do this to her, make her want and need him to the point where his thrusts into her body and roll of his hips against hers had her shuddering inside out? His head dipped to her breasts and when he captured the other nipple in his mouth, she fought back a scream. He should know by now that his mouth on her breasts did things to her. It was her hot spot. That was fine, because she had discovered his.

Reaching her hand up, she caressed the side of his face,

right below his ear. He released her breast to stare down at her, and when her fingertip caressed him in that spot again, she saw the glaze of intense desire in his eyes just seconds before he let out a deep groan. Then he threw his head back as he increased his thrusts, pushing her to heights of rapture she'd only ever experienced with him.

"Saint!"

"Zara!"

His hips rocked against her as he thrust harder, over and over. Together, they came before he collapsed on top of her. Prior to him shifting their bodies to lie side by side, she had felt his heart pounding against hers. Now the room was filled with a deep silence, except for their heavy breathing. That had been some lovemaking. Every woman should have such an experience in her life at least once. She'd never felt this hot for a man before and wanted more.

He held her in his arms, kissing the dampness from her forehead. "I'm so glad our paths crossed again today."

"I'm glad, too, Saint."

She was certain he didn't know the half of it. He hadn't a clue just how much she'd meant those words. Her cautious side warned her to pull back some, slow down and think logically of where she might be headed if she didn't. But then another part of her knew she would be fine since no man would ever have her heart again. No emotional attachment, no commitment and no expectation of anything other than the moment.

As he gathered her closer into his arms, Zara knew while it lasted, she wanted many more moments with him.

Saint slowly opened his eyes to the bright sunlight coming through the cottage's bedroom window. Glancing at the clock on the nightstand, he saw it was a few minutes past seven.

The bed was empty, but he could smell coffee. He could also smell the scent of Zara all over him. He closed his eyes and bit back a groan as he remembered all they'd done last night. When they'd made love a second time, he had barely slid inside her before she began raising her hips to entice him into a fast rhythm. Then there was the time the tip of her tongue had grazed the head of his shaft. And he definitely couldn't forget when she'd ridden him. Hard.

Stepping out of bed, he slid into his slacks and left the bedroom to head for the kitchen. She wasn't there and he looked up when he heard movement in the loft. After pouring a cup of coffee he went up the stairs and paused when he saw her sitting in front of an easel with her own cup of coffee close by. She was wearing his T-shirt again and he thought her sitting there, with the hem having ridden up her thigh, looked so damn sexy and he felt another boner coming on.

When she'd opened the door yesterday wearing that shirt, the first thing that crossed his mind was that since that shirt was his that she was his, too. But he quickly quashed that notion. Zara was a free spirit who didn't belong to anyone. She'd played that game before with some asshole and she wouldn't do it again. He thought that was a pity. She was a beautiful, warm and loving person who had a lot to give a man. The right man.

"Good morning."

She jerked her head around and smiled. "Good morning, Saint."

He loved hearing her say his name. "Did you plan to wake me up?"

She shook her head, making a mass of hair spread around her shoulders. He could recall exactly when he'd set it free and had run his fingers through the glossy tresses. "I figured you would eventually wake up on your own. Besides, you looked good sleeping in my bed."

He wondered if she knew that sounded pretty much like an invitation for another time. But then hadn't she practically insinuated that at breakfast yesterday morning? "Thanks." He took a sip of his coffee, tempted to say he would love to see how she looked in *his* bed one of these mornings.

Instead, he asked, "What are you painting?"

She smiled at him. "Come see."

In his bare feet he crossed the room to stand beside her and gaze at the picture. "That's one of your shops?"

"No," she answered. "On my walk to the Witherspoon Café yesterday morning I passed this storefront. It was vacant and for sale. My mind suddenly envisioned how it would look if I were to turn it into one of my boutiques."

He lifted a brow. "I didn't know you were entertaining the idea of opening a shop here."

"I'm not. I just saw it vacant, and my mind went to work."

"Well, you did a great job. You're a gifted artist, Zara."

"No, I'm not."

"Yes, you are. I pass by that vacant storefront all the time and never envisioned it looking like this. You've painted it to look like a shop that would be in Paris somewhere."

"That's the way I imagined it."

Saint studied the painting again. She had used radiant colors, and the flowers in the box looked real. Just knowing she had painted this from an image derived from her thoughts was both impressive and amazing.

And it had him thinking.

"Are you sure you don't want to consider purchasing it?"

She tilted her head to look at him. "Purchasing what?"

"That vacant storefront." He figured the thought must have crossed her mind.

She shook her head. "I'm not interested."

"Why not?"

She shrugged. "Why would I be?"

"Long-term investment. You would qualify for Reid's low-interest loan if you decide to go that route. I personally think it would be a good move with the interest rates as low as they are. For you it would be a win-win situation."

She continued to paint, and he had a feeling she would give his suggestion some thought, although she hadn't said that she would. He'd discovered Zara was a good businesswoman, and he appreciated that whenever he gave her advice, she listened. On that note, he decided to give her more to think about. "I think it would make good business sense to place another boutique in this area instead of everything being in the New England area."

She set aside her paintbrush and turned to him. "I have a boutique in New York."

"Yes, and that, too, was a great business move. Why did you do it?" He knew his question would get her to thinking.

"It was time I branched out into an area other than New England. That also gave me an opportunity to diversify. In addition to my fashion designs, that particular boutique also sells shoes and handbags."

"I see." He did and had a feeling she eventually would, too.

When she remained silent, he then said, "Then you can make that dream you've put to canvas a reality, Zara."

She frowned. "This is not a dream, Saint. Catalina Cove stopped being my home a long time ago."

"For years I thought the same thing. I bet so did Vaughn,

Kaegan, Sierra and Vashti. But we all came back, and you know why?"

"I know why Vaughn came back."

"Let's look at Vaughn, then, as well as the others. I think at some point they realized something they'd heard for years was true."

"And what's that?"

"When the going gets tough, there's no place like home." He leaned down and placed a kiss across her lips. "I'll be leaving town later today for New York. I won't be back until Saturday."

"In time to attend Jaye and Velvet's engagement party?" she asked.

"Yes, and I hope to see you there."

"You will," she said, sliding off the stool.

He stroked his knuckles across her cheek and said, "There's something I'd like to do before I leave, though."

"What?"

"Make love to you again."

She wrapped her arms around his neck. "Then do it, Saint."

13

"Are you getting excited about your trip? Part two of your honeymoon?" Zara asked her sister-in-law. After dropping Teryn at school that morning, Sierra had called and suggested they have breakfast at the Witherspoon Café.

Sierra's lips spread into a huge smile. "Yes, and I think Vaughn is even more so. I can't wait."

When they got married in March, Vaughn and Sierra had only taken a weeklong honeymoon to the Caribbean, which had coincided with spring break. That way Teryn got to spend a week with Sierra's sister Dani and her family in Atlanta. They had made plans to have a second honeymoon—a continuation, so to speak—at the end of the school year and would leave right after Memorial Day. This one was for three weeks, and they would be traveling to the Maldives. Sierra's parents would be taking Teryn and their grandkids on a month-long vacation.

"How's the painting coming along, Zara?"

Zara arched a brow. "Painting?"

"Yes. When I dropped by the other day to bring you lunch, you were painting. And when Vaughn and I didn't hear from you yesterday, other than your text canceling our lunch date, I figured you were still doing it."

Zara tried to keep the blush off her face. She'd still been doing it alright. Doing it with Saint. When he'd taken her back to bed, they'd made love for hours until he had to leave to check on his parents before packing for his trip to New York.

After he'd left, she'd been too weak from lovemaking to do anything but remain in bed for a while. There was no way she could have joined Sierra for lunch. She'd finally gotten up around two, showered and gone to LaFitte's Seafood House, a popular restaurant on the boardwalk. "I finished the painting yesterday."

"That's great! So, what did you paint?"

Zara bit into her muffin and decided to be truthful with Sierra. She adored her sister-in-law and thought she was the best thing to happen to her brother. Vaughn might have gained a beautiful wife, but Zara had gotten the sister she'd never had and always wanted. It was great that they were the same age and their birthdays were just months apart.

"The other day when I had breakfast here, I parked near the shipping district and decided to walk. I passed a vacant building between the Ellorans' ice-cream shop and Jenkins's Florist."

Sierra smiled. "I know the building you're talking about. It is huge and, like my place, it's two-story. In fact, it has more square footage than the Green Fig. What does that building have to do with you painting?"

Leaning over the table Zara lowered her voice and said, "Well, I wanted to paint but wasn't sure what. Then my mind led me to paint that storefront. I painted what I envisioned for that vacant building. My boutique. It had more of a French look than any of my others and it looked pretty." She beamed. "Even Saint said so."

"Saint? He saw it?"

Zara wanted to swear under her breath. She hadn't meant to let any mention of Saint slip. But she would own up to it. "Yes, he saw it."

"Hmm." Sierra picked up her coffee cup and after taking a sip, she lifted a finely arched brow and said, "I hope you know that bit of information only has me thinking. And just like we told you the other day, our conclusions might be hotter and more erotic than the real thing."

Zara grinned. "And like I told you and the others, there's no way they could be hotter and more erotic than the real thing. Without giving any details, I thought I'd pretty much made myself clear as to what was going on between me and Saint."

Sierra laughed softly. "You did, but now I'm wondering if things are getting serious between the two of you."

Zara was aghast at the suggestion and figured her expression showed it. "Of course not."

"Oh."

Sierra honestly sounded surprised, and for that reason, Zara wanted to explain. She sipped her coffee, then said, "Like I told you, I honestly didn't think I'd see Saint again after our one night together two and a half years ago. Now I've seen him practically every time I've returned to Catalina Cove. First at your and Vaughn's celebration cookout when I learned his real identity. Then again at your wedding. Now I'm back and it seems natural for us to be together while I'm here. But trust me when I say that it is not, and I repeat, not, a serious involvement."

"So, the two of you are friends with benefits?"

Zara paused a moment before answering. "To me that denotes a more structured relationship than the arrangement we have. Saint and I have reasons not to want to get seriously involved with anyone, not even with each other. We like spending time together and nothing more than that. It isn't serious or permanent. In fact, we don't even have each other's contact information. If I happen to be in the cove and we run into each other, that's fine. If we don't, that's fine, too."

Sierra nodded. "Well, just like we told you the other day, people in the cove have always liked and respected Saint and considered him a nice guy. He's always been courteous, thoughtful and respectful. Back in the day, mothers would always try fixing him up with their daughters because they knew he was a perfect gentleman. He wasn't one to lead a girl on, and he wouldn't become involved with one unless he meant it."

Sierra bit into her muffin as if giving what she'd said time to sink in. "Saint's mother and mine are friends," she continued, "and according to Mom, Ms. Irene always wanted a house full of kids. However, due to medical reasons she only had Saint. She thinks she can remedy that by having a bunch of grandkids instead. That's why she's set her mind to finding him a wife."

"He told me about his mother's determination to do that, and he's not happy about it," Zara replied.

"And he has a right not to be," Sierra said. "From what Vaughn said, he can barely eat a meal anywhere without some woman inviting herself to join him or deliberately walking by his table to speak to him. There are one or two who know his whereabouts before and after work hours and show up where he is, hoping to get noticed. I understand Saint's mother is feeding them that information."

Zara frowned. "That's a bit much for those women. To run behind a man that way."

"I totally agree. But I guess if you're a woman in the market for a husband, especially a handsome man who doesn't have commitment phobia, you'd see the chase as worth it. I bet some are even taking his disinterest as a challenge."

The thought of that bothered Zara. "They are wasting their time. I know for a fact that a serious relationship with a woman is the last thing Saint wants."

"Why? Because he's still in love with his old girlfriend?"

"That's not it," Zara said without much thought and in a tone that she regretted sounded annoyed.

Sierra eyed Zara speculatively. "If you and Saint aren't friends with benefits, then what are you?"

Zara honestly couldn't answer that, other than saying, "We're two people who have decided we enjoy each other's company whenever we want without the trappings of an emotional attachment, commitment and any expectation of anything other than the moment. I guess you can say that we're hookup partners."

Sierra bit into her muffin, chewing thoughtfully. Then she asked, "Whose idea was that?"

"Mine, but he agreed to it."

Sierra stared at her for a moment before asking, "And how is it working for you? This hookup-partners thing?"

Zara shrugged. "I think it would work better if I wasn't planning on being in Catalina Cove for a longer stay this time. The other two times I was in and out within days. For this visit I'm here for six weeks. Now I want to…"

Sierra gave her a curious stare. "Want to what?"

"Spend more time with him." Zara let out a deep sigh. "I look forward to being with him, Sierra."

"So, for you it's only sexual."

Zara noted Sierra had said it as a statement and not a question. "Maybe it was at first. I like being with him in every sense of the word. The lovemaking is wonderful, off the charts, the best I've ever had. And then we communicate on a level that I'd never experienced with Maurice. I run stuff by Saint for his ideas, thoughts and suggestions. He even thinks I should consider buying that vacant building."

"He does?"

"Yes. He feels it will be a good investment move for me."

"He's probably right, Zara. Buying that building when I did and turning it into the Green Fig was the best business decision I could have made. Vaughn and I have even talked about expanding to the second floor to include banquet rooms when we move out and the upstairs living quarters are no longer needed."

"Wow, that will be a huge undertaking."

"Yes, but a good business decision for us. We'll promote Levi from assistant manager to manager when we start a family."

Zara beamed. "The two of you are thinking about starting a family sooner rather than later?"

"Yes," Sierra said excitedly. "Definitely sooner than we originally planned. We've chosen a house plan and hope that by the time we move in I'll be pregnant."

"That's wonderful, Sierra." The thought of being an aunt made Zara happy. "How soon do you think it will be before they start building your house?"

"Not sure. The builder for the development has been selected, and I understand he'll be moving to town in a few weeks. It's Jaye's youngest brother, who owns a construction company." Sierra remained silent for a moment. Then she said, "You know what I think regarding the situation with you and Saint?"

Zara lifted a brow. "No. What do you think?"

"I understand you guys wanting to keep your involvement private from prying eyes. That's your right. However, I'm not sure that will work for long."

"Why not?"

"Sexual chemistry is something you and Saint can't seem to hide."

On Saturday afternoon, Saint turned his car onto Buccaneer Lane, the scenic tree-lined road that led to the bed-and-breakfast inn, Shelby by the Sea. Although he'd been back in Catalina Cove for almost six months, it had been years since he'd been here. This place held so many fond memories for him. He couldn't help recalling that it had been Ms. Shelby who'd given him and Brody their first summer jobs at the age of fourteen. Namely, to keep the area leading to the inn immaculate. They had no problem picking up trash and the empty wine and beer bottles. It had put coins in their pockets to play the video games at the local recreation center.

When the historic mansion came into view, he thought it was as massive, stately and majestic as ever. Even more so since Ms. Shelby's niece, Vashti Alcindor Grisham, had resurrected the inn a few years ago. From here he could hear the sound of the ocean, which was directly behind the inn.

The twenty-guest-room mansion was built in 1905 and had been owned by the Barlowe family for generations. Some claimed the original Barlowe had been Jean LaFitte's right-hand man, and for his loyalty LaFitte had awarded the man the land the mansion sat on.

Close to forty years ago, Hawthorn Barlowe, upon his death, being the last of the Barlowes, had bequeathed the mansion and all the land surrounding it to his loyal and trusted nurse,

Ms. Shelby. With no need of a house that big, Ms. Shelby had turned it into a bed-and-breakfast inn and named it Shelby by the Sea.

Shelby by the Sea was one of the most popular places in Catalina Cove, a hallmark. It was always brimming with business, particularly newlyweds from all over the country on their honeymoon, and married couples reigniting the flame in their marriage. Even as a kid, Saint would admit he'd envisioned himself getting married here. Today he was attending the engagement party for Jaye and Velvet.

He parked behind the car he knew was Vaughn's, which made him wonder if Zara had arrived. When he'd seen her two days ago, she'd said that she would be attending. Since he didn't have her contact information, he had no way to check if that was still her plan.

He hated admitting it, but not having her phone number was annoying the hell out of him. He understood that she didn't want anything other than hookups—that was how he felt as well—but that shouldn't keep them from exchanging phone numbers.

He had intended to broach the subject with her the last time they were together, but it had slipped his mind. However, he resolved to talk to her about it, and soon.

As he walked toward the perfectly landscaped yard, he saw uniformed attendants greeting arriving guests and guiding them to a welcome table where names were checked on a list. Then they were escorted to the backyard where the outdoor festivities were being held.

Saint understood why names were being checked. This was a private affair and there were those in the cove who felt they were entitled to be invited, regardless of whether they received an invitation or not. Jaye had a long memory and anyone who'd slighted Velvet when they hadn't known she was an heiress did not receive an invitation.

The sky was a stunning blue and the temperature was the best it'd been since spring had arrived. Jaye and Velvet had certainly picked a good weekend for their party. It was Memorial Day weekend and, as usual in the cove, school had ended yesterday. He'd heard from Jaye that Velvet had wanted to finish out the school year before celebrating their upcoming nuptials. A second engagement party would be held next month in Phoenix.

As he followed the attendant through the flower gardens, he was glad to see the huge gardenia bushes and magnolia trees were still there and more had been added. Anyone who'd known Ms. Shelby knew that gardenias and magnolias were her two favorite flowers and the older woman had planted special gardens of both on the sides of the mansion.

He had to hand it to Vashti. Not only had she restored the inn to the grandeur of yesteryears, but she had also remodeled it with all the honor and magnificence that her aunt Shelby would be proud of.

The scent of the blossoms was strong, and he was escorted toward an area where a large gazebo sat facing the ocean. When he rounded the corner, he saw the crowd of people. Some he knew and others he didn't recognize. He had met Jaye's father and brothers and some of his closest friends from Phoenix last month when they'd come to the cove to visit Jaye and Velvet.

A huge "Congratulations, Jaye and Velvet" streamer extended from one side of the gazebo to the other, anchored by black and gold balloons. Even the pier that led out to the beach was decorated. He accepted a drink off a passing waiter's tray, then looked around the yard. From the sensuous stirring he felt in the pit of his stomach he knew that although he hadn't seen her yet, Zara was here.

He'd given up trying to figure out why there was such an intense physical attraction between them. All he knew was that she could set his entire body on fire, and it would burn for days even when she wasn't in his presence. Just from thinking about her. That was how it had been for the past two days when he'd been out of town. She had been on his mind a lot.

He scanned the crowd for her as his heart began beating faster and faster. When a group of people shifted, he saw her standing and talking with several women. Some he recognized, some he didn't. Ashley Sullivan had walked up and was happily twirling around, proudly displaying her rounded belly, which had grown a lot since he'd last seen her.

He took a sip of his drink with his gaze trained on Zara. She looked sexy with her purple sleeveless, high-neck short dress that displayed those alluring shoulders he loved licking, and her gorgeous legs he loved caressing. She had a pair of cute black stilettos on her feet and her hair was flowing around her shoulders, just the way he liked. She had the body for that dress, all the right curves, and it looked damn good on her. Totally ravishing. One of the ladies must have said something amusing because Zara threw her head back and laughed.

He wondered how long it would take for her to feel his presence. Somehow, it seemed that she could with him, the same way he could with her. He watched and waited. The moment she began craning her neck to scan the crowded yard, he knew why.

Then their gazes met.

14

Zara was laughing. Ruthie, Velvet's best friend from Phoenix, who was getting married next month, had just told them about some of the things that had happened at one of her bridal showers. Suddenly, quivers of intense heat raced up Zara's spine, making every cell in her body sizzle. For her, that was a stark indication that Saint had arrived.

She no longer tried to understand this thing between them. It was one of those phenomena that had no real name, just a ton of energy. In their case, it was sexual energy. Even without seeing him, her body was reacting to his presence. Even the air she breathed pricked her awareness. Moments ago, her nostrils had been pulling in the scent of the sea. Now it was inhaling the scent of him.

"Are you alright, Zara?"

She looked over at Sierra. That was when she noticed all the other women had walked off. "Yes, I'm fine. Where did everyone go?"

"To the buffet table. Bryce asked if you wanted anything, but you were too busy looking around to give her an answer.

Are you expecting someone?" her sister-in-law asked with a sheepish grin.

Instead of answering, Zara craned her neck again, glancing around. Then she saw Saint. He was standing across the yard with a drink in his hand and staring at her. At that moment, she could not ignore the heat of attraction flowing between them. Even from the distance, she could see desire in his eyes. He began walking toward her.

"Well, wouldn't you know. There's Saint coming this way," Sierra said with a mischievous grin.

Without taking her eyes off him, Zara said, "Yes, wouldn't you know."

"And do you remember what I said the other day about sexual chemistry being something that you and Saint can't seem to hide?"

Without breaking eye contact with Saint, Zara said, "Yes, I remember."

"Just thought I'd remind you."

Zara acknowledged Sierra's words with a nod. That was all she was willing to do since her full attention was on Saint as he approached. He was dressed in a pair of slacks and a button-up shirt over a pair of broad shoulders and a muscular chest. He looked so good, and the way his slacks fit him, they appeared tailored to his hips and thighs. She noticed that about all the pants he wore, whether dress slacks, trousers or jeans.

She remembered the last time they were together, how her hands had explored up and down his bare chest and sculpted abdomen. She took a sip of her wine and then licked her lips.

He was now less than ten feet away from her and their gazes still held. Suddenly, a woman appeared out of the crowd and grabbed his arm, halting his stride and forcing his eye contact away from her. Zara saw intense annoyance on his face when he glanced down at the woman.

"In case you're wondering who she is," Sierra said, "that's Samantha Groover."

Zara couldn't recall having ever seen the woman before. "She lives here?"

"She was born in Catalina Cove and like the rest of us didn't return after college. She was living in Tulsa and working in management at the Colfax Bank. When a branch opened here, she put in a transfer to return home. She graduated from Catalina Cove High School the same year Saint did."

Zara felt a knot form in her stomach—a knot that shouldn't be there, but was. She and Saint weren't exclusive. They were just hookup partners. Yet, she wanted to know more about the woman. "Was she his girlfriend?"

"Nope. Although that was six years before our time, I remember her because she used to babysit me and Dani, until my parents found out she was letting her boyfriend come over and spent more time kissing him than watching us.

"She dated Oscar Belkins all through high school. They broke up after they left for college," Sierra said.

"Oh." Zara noticed the woman, grinning and getting all in Saint's face, and didn't like it one bit. "Maybe I should just go over there and—"

"Do what?" Sierra asked, tilting her head to study her. "Didn't you tell me that you and Saint were just hookup partners? That the two of you don't share any emotions, commitment or expectations of anything other than the moment?"

Zara breathed in deeply. Yes, she had said that, and she'd meant it. So why was she allowing emotions she shouldn't have intrude now? Seeing him with a woman—a very pretty woman—shouldn't bother her. So why was she letting it?

"According to what Samantha is telling people, she thinks she has an advantage over any woman who might want Saint."

Zara couldn't stop the irritation from showing in her eyes. "Really? And just what is this advantage?"

Sierra fought back a grin when she leaned in and said in a low voice, "She claims Saint had a crush on her in the sixth grade."

Zara threw a hand over her mouth to keep from laughing out loud. "And she honestly thinks that counts for something? A crush that happened over twenty years ago?"

"I guess so," Sierra replied with amusement in her voice. "Come on." Taking Zara's hand, she led her toward the buffet table. "Be prepared. Samantha isn't the only one with her sights on Saint. Like you, there are a few other women here who've been waiting for him to show up."

"I haven't been waiting for him to show up," Zara said, maybe a little too quickly.

"Sure you haven't. I guess neither have Robin Dyer, Kassie Fisher and Peggy Fulton. But it seems Samantha got to him first."

Zara knew that Robin and the other women Sierra had named were coworkers of Velvet's. Single teachers in town. She shrugged and said, "Whatever."

Sierra smiled in an assuring manner. "I suggest you let Saint handle Samantha, Robin and any others who try to claim his attention. There is no doubt in my mind that he will find you after he does."

Saint did find her.

Zara had known the moment he'd joined the group and greeted everyone. When conversations started up again, she tried not looking over at him but knew his eyes were on her the entire time. She felt his gaze like a physical caress, which heightened the beat of her pulse.

The party planner got everybody's attention to announce that the first dance would be the official engagement dance for Jaye and Velvet. Everyone looked toward the huge portable dance floor as Jaye took Velvet into his arms in a slow dance. He wrapped her in his embrace like he never intended to let her go.

Zara and the other ladies around her fought back tears as they watched the couple. It was so obvious they were deeply in love and wanted everyone to know it. She pushed the thought to the back of her mind that she would never take part in that kind of love with a man. Mainly because she would never let one get that close to her heart again.

She peeked over at Saint. Like her and everyone else, he was watching the couple. But then, as if he felt her eyes on him, he switched his gaze to her. The intensity in his eyes made her feel as if she was burning alive from the inside out. How did Saint have the ability to do that to her?

She broke eye contact to watch the couple again just as they ended their dance with a kiss, which had all the teary-eyed women fanning their faces with their hands. When they ended their kiss, everyone clapped and cheered.

The DJ played another song, and everyone was invited to the dance floor to join the couple. "I want to dance," Sierra said, taking Vaughn's hand and tugging him toward the dance floor.

"So do I," Bryce said, grabbing her husband Kaegan's hand.

It was obvious Vashti thought her two friends had the right idea as she took Sawyer's hand and led him to the dance floor, too. That left Zara and Saint standing there alone.

He inched up beside her. "Do you want to dance, Zara?"

She met his gaze and recalled that night when he'd taken her dancing in New Orleans. Just the thought of her body pressed up against his had her pulse pounding. Whenever she was in Saint's arms, whether it was on the dance floor, flat on her back with him above her or stretched out on top of him in bed, she had a tendency to lose herself.

"Do you honestly think that's a good idea?" she asked.

She knew he understood her meaning when a grin touched his lips. "I guess you're right."

She chuckled softly. "You know I am." She took a sip of her drink as they stood there watching the dancers as a slow song played.

A short while later, because she couldn't let go of something Sierra had said, she asked, "So you used to have a crush on Samantha Groover?"

He looked at her. "That's what I've been told by Samantha and pretty much verified by my mother. Mom claims I insisted on buying Samantha a box of Valentine candy one year."

Zara tilted her head. "Don't you remember?"

"No. That was a long time ago. I didn't even recall her name until she told it to me the other day."

"She evidently remembers," Zara said.

"Doesn't matter since I'd forgotten." He studied her features for a minute and asked, "Is there something we need to talk about, Zara?"

The last thing she wanted was to come across as emotionally attached—especially not jealous. "No, there's nothing we need to discuss."

"You're sure?"

"I'm positive."

He was about to say something when everybody returned

from the dance floor. She regretted even bringing up Samantha. What he did was his business just like what she did was hers.

Saint tried not to notice the man dancing with Zara. He didn't recognize him from the cove, so he figured he was one of Jaye's friends from Phoenix since a number of them were here. So far, Zara and the guy had only danced to fast songs. Why did it matter to him if they danced to a slow one?

He of all people knew how much Zara liked to dance and, so far, she hadn't missed a chance to be on the dance floor, except for the one time she turned down his offer to dance. She hadn't exactly turned him down, but wisely suggested they didn't dance together. Remembering how they'd danced that night in New Orleans and the seductive moves they'd made to each other, she was right. Dancing with her was sensuality in motion. Sharing a dance wasn't a good idea. Still, it bothered him that that one guy was claiming all of her time.

The song ended and he watched as Zara walked away from the dance floor. More than one man stared as she passed. There was something pulse-throbbing about the elegant sway of her hips and those gorgeous legs as she strolled to one of the open bars. The guy who'd dominated her time was still with her, right on her heels. Saint frowned, wondering who the hell he was. If he were to ask Jaye that would be a dead giveaway that he was asking for a particular reason.

"Why are you standing over here by yourself and not out there on the dance floor?"

Saint looked at the man who'd entered his space under a cluster of cypress trees. It was the perfect spot where he could observe unnoticed. Several women had approached him to dance and he'd politely turned each one down.

The man who'd interrupted his private moment was one

he'd known his entire life, Levi Canady. Levi, who was the assistant manager of Sierra's café, the Green Fig, was highly respected in the community. He was good friends with Saint's parents as well, and he and Saint's father often went fishing together.

When Saint was growing up, Levi had been a part of Catalina Cove's police force. One night while patrolling the outskirts of town, Levi had encountered a group of bikers who had been speeding.

He pulled them over to give them tickets and the four bikers overpowered him, took his gun and shot him in the leg.

The bikers were apprehended less than a month after the incident. Levi turned in his badge after that and for years had taught drivers education at the high school. When Sierra returned to the cove to open her café, she offered Levi the position as her assistant manager.

More than once, Saint had heard his mother express her concern that Levi refused to open up his heart to love again after losing his wife to a sudden heart attack some years back. These days, when he wasn't working at the café or out in his boat fishing, Levi preferred spending his free time with his dog, Chip.

"Tonight I just want to watch," he said to Levi. "What about you? I haven't seen you on the dance floor."

"My leg's been bothering me today."

"Oh." Saint recalled due to trauma after his injury, there were times he walked with a slight limp.

"I only plan to hang around a little while longer. It will be time to feed Chip and take him out."

"And how is Chip?" He would often see the dog when Levi, along with Chip, visited his parents.

"Chip is great and the best companion a man could have. Tell your dad I'll be calling him next week, Saint. I heard from

Kaegan that the trout and whiting are all but jumping out of the ocean. It's time for us to go fishing." Kaegan Chambray owned a seafood shipping company in town.

"I'll be sure to tell him."

"It was good seeing you, Saint. Have a good night."

"You do the same, Levi."

When Levi walked off, heading toward the buffet table, Saint turned his attention back to the dance floor. A different song was playing, and Zara was out there dancing with that guy again. A part of him was glad that so far, the DJ was playing fast songs.

Deciding not to stand there and stare at Zara a moment longer, he headed over to the buffet table, hoping he didn't run into Samantha again. The other women had taken his hint that he didn't want to be bothered, but it seemed Samantha was slow to catch on.

He had filled his plate with what he knew was Kaegan's mouthwatering seafood dip when a feminine voice behind him said, "There you are, Saint. I've been looking for you."

He cringed. It was Samantha again.

"I was wondering if you and that guy were going to ever get off the dance floor," Vashti said, grinning.

"And Saint had his eyes on you the entire time," Sierra said, as if also amused.

Zara sipped her wine, refusing to comment. To be honest, although she hadn't seen Saint's eyes on her, she had felt them with each and every dance move she'd made. She didn't want that to mean anything to either of them... Just like it didn't mean anything every time she'd seen Samantha, Robin or several other women sidle up to him tonight.

But it had meant something to her.

She reasoned that since he'd been the only man she'd slept with since her breakup with Maurice, she was due to feel some kind of possessiveness, even if it was unwarranted.

"I'm surprised you and Saint haven't danced together yet," Vashti said.

Zara knew what Sierra and Vashti were doing. They'd never seen her and Saint dance before, but they had been witnesses to the strong sexual chemistry they could emit. Although they figured anyone watching her and Saint dance would witness it as well, they were encouraging her to do whatever the hell she wanted to do when it came to Saint. If others picked up on the crackle of sexual energy passing between them, it was her and Saint's business and nobody else's.

Speaking of Saint, she looked around for him and didn't see him anywhere. Had he left the party? Now that it had grown dark, lanterns had been lit, giving the area a romantic feel. The DJ had taken a break and a number of people who'd been dancing were at the buffet table to refuel. More guests had arrived, and additional food and drinks were being served.

A short while later the music began again. Now the DJ was playing a slow song. Earlier, Sierra had rescued her from Keith, who'd seemed intent to hang by her side. Although Zara had enjoyed dancing with the man and thought he was nice, the last thing she wanted was for anyone to assume something was developing between them. It wasn't. The only man she'd wanted to dance a slow song with appeared to have left the party.

Fighting back the disappointment she knew she shouldn't be feeling, Zara headed for the buffet table. She figured since most people were now back on the dance floor, it wouldn't be as crowded as it had been earlier.

Zara was halfway there when suddenly a jolt of energy

rocked her to the bone and made her pause. Even before glancing around, she knew why. Obviously, Saint hadn't left the
party after all. She craned her neck, determined to find him
among the crowd of people in the yard. She finally saw him
and, the moment their eyes met, they began moving toward
each other, as if a magnet was pulling them together.

When she came to a stop in front of him, she said, "I thought
you had left."

"I was about to leave. I'd made it to my car, and then decided there was no way I could go until I did the one thing I
truly wanted to do, Zara."

The sound of his voice, deep, husky and sexy, always made
her want to lean in closer. So she did. "And what is it that you
truly want to do, Saint?"

"Dance with you."

15

Saint studied Zara's expression and noticed her thoughtful look. He figured she was recalling their earlier conversation about why they shouldn't dance together. While watching that guy dance with her, song after song, he'd recalled it as well. That was why he hadn't crossed the yard and cut in for a dance like he'd been tempted to do.

When he'd gotten so irritated that he couldn't dance with her and someone else could, he had decided it was time to call it a night. Upon reaching his car he decided not to leave but to go back and do what he would hate himself for not doing in the morning. That was to dance with Zara and damn the consequences. But he knew it would be her decision to make. More than anything he hoped that she would dance with him.

She held his gaze for what seemed like a long moment before she smiled and said, "Yes, I'll dance with you."

"Are you sure?" There was no doubt in his mind she knew why he'd asked.

"Yes, I'm sure. I want to dance with you, too, Saint."

Pleased, Saint took Zara's hand and led her to the dance

floor just as the DJ started playing another slow song. The moment he drew her into his arms, intense heat rushed through his body. It had been two days since he'd seen her, and he had missed her. That in itself was odd, given that until she'd returned to Catalina Cove this time, he hadn't seen or talked to her in two months. Yet, while holding her in his arms with her body pressed to his and inhaling her scent, it just felt so right.

As they swayed to the music, of their own accord, his hands moved from her waist to float across her back, and he didn't give a damn who was watching. Nothing mattered other than the two of them wrapped in each other's arms, dancing to this slow song.

He wanted to pull her closer but knew he had to at least keep things decent. When they were alone then they could get as indecent as they wanted. Usually, they did. They always managed to take hooking up to a whole new level. Heat curled his insides when he thought of some of those times. Making love to her was always an adventure. Neither held anything back in the bedroom.

As they continued to dance, her hips hit up against his front. Each time, he sucked in a groan from the sinfully erotic friction. After a while, he suspected she was doing it deliberately. He leaned down and whispered close to her ear, "Behave."

She looked up at him, smiled and whispered back, "Make me."

With her challenge, sexual excitement curled his stomach. When he gazed down at her something happened. First, he recognized the song being played. His mind became flooded with memories of the time he'd seen that look, when they'd danced to the same song that night in New Orleans.

He was fully aware when she'd remembered it, too. That was when she shifted her hands from his shoulders to place her arms around his neck. But he hadn't expected her to lean in on tiptoes and kiss him. He'd been so taken by the way her lips felt pressed against his that he hadn't hesitated in kissing her back.

It was only when he heard the catcalls and whistles that he realized what they were doing and broke off the kiss. By then the damage was done. Just like that night in New Orleans, they'd kissed in the middle of the dance floor. Unlike that night, when the observers had been strangers, their very public display of affection had been witnessed by a number of people who knew them.

Aww hell.

Saint was a man with a strong protective instinct, especially when it came to people he cared about. He knew that Zara could take care of her own business and that she resented anyone who tried to handle it for her. But he could foresee that kiss impacting her reputation, and not giving a damn about what people thought wouldn't cut it.

This called for some form of damage control. Over her shoulders he'd caught a glimpse of a fuming Samantha. Some women could be catty—deliberately so. They wouldn't like the fact that he had refused to dance with them yet had not only danced with Zara but kissed her for all to see. She might not have a problem with anyone gossiping about her, but he did. He knew his and Zara's history. Others did not.

Her arms were still draped around his neck, and he could feel the intense energy crackling between them. Their bodies were in sync, and she was back to brushing her hips against his front. Each time she did so his heart rate increased.

He was just about to suggest they stop dancing after the song ended, when he gazed into her eyes. The ones staring back at him were intense and seductive. His eyes moved to lips still wet from their kiss. "Saint?"

There was a deep pounding in his chest just from the sound of his name from those lips. "Yes?"

"I won't apologize for kissing you."

He lifted his gaze back to her eyes. "And I won't apologize for kissing you back."

"Good."

Zara and Saint stayed on the dance floor through a few more slow songs before he finally said, "I think we need to leave now."

"Alright."

"I'll follow you home because we need to talk."

After passing through the security gate, Zara drove down the access road toward the pier. A glance in her rearview mirror indicated Saint was still behind her. He'd said they needed to talk, and she had a feeling although he said he didn't regret it, the talk would be about their kiss.

Zara brought her car to a stop and drew in a deep breath when Saint parked beside her. Knowing she'd be coming in late, she had left the floodlights on around the cottage and it looked impressive sitting there across the pier.

She'd been so absorbed in how awesome the cottage looked that she nearly jumped when Saint tapped on her car window. He was probably wondering why she was just sitting there staring across the water. She unlocked the car door, and he opened it for her and offered her his hand.

He was forever the gentleman. Maurice had only done such chivalrous things for her when they were seen in public, for show. With Saint, it was the norm.

He took her hand as they walked toward the pier. When

he laced his fingers through hers, heat drummed through her. She peeped over at him. He was quiet. The only sound was the clicking of the shoe heels against the cedar planks.

She decided to break the silence and said, "It's a beautiful night, isn't it?"

He met her gaze. "Yes, it is, and you look radiant." He then added, "You look gorgeous all the time."

Touched by his words, she stopped walking and he stopped as well. "That was a nice thing to say, Saint."

Facing her, he reached out and softly stroked a finger down the side of her face, then traced the corners of her mouth. "I meant it. Every word."

"Thanks."

"No need to thank me, Zara. I'm just keeping it honest."

Saint's finger traveled down to her neck. "You have tense muscles here," he said, gently rubbing the back of her neck. "You okay?"

"I'll be a lot better once we have that talk. It's about our kiss, right?"

He released a deep sigh. "Yes, it's about the kiss."

She lifted her chin. "I told you that I don't regret kissing you, Saint. And you said you didn't regret kissing me back."

"And I meant it."

If that was the case, why did they need to talk about it? When he moved his hand from her neck down to her waist, she inched closer to him and gripped the elbows of his powerful arms. The naked desire she saw in his eyes warmed her all the way through.

She slipped her arms around his muscular back. From the way he was staring at her through heavy-lidded eyes, intense desire rocked her body, like always. Granted, she hadn't meant to kiss him on the dance floor but, like she'd told him, she had no regrets.

Saint leaned down and captured her mouth with his. He definitely knew how to take a kiss from good to off-the-charts scandalous. The way he could maneuver his tongue to consume every part of her mouth, while easing into every nook and cranny like he knew all the intimate details.

She moaned in protest when Saint ended the kiss. To appease her, he ran the tip of his tongue across her lips, from one corner to the other, then whispered in a deep, husky tone, "Come on."

Taking her hand again, they resumed walking across the pier to the cottage.

16

"Is there a reason why you're suggesting we need to do something, just because we kissed in public, Saint?"

Saint could tell by Zara's expression she hadn't fully grasped the magnitude of what he'd said or what they'd done. Her statement confirmed it. When they'd reached the cottage, she'd suggested coffee and he'd agreed. Now she was sitting on the sofa and he'd eased into the wingback chair across from her.

It was getting late, not quite ten o'clock. When they'd left, the party was still in full swing. Because Jaye and Velvet had reserved all twenty guest rooms at Shelby by the Sea for their guests, Saint had a feeling the party would be going on way past midnight.

Now to address Zara's question. "Yes, there is a reason. Our open display of affection will cause tongues to wag."

Zara rolled her eyes. "Like I care. I'm a grown-ass woman and although I'd preferred keeping our affair private, I don't answer to anyone other than myself, and how I live my life—and with whom—is nobody's business."

"Kissing the way we did is a whole new ball game and has nothing to do with anyone getting into our business. Now it's a question of respect. I refuse to let anyone sully your good name just because of what we did."

She rolled her eyes again. "We kissed, Saint, not stripped naked and made love in front of everyone. No harm done. And as far as anyone sullying my good name, then let them. I don't live in the cove, so it doesn't matter what people think of me."

"But I do live here, and I care what they think of you, Zara. I also care about what they think of me."

She held his gaze as if considering his words. "You're right, Saint. You're well-liked in the cove and the last thing I want is anyone thinking you're no longer a nice guy."

"It's not that they'd think I'm no longer a nice guy, Zara. They will assume my values have changed. Like I told you, I've never just dated a woman for the hell of it. For me to openly kiss one the way I did tonight, they would assume she meant something to me."

She placed her coffee cup on the table and met his gaze. "Okay, Mr. Problem Solver, what do you suggest we do for damage control?"

He set his coffee cup down as well and leaned forward with his elbows resting on his thighs to make sure he had her absolute attention. "I suggest we fake an affair."

Fake an affair? He had to be kidding. "You're joking, right?"

"No, I'm not joking, and the more I think about it, the more I like the idea."

"Why?" She couldn't wait to hear his answer because she thought the idea was ridiculous.

He smiled. "For starters, it will baffle those who saw us

together tonight. Especially those busybodies who have been trying to keep tabs on me since I returned."

"What kind of tabs?"

After taking a sip of his coffee, he said, "Trying to figure out which of the women who've been trying to wear down my resistance will succeed. I understand there are some who have compiled a list. You weren't on the list yet. After tonight it will appear you're the one I've chosen. Most are wondering when, where and how, since other than that one time we ate breakfast together at the Witherspoon Café, we haven't been seen together."

She knew that was true. They spent most of their time here in the cottage, mainly in the bedroom. Few people knew they were hookup partners. She hadn't told anyone other than those she considered as close friends. Vaughn didn't even know. She couldn't help but wonder what he thought about her and Saint's open display of affection. He wouldn't say anything to her about it, but still, he had to be wondering about what was going on between them. If he'd suspected anything before, he definitely knew it now.

When she remained silent, he continued, "Hooking up with you was working fine for me. Although we weren't sneaking around, we were keeping things private and between us, and we had every right to do so."

Zara met Saint's gaze and sighed deeply. "It's no longer private and between us, is it?"

"No. I think we both knew dancing together would raise a few brows. Sexual chemistry between two people who'd never had contact before is not unheard-of. However, the way we danced, with clear familiarity, topped off by that kiss, was a strong indication we're sleeping together."

She took a minute as she absorbed what he'd said. He had

tried to keep things under control with that dance and had even tried keeping a decent amount of space between them. But her body had wanted a connection with his even with their clothes on. He'd whispered for her to behave but she'd been naughty anyway.

That physical contact hadn't been enough. Desire for more had rocked through her veins. She'd been the one to rise up on her toes and plant a kiss on his lips. Of course, he'd kissed her back.

"Tonight was all my fault," she said, disgusted with herself because even with this turn of events, she still didn't regret kissing him.

"It wasn't your fault. I was a willing participant."

"But I'm the one who initiated the kiss and kept intentionally pressing my body against yours. I got us in this mess, and I'll do what's needed to get us out. But I'm only going to be here for six weeks, Saint. I'm leaving the day after the Fourth of July. What happens when I return to Boston?"

He shrugged. "For a while people might assume we'll engage in a long-distance affair. When they discover that's not the case, they'll figure things didn't work out between us and that we ended things."

She agreed with his logic. "What will a fake affair entail?"

"The same thing we're doing now. However, you can join me for breakfast or lunch on occasion, and I'll take you out to dinner, movies and even dancing."

Zara thought about all he'd said. She didn't live in Catalina Cove, but he did. What repercussions would her behavior tonight have on him? Just the other day, Sierra had told her how people in the cove liked and respected Saint and considered him a nice guy. She'd also said he wasn't one to lead a woman on and wouldn't become involved with one casually. But he was involved with her. She'd made that pretty clear tonight.

In a few weeks, she would be leaving for Boston, returning only on occasion to visit Vaughn, Sierra and Teryn. Would it be so bad for people to think something romantic was going on between them? Who would it hurt? He'd said it would work in his favor, but it would also benefit her as well.

She liked spending time with him. Although she was in town to pack up her things at Zara's Haven, she had envisioned spending time with him here at the cottage, in private. They would still have opportunities for that; however, by pretending an affair, their time together wouldn't be limited—they'd be free to go anywhere they wanted.

She would admit that she missed doing things that couples normally did. Mainly going out on dates to dinner and movies. She had no problem doing those things while she was here, and she wanted to do them with Saint.

"Okay."

He lifted a brow. "Okay?"

"Yes, I'll go along with your suggestion that we fake an affair."

It was a six-block walk home from Shelby by the Sea, but Levi Canady didn't mind. Like he'd told Saint, the ache in his leg was more profound tonight. He'd discovered the best way to overcome the pain was to walk it out. Besides, he liked walking, inhaling the scent of the sea, looking up in the sky and seeing the stars, appreciating how quiet the town was at night. Using his legs made him also appreciate life when he recalled there had been a time when he thought he would lose one of them.

He pushed those thoughts to the back of his mind as he

increased his pace a little. There was no reason to keep Chip waiting. There were times he believed his dog could actually tell time and expected him to walk through the door at a certain hour. If he arrived late, Levi would find Chip pacing the floor, actually looking worried. Whoever said a dog was a man's best friend knew exactly what they were talking about. Chip was certainly his.

One street away from his home, Levi turned the corner and heard a sound. He slowed his pace, remembering there was an alley between the two houses. He had walked this way many times and never thought much about it. Since Sawyer Grisham took over as sheriff, crime had become almost nonexistent. Although, he would have to say, there was never a time when there had been any real crime in Catalina Cove. And when rare incidents occurred, it was usually outsiders coming to the cove causing trouble. Like a couple years ago when Bryce Witherspoon had gotten kidnapped. Luckily, she'd been rescued unharmed.

He stopped walking when he heard the sound again and recognized a feminine voice calling out in a low tone. "Dad? Dad? Where are you?"

The former cop in him had him moving in that direction. That was when he saw a woman with a flashlight in her hand, scanning the area as if she was looking for something or someone. "May I help you?"

His words made her jump, and she threw her hand to her chest, nearly dropping the flashlight. "You scared me."

"Sorry," he said. Fortunately, he was able to make her out in the dark because of the full moon in the clear sky and a nearby streetlamp. He knew most of the people living in Catalina Cove and she didn't look familiar. "I didn't mean to scare you. I was on my way home and heard a sound and decided to investigate. I couldn't help it. It's the ex-cop in me."

"Oh. I was looking for my father. His cat got out and when I was in the kitchen Dad left to go looking for him."

"Let me guess. Mr. Chelsey and his cat, Butterball."

"Yes. You know them?"

Levi barely held back a laugh. "I think everyone living in Catalina Cove does. That means you're his daughter, Margarita."

"Yes, I'm Margarita Chelsey Lawson, although most people now just call me Margie. And you are?"

"Levi. Levi Canady. As a teen I would cut the Chelseys' yard during the summers. I recall they had a daughter, but you were way younger than I was." If he remembered correctly, she was eight to ten years younger. "I didn't know you had returned to town."

"I moved back last month when I retired from my job as a nurse in Dallas. Dad turns eighty-four this year and I wanted to be here to take care of him." She glanced around. "Now, if I can only find him."

"Mr. Chelsey usually doesn't go far in his search for Butterball. I'll help you look."

"I hate to cause you any bother."

"You won't. I have my dog, Chip, waiting at home for me, but if he needs to go out before I get there, I had one of those doggy doors installed, so he can go in and out whenever he needs to."

"Well, if you're sure you don't mind helping me look."

He smiled at her. "No, I don't mind. I'll be glad to help."

17

Saint entered the Witherspoon Café on Tuesday morning and smiled at the waitress who greeted him. "Good morning, Saint. Sitting alone this morning?"

"No, Presley, I'm expecting someone."

"Okay, I have a booth this way."

"Thanks." He liked Presley. Saint knew the main reason his mother hadn't included Presley's name as one of the eligible single women in town was because people knew she was still grieving the loss of her husband. The man had gotten killed in a motorcycle accident last year.

After he was seated, Presley asked, "Do you want to order now or wait for your guest to arrive?"

"I'll wait."

"Okay then, I'll be back."

When Presley walked off, Saint checked his watch. He was early. He and Zara had made plans for this week. They would meet for breakfast on Tuesday and lunch on Friday. They didn't set a particular day to meet for dinner. They figured they could combine dinner with a night of dancing or a movie date. Their goal was to be seen together a few times during each week.

Since Vaughn was out of town for the next three weeks on the second phase of his honeymoon, there was a possibility Saint would have to work late on some days. If that happened, they would adjust their schedule accordingly.

He'd spent Memorial Day with his parents. His father had taken the grill out and Saint had helped cook the meat. Later, they had gone out on his father's boat. His parents had been pleased that he had spent the entire day with them.

Of course, the news of his and Zara's kiss had wasted no time reaching his mother's ears. He wasn't surprised, since the head bank teller at the Colfax Bank, Selma Bivens, was a friend of his mother's. Jaye had invited the bank employees, so Selma had been at the engagement party.

Saint figured his mother would have been overjoyed with the news that he was interested in someone. She wasn't. Although she thought Zara was a nice girl, she felt he was wasting his time dating her. To Irene Toussaint's way of thinking, he should concentrate his time and attention on one of the women living permanently in the cove, instead of someone who was just visiting. For him to do otherwise, to her that didn't make sense.

To his way of thinking, it made perfect sense, although he couldn't tell his mother that. The last thing he wanted was to give his time or attention to any woman. Instead of telling her how he really felt, he told her that of all the girls he'd met since returning to the cove, he liked Zara.

Then she'd asked why he hadn't invited Zara to officially meet his parents. He'd told her Zara had made other plans for Memorial Day. That was true. She had told him Saturday night she would be meeting a girlfriend in New Orleans.

He and Zara had decided if anyone were to ask that they'd become interested in each other a few months ago, February to be exact, at Vaughn and Sierra's celebration cookout. He went on to say that the reason he hadn't mentioned it to anyone was because they'd started off as just friends and had only recently decided to date. None of what he'd told his parents was a total lie. He just hadn't divulged details of what kind of *friendship* they'd been sharing before deciding to date.

Saint knew the moment Zara arrived at the café. He gazed at the entrance and saw her. When she saw him, she smiled and immediately he felt sexual vibes flow between them. As she walked toward him, he felt like he was drowning in the sight of her.

She was wearing a pair of jeans and a pretty green printed blouse. Her hair was windblown, and she was pushing it back from her face as she approached the booth. He'd noted the wind off the ocean was brisker than usual this morning. He stood when she reached his table.

"Good morning, Saint," she said, smiling brightly.

"Good morning, Zara." He waited for her to slide into the seat across from him before sitting back down. Looking across the table at her, he felt what he always felt whenever they were together—a primal attraction that he couldn't explain, but wholly accepted.

"You've been waiting long?" she asked him.

"Not at all."

Before she could say anything else, Presley came to take their order. He wasn't surprised that Presley and Zara knew each other because they'd graduated from high school the same year. But then he figured she would know Presley since she was Juanita Beckett's daughter. Zara had told him how in secret she had helped Ms. Beckett make her cheerleaders' uniforms.

He'd heard from a number of people living in the cove that although Zara had come from one of the wealthiest families in town, and while growing up her parents were considered snobs, that term had never extended to Zara or Vaughn. Both had been friendly, down-to-earth and well-liked in school.

After Presley had taken their orders and left, he looked at Zara. "So how was your Memorial Day in New Orleans yesterday?"

She gave him a huge smile. "It was wonderful. Eugenia and I attended the same fashion design school. I hadn't seen her since moving from Paris. I'm glad I was able to meet up with her in New Orleans. It's been on her bucket list for years, and she finally got to travel to the States to visit the French Quarter."

"Well, I'm glad you enjoyed yourself. What do you have planned for today?"

She released what sounded like an excited sigh. "I start packing up things, so I'll spend most of my time at Zara's Haven."

"Don't try lifting any heavy boxes. Leave them. I'll help you move them when I get off."

"Thanks, Saint."

"No problem. Just call me." Saturday night, after their talk, they had finally exchanged phone numbers. He was glad of that, and to think it had taken a fake affair to make it happen.

Presley returned with coffee and blueberry muffins. When Zara closed her eyes and inhaled deeply, one of his brows arched in amusement. "I take it you like the aroma of Ms. Deb's muffins."

She opened her eyes and grinned. "Yes. Especially now

since you've set me straight that it's Ms. Debbie who bakes them and not Mr. Chester."

Saint fought back a laugh. "I'm sure he has the recipe, as well as their sons, Ry and Duke. But I hear Ms. Debbie considers the blueberry muffins as her baby."

"And I'm not mad at her for doing so."

He did laugh this time. It couldn't be helped. In or out of bed, he enjoyed Zara's company. Faking a serious affair with her would definitely be easy to do. "Did Vaughn and Sierra get off okay yesterday?"

"Yes. He called me from the airport right before their flight left. Sierra's parents have Teryn, and Levi will be handling things at the Green Fig until Sierra returns."

"Then the café will be in good hands."

Since Zara had ordered blueberry pancakes as well, she'd only eaten one muffin and had left the others for him. He had no problem eating the rest. "Have you given any more thought to that vacant building on Main Street?"

After sipping her coffee, she said, "No, why?"

Saint looked at her over the rim of his cup. "Just wondering."

He was doing more than just wondering. He had walked by the building this morning, and after seeing that picture she'd painted of how the place could be transformed into one of her boutiques, he could visualize it just as she'd painted it.

After Presley refilled their coffee, he couldn't help but notice how much attention he and Zara were getting. Evidently, most people had heard of their kiss by now, so in their minds seeing them together made sense. Like he'd explained to Zara, not to see them together would warrant speculation and unnecessary talk.

After breakfast, he walked Zara to her car. When they

passed by the vacant building, she didn't say anything about it, and he didn't, either. He noticed she hadn't glanced in the window to see if the For Sale sign was still there.

After opening the car door for her, he leaned in and brushed a kiss across her lips. That hadn't been part of their plan, but for some reason, it felt right doing so at the moment. "Have a good day, sweetheart."

"Oh, alright."

Saint could tell the kiss had caught her off guard, as well as the term of endearment. He smiled at the thought of that as he turned and walked off.

Zara didn't immediately start her car. She sat there and watched Saint until he was no longer in sight. She understood the brush across the lips since you never knew who might have been watching. But why the term of endearment?

And why was a smile spreading across her lips that he was really getting into this fake affair? More than likely, he was trying to get into the role, so calling her that would come naturally if they were around others. That made sense.

She started the car and drove toward Zara's Haven. Vaughn had delivered a lot of empty boxes to her on Sunday. Although he hadn't mentioned anything about what she now thought of as "the Kiss," she knew Vaughn had to have seen it.

Instead, he talked about the trip he and Sierra were taking and how excited they were about it. He said he felt bad about her being in Catalina Cove when he wouldn't be around. However, she had assured him she would be fine and had plenty to keep her busy. And just for good measure—and to answer any unasked questions—she told him since she and Saint would be spending time together, she would be okay while he was gone.

Zara knew Vaughn would assume, like others, that she and Saint were a couple. That wasn't a lie since for the rest of her time in Catalina Cove, they would be.

Earlier that morning she had checked in with Sherri to see how things were going with her boutiques. All the store managers had checked in and inventory was good, and three of the boutiques had held successful sales over the weekend. It felt good knowing she could be away and she had capable people in charge of her shops.

Her thoughts shifted to how nice it had felt sharing breakfast with Saint. He had looked good in his business suit. When she'd entered the café, she couldn't help but admire just how handsome he was. Her gaze had done a leisurely scan of his impressive body.

Visions of how they'd spent Saturday night after their talk—enjoying wild, raging sex—had her mind spinning. Even now, she felt desire clawing inside her. She'd never considered herself a particularly passionate being—until Saint. With him she was doing things in the bedroom that she'd never done before and hadn't realized *could* be done. With Saint, she held nothing back and let all inhibitions go. Usually, that was when things got wild.

A short while later, with a smile from those memories still on her face, she pulled into Zara's Haven, ready to roll up her sleeves and get to work. Before she could exit the car, her cell phone rang.

"Hello."

"Zara, this is Vashti. Ray and Ashley's son arrived before daybreak this morning, weighing almost ten pounds."

"Ten pounds? No wonder we thought she was having more twins. What did they name him?"

"Logan Ashton."

"Logan Ashton Sullivan. I like it."

"I do, too. I just wanted to let you know. We're all happy with the news. I texted Sierra, but if you talk to her, make sure she knows. I'm not sure how the text messaging will work over international waters."

"I will."

After ending the call, Zara stepped out of the car, pushing the disheartening thought out of her mind that although she loved kids, thanks to Maurice's betrayal and her inability to love and trust again, she would never have any of her own.

Margie Lawson checked her watch as she entered the room and looked over at her father. After eating the breakfast she'd prepared and saying over and over how good it was, he had left the kitchen to watch his favorite game show on television. It wasn't even noon yet but now he was stretched out asleep on the sofa with Butterball lying on his chest.

More than likely, he was still exhausted from last night's Memorial Day fireworks show. It had been years since she'd last been in Catalina Cove for Memorial Day. Not since she'd left for college. Her father had been excited about going and she was glad that this year she had been with him.

She'd made the right decision to move back home. Like she'd told her son and daughter, with their father gone, there was no reason for her to remain living in Dallas. It wasn't like they lived there. David, who was thirty-two, and his wife, Cheryl, were living in Wisconsin. Her daughter, Bellamy, who was twenty-seven, and her husband, Sam, lived in Syracuse.

Both of her children had followed in their father's footsteps and become medical doctors. Both David and Cheryl were neurosurgeons, and Bellamy was a cardiologist. Her husband, Sam, was CEO of his own finance company. She was proud that both her kids were happily married and doing well in their chosen careers.

When Margie's husband, Ronald Lawson, had died of an aneurysm three years ago, her adult children were both married with lives of their own. Although they had invited her to move in with them, the thought of moving to New York or Wisconsin hadn't appealed to her. Of course, if either David or Bellamy had given her grandkids by now, she might have reconsidered.

She looked at her father and thought, maybe not. Her father needed her more. It had made perfect sense to move back to the town she'd always loved. The only reason she hadn't done so before now was because when they'd married, Ron already had a medical practice in Dallas. Still, they brought the kids to the cove to visit their grandparents every chance they got. There was a time when David and Bellamy would spend the entire summer here with her parents.

Her mother had died fifteen years ago, and her father had pretty much accepted a life alone. For years he'd been active in his church. Now he was six years from turning ninety, and although he'd always had a sharp mind, he'd been hospitalized twice the previous year because he had forgotten to take his medicine. When she retired recently, she made the decision to sell her home in Dallas and move back here.

It didn't take long to get reacquainted with former friends in Catalina Cove. Most of her classmates had moved elsewhere. Like her, they had left for college and never returned other than to visit loved ones during holidays.

Margie had always intended to return after college to work at the hospital here as a nurse practitioner. But then she'd met Ron and fallen in love. They had been married for thirty-five years, and they had been good years.

She went outside to the backyard to check on the plants in her father's flower garden. Originally, it had been her mother's garden and had been the pride of the cove, winning all kinds of awards at the Best of the Flowers Show held each spring.

After her mother's death, her father had made it his life's mission to keep the flowers as beautiful as her mother had. Lately, doing so had become a major challenge for him. He couldn't get down on his knees like he used to do. But she knew this garden brought him a lot of joy and was filled with a lot of good memories for him.

On warmer days, he would often come out and sit on the bench and stare at the rows and rows of immaculate flowers of all kinds and colors. It was during those times that she knew he was probably remembering sitting in that same spot and watching her mother take care of the flowers.

It was only after losing Ron that she fully understood the loneliness her father had faced. Those times when she would call and he would tell her that he was okay, she now knew that he probably wasn't really okay. But then, for the past three years after Ron's death, hadn't she said the same thing to her kids whenever they called to see how she was doing?

A half hour later she went inside to find both her father and Butterball in the kitchen. Her dad was sitting at the table reading one of those sales magazines with Butterball at his feet. Her father often told her how glad he was to have her home, and she'd tell him how glad she was to be here.

He had married her mother late in life and there had been a twelve-year difference in their ages. For years he'd said her mother had kept him young. Eventually, she believed him because just a few years after she died, he seemed to have aged tremendously.

These days, attending church was the only time he left the

house, and his constant companion was Butterball. All of them were convinced that cat had more than nine lives. Butterball had to be at least twenty years old, if not older. Some days Margie thought the cat was slowing down and finally showing signs of his old age. Then on other days, he seemed just as spry as a cat half his age. That was when Butterball would take to roaming the neighborhood and disappear, only to have her father out during all hours of the night looking for him. Margie had always been fearful that someone would mistake her father for a burglar one of those times and—

The doorbell sounded. In a way, she was glad. She didn't want to continue her train of thought. She'd only been back home a month and was grateful some of the neighbors and his church family checked on him periodically.

He'd often told her how his next-door neighbor, a young woman named Bryce Witherspoon, would also check on him and Butterball, and that she would frequently bring him meals from her family's café. Although Bryce had gotten married and moved to the bayou, she still occasionally visited to make sure he was okay.

"It's probably Pastor Dawkins," her father said. "Sometimes he drops by to check on me."

"That's nice of him," Margie said as she headed for the door.

"That's what pastors are supposed to do," was her father's response.

She couldn't help but smile. She was finding out that her father was speaking his mind a lot more these days. But she figured if you lived to be almost eighty-four, you've earned that right.

When she reached the door, she asked, "Who is it?"

"Levi Canady."

She smiled upon opening the door. He was the nice man

who'd helped to find her father and Butterball on Saturday night. Of course, her father had declared he had not been lost and hadn't understood what all the fuss had been about.

"Levi, what a pleasant surprise," she said, inviting him in. She hadn't seen much of him that night because it had been dark, but today she could clearly see that Levi Canady was a very good-looking man. She'd known he was tall, but she hadn't noticed the color of his eyes was a stunning shade of green or that the color of his skin was a coffee-bean brown.

"I just wanted to stop by to check on Mr. Chelsey to see how he's doing and to bring him something that I picked up at the store earlier today."

"Dad and Butterball are in the kitchen," she said, leading the way.

When they reached the kitchen, her father looked up and she said, "Dad, you have a visitor and it's not Pastor Dawkins."

Her father actually smiled when he saw Levi. "Levi, how are you doing?" he asked warmly.

"I'm fine, thanks. I came by to bring you something I think might work whenever Butterball decides he wants to take a little stroll without you."

"What is it?"

Levi pulled something out of the bag he was carrying. "This is a lighted collar. If you turn it on at night and Butterball gets out, it will make finding him easier because the collar lights up. And with this little remote here," he said, showing the gadget he held in his hand, "it makes the collar flash as long as Butterball is within forty feet of you."

"Well, I'll be," her father said, clearly fascinated. "Thanks, son. This is really nice, and it was kind of you to get it for me."

"Don't mention it."

"Dad and I were just about to eat lunch. Would you like to join us?" Margie asked.

"No, thank you. I took Chip into the vet for his regular checkup and now I'm on my way to work."

"I want to again thank you, Levi, for helping me look for Dad the other night and—"

"You didn't have to look for me, Margarita. I was not lost."

Whenever her father used her full name, she knew he was not happy with her. "Oops," she said, sharing a grin with Levi because the two of them knew better. "You are right, Dad. Sorry about that."

Levi hid a grin and said, "I'll be going now. Goodbye, Mr. Chelsey."

"Goodbye, young man."

"And I will see you out." Margie led him from the kitchen.

When they reached the front door, Levi grinned and said, "I need to come by more often. I can't remember the last time someone called me a young man."

Margie laughed. "Compared to Dad you are a young man, and feel free to drop by anytime."

"Thanks. I'll keep that in mind."

Again, she noted how tall he was. He had to be at least six-two, compared to her five-seven height. And he had a head full of hair with gray streaks at the temples. She was tempted to ask his age, but figured that wouldn't be a nice thing to do. If she had to guess, she estimated he was maybe three or four years older than she was. However, he'd said that he cut her parents' yard during the summer as a teen, which would make him older than that.

Another thing she noticed was that whenever he smiled, laugh lines appeared around his eyes and mouth, and they seemed to light up his entire face. No doubt about it, Levi

Canady was a handsome man. The one thing her father had mentioned was that when Levi had been a cop, this area of town was his beat. Her father had also mentioned Levi was a widower. His wife had died a few years ago, but her father couldn't recall what she'd died of.

"Goodbye, Margie." He smiled, showing those laugh lines again.

She smiled back. "Goodbye, Levi."

He was about to turn to leave, but then he said, "If you're ever out and about, why don't you drop by the Green Fig one day this week. We open for lunch and dinner, Mondays through Fridays, and just for lunch on Saturdays."

She raised a brow. "The Green Fig?"

"Yes. It's the restaurant where I work. It sells the most delicious soups you've ever tasted."

"You cook for them?"

He shook his head, chuckling. "No. A young lady by the name of Sierra Crane does most of the cooking. She uses her grandmother's recipes. I'm her assistant manager."

Margie's forehead bunched. "I remember some Cranes from years ago. I graduated with Sidney Crane."

"That is her uncle. Her father's younger brother. He's living in Florida now. Sierra's father, Preston, is a good friend of mine—my best friend, in fact. He and I finished school together. For years Preston managed the only gas station in town."

"I remember Sidney's older brother, Preston," she said. "He began working at that gas station when he was still in high school." And if she recalled, there was a seven-year difference in their ages. If Levi graduated with Preston Crane, did that mean Levi was about seven years older than she? If so, he definitely didn't look it.

"You have a good memory," Levi replied.

Margie thought Levi was friendly and easy to talk to. "I recall his mother, Ms. Ella Marie, too," she said. "She used to make soup from her house and sell it in these cute containers that looked like kegs. I remember Mom and Dad buying her soup all the time. It was delicious."

"Well, Ms. Ella Marie passed her soup recipes on to her granddaughter, and she came back to town a couple of years ago and opened the Green Fig Café, which specializes in all Ms. Ella Marie's soups."

"That's wonderful."

"We even put the take-out orders in those little kegs. Only thing, due to health department rules and restrictions that are now in place, we can't use them for refills."

"Thanks for telling me about the Green Fig, Levi. I might stop by one day this week."

"I hope you do. Sierra and her husband, Vaughn, got married back in March and took a short honeymoon. They left yesterday for a longer one. As assistant manager, I'm in charge while she's gone. That means I'll be working longer hours for the next three weeks. I'll be glad to see you again if you do drop by. Goodbye, Margie."

"Goodbye, Levi."

She closed the door and from the window she could see him walking down the sidewalk and noticed his slight limp. The nurse in her had picked up on it and wondered if it was due to an old injury. But then it just might be arthritis, or Father Arthur, as her dad liked to refer to it. That was one of the reasons she liked staying active and took walks every morning.

Margie smiled when she moved away from the door thinking she would make it a point to patronize the Green Fig one day this week like she'd told Levi she would do.

18

The buzzer on Saint's desk sounded. "Yes, Mrs. Dorsett?"

"Saint, your three o'clock appointment has arrived."

"Please send them in."

After ending the connection, Saint stood and reached for his jacket to slide it on. This appointment was one he was handling in Vaughn's absence. He was meeting with Jaye's brother, Franklin Colfax, whose construction company Reid had chosen for his housing project; and with Colfax's planning manager, a man by the name of Keith Vickers.

Mrs. Dorsett escorted both men into his office. Although Saint hadn't met Keith Vickers before, he immediately recognized him as the guy who'd tried dominating Zara's time on the dance floor Saturday night.

He came from around his desk to shake Franklin's hand and then Keith's after introductions were made. Saint knew the moment when Keith recognized him as the man who'd replaced him with Zara for all of the slow songs. That meant, more than likely, he'd seen the way they danced and their kiss. Hopefully, this guy would assume Zara was taken.

Saint gestured the two men to the chairs in front of his desk. After they were seated, Saint's suspicions were proved correct when Keith said, "I believe I met your girlfriend at Jaye and Velvet's engagement party Saturday night."

If the man expected him to say Zara wasn't his girlfriend, then he would be disappointed. While they were playacting their affair she was off-limits. "Yes, Zara loves dancing. I saw you managed to keep up with her, which isn't always an easy thing to do on the dance floor," he said, grinning.

There…he had let Keith know he'd been aware of him dancing with Zara, and that he didn't have a problem with it. What if he'd left the party like he'd almost done? Would Zara have danced those slow songs with Keith?

Saint leaned back in his chair. The thought that she might have bothered him. But who she danced with shouldn't have been any of his business. Yet, that was before. The reason he could make it his business now was because of their fake affair. So far, it was working. When he'd arrived at the Witherspoon Café this morning, Debbie Witherspoon had commented on how good he and Zara had looked dancing together and she thought they made a lovely couple.

"I understand your entire work crew will arrive in town in a week," Saint was saying.

Franklin smiled. "Yes. Keith and I are ready to get things started."

Saint knew all about Reid's vision. It would be a luxurious gated community of grandiose homes. Although each property owner could build the house of their dreams, all the houses had to be energy efficient and have smart home features. Also, the architectural design had to blend in with Catalina Cove's French, Spanish, Creole and American style.

A number of celebrities had made purchases. A few had inquired but hadn't liked the restrictions on the style and design of house they could build. Reid had no problem telling them, in that case, Catalina Cove wasn't for them. His intent was to retain the grace, beauty and classiness of the cove. Reid and his wife, Gloria, had purchased the largest oceanfront lot for themselves. Like Vaughn, the older man would be listing his mansion with the Historical Society sometime within the next two years.

Less than an hour later the meeting ended. It had gone well. He liked Franklin and soon discovered that he liked Keith as well. There was no reason not to. After the men left, he wondered how things were going for Zara with packing. He picked up his cell phone to find out, appreciating that he had her number and could now call her whenever he liked.

"Saint?"

She must have added him to her phone contacts already or had assigned him a special ring. Why did the thought of that please him?

"Yes, Zara. I was wondering how the packing is going?"

"Great. I decided to start on my parents' room first. A part of me wished I'd done so long ago, but after packing up their home in Paris, Vaughn and I put off going through any of their belongings here. I've packed up a lot of stuff. I will be donating some of the boxes to Goodwill."

"It sounds like you've been busy. I planned to leave work in a couple of hours and wondered if you were hungry. I can grab takeout for you."

"That's kind and thoughtful of you, Saint, and that would be wonderful. I finished all the packing that I intend to do today and will be heading to the cottage in an hour. That will give me time to shower and change before you arrive."

At the mention of a shower, he vividly recalled the times they'd showered together and felt a heated rush at those memories. "Do you have a taste for any particular thing?"

"Yes, crab cakes, fries and coleslaw from LaFitte's Seafood House."

He chuckled. "Sounds good. Next time you have a taste for crab cakes, I have my grandmother's recipe and will be happy to prepare them for you."

"So, you're good in the kitchen?"

"Not to sound boastful, but haven't you realized by now that I'm good at a number of things, Zara?"

She was quiet for a moment and then she said, "Trust me. I have realized it, Saint."

It pleased him that she had. "I'll see you in a few, sweetheart."

"Okay. I'll be at the cottage waiting."

When he ended the call, he noted that he'd used a term of endearment for the second time that day. The thought that he'd done so didn't bother him. Besides, for the time being while engaged in this fake affair, she was his sweetheart.

He leaned back in his chair thinking that earlier that day, he'd gone to the Green Fig for a late lunch. Every once in a while, Levi would drop by his table to shoot the breeze. At some point Levi mentioned running into a woman Saturday night on his walk home from the party by the name of Margarita Lawson.

The woman, who went by Margie, was the daughter of Mr. Chelsey. Everyone in the cove knew Alton Chelsey since he'd been Catalina Cove's mailman for years before retiring. Saint observed Levi's features when he talked about Margie.

He wondered if that sparkle in the older man's eyes meant he liked her. It definitely sounded that way.

As Saint got back to work, the thought that Levi might be smitten at his age was good news. It couldn't happen to a nicer guy.

Zara knew the moment Saint punched in the access code to her property. It had been thoughtful of him to offer to bring her dinner. She had accomplished a lot that day and hadn't bothered to stop for lunch since she'd eaten a hearty breakfast with Saint.

She smiled when thoughts of him filled her mind. Although he hadn't mentioned it, she had noticed several people in the restaurant staring at them this morning. That meant word had gotten out about their kiss. At first, the thought of a fake affair had turned her off, but then she had to admit she had no problem keeping the women out of Saint's face while she was in town. In other words, she liked having him all to herself. The women could resume competing for his attention after she returned to Boston.

Before leaving her bedroom, Zara briefly inspected her reflection in the full-length mirror. She was wearing a pair of shorts and a floral print top. Beneath her shorts was her two-piece bathing suit. Before leaving Zara's Haven she had sent Saint a text inviting him to go swimming with her if he was interested. He had texted her back that he was definitely interested.

When she got to the living room, she glimpsed out the window and saw Saint walking across the pier. He had changed from his suit and was wearing a pair of khaki shorts and a T-shirt. In one hand was a big bag with the take-out food. In the other was an overnight bag. She never had to invite him to spend the night since she'd told him he was always welcome to do so. To the outside world, those intent on getting into their business, they were pretending to be girlfriend and boyfriend. In essence, they were lovers in every scope of the word.

While watching him, she saw the swagger in his walk and thought it was sexy as hell. She fully understood why the single women in the cove would be vying for his attention. He had a lot going for him. Good looks, good job, nice personality, respectability and every single thing any sound-minded woman would want in a man. She also knew he had the ability to rock a woman's world in the bedroom.

Deciding not to wait for him to knock on the door, she went outside to stand on the porch. When he reached the end of the pier and saw her, a huge smile spread across his face. That Evans Toussaint smile almost took her breath away. She then recalled during their earlier phone conversation he had used the term of endearment again. It sounded natural and she'd liked it.

"You must be starving," he said.

Zara tilted her head and grinned. She was starving alright, and it wasn't just for what was in that take-out bag. "Yes, you can say that. I notice there's only one food container in that bag."

"I ate a late lunch at the Green Fig. Besides, I got a lot of barbecue ribs left from yesterday when I grilled for the folks," he said.

He'd told her it had been years since he'd been in the cove on Memorial Day. Usually, he waited to come home for two weeks around the Christmas holidays and for three weeks during the summer in July.

Maurice had only visited Catalina Cove once. It had been the year Vaughn had moved back, and she'd wanted to spend the holidays with him. Maurice had wanted her to spend the holidays in Paris with him. When she'd refused and told him it would be a good opportunity to meet her brother, he had relented. Although Vaughn never said anything to her, she knew he hadn't cared for Maurice. His arrogance was a turn-off for most people. He came from money and wanted everybody to know it.

When Saint reached her, she patted his chin. "Thanks for bringing this to me. You're such a nice pretend boyfriend," she said, taking the bag he handed to her.

"You think so?"

"I most certainly do. Come on inside. You can keep me company while I eat since you're not hungry."

The look he slanted her had heat curling up inside her. Without saying a word, that look let her know that he might not be hungry for food, but he was definitely hungry for her.

He followed her inside, placing his overnight bag on the coffee table then trailing her to the kitchen. "You sure you don't want anything? I have no problem sharing," she said.

"I know you don't. You're the most giving person I know, Zara."

She thought that was a sweet thing for him to say. She looked at him over her shoulder and smiled as her body heated up a little more under his regard. "If you don't mind, please pour us glasses of wine," she said.

"I don't mind."

As she sat at the kitchen table, she saw how easily he moved around her kitchen and with such familiarity. That was understandable since he'd been there several times, and she always relished his presence in the cottage.

"Did you finish that painting?" he asked.

She knew which one he was asking about. The one of the vacant building. "Yes, I finished it and I plan to give it to you as a gift before I leave."

When he headed toward her with the full glasses, she said, "It's such a pretty day. Let's sit outside on the back porch."

"Okay."

Settling into the chair at the patio table, she was glad she suggested they sit out here. The view of Pelican Bay was gorgeous, and this time of year was when the pelicans returned from their winter trip south. They were breathtaking and she understood why her mother liked painting them so much. Across from the table were wooden patio chairs and chaise lounges that faced the shimmering blue waters of the bay. On nice evenings she would sit in one of the chairs and read a book while drinking a glass of wine.

"You were right. It's nice out here," he said.

She glanced at Saint. "I will admit this is the one thing I miss about living in Catalina Cove. The number of beautiful days there are. I talked to Sherri this morning and it's been snowing in Boston every day since the weekend."

His brow arched. "Is that normal to get snow this late in the year there?"

"Not normal, but it snowed in May years ago. I'm glad I'm here and not there."

"I'm glad you're here, too."

An unexpected measure of appreciation flowed through her. He probably hadn't meant anything with his words, but they made her heart thump in her chest anyway.

He took a sip of wine and she watched him. She grew aroused watching how his lips fit on the glass. Then she recalled all the things those hands holding the wineglass could do to her, had done to her. Just thinking about it made her body throb.

"I saw that guy today."

She switched her gaze from Saint's hand to his face. "What guy?"

"The one you danced with on Saturday."

"Keith?"

"Yes."

Did she detect irritation in his voice? "Where did you see him?"

"I had a meeting with him and Franklin Colfax. He's the planning manager for Colfax Construction Company."

"That's right. I recall he had mentioned that." She also recalled what Sierra had said about Saint watching her and Keith dance.

"He did a good job of keeping up with you on the dance floor."

She grinned. "Yes, he did." Wanting to drop the subject of her and Keith dancing, she said, "These crab cakes are delicious. You sure you don't want one?"

He looked down at her plate. "I guess you can give me a tiny piece of one."

"No problem." She broke off a section of crab cake and offered it to him.

"Feed it to me, Zara."

Lifting the morsel, she placed it to his lips. When he opened his mouth to accept it, she drew in a sharp breath when the warm tip of his tongue licked her fingers. He held her gaze as he slowly chewed the food. "You're right. It's delicious."

She sat there transfixed and only blinked when he said, "Look over there."

Her gaze followed where he was pointing and saw the sun

going down across Pelican Bay. It was an awe-inspiring sight. "It's beautiful, isn't it?" she asked him.

"Yes, and so are you."

She looked at him and smiled. "You say the nicest things to me."

"And all of them are true."

"Thank you."

When she finished eating, she asked, "Are you ready to go swimming now?"

He stood as she gathered up the trash. "When it comes to you, Zara. I'm always ready."

Since he was standing, her eye level was below his waist. She saw what he meant when she took note of his aroused body.

She met his gaze. "I'm always ready, too."

When he smiled, she knew he'd gotten her meaning just like she'd gotten his. They weren't talking about swimming.

Levi settled into his favorite wingback chair in front of the television. The national news from the station in New Orleans was about to come on and he was ready to watch it. Chip had been fed and walked and he was ready, too.

He took a sip of beer while thinking that today things had run smoothly at the Green Fig. He figured a number of people were still in town for the Memorial Day weekend, which accounted for the increase in business for a Tuesday. All the waitresses and waiters had reported to work today, and knowing he had a full staff was always good.

Like most mornings, he'd gotten up around eight and walked Chip before getting dressed for work. Today he had left early to take Chip to the vet. Then he'd stopped by the pet shop to get that lighted cat collar for Mr. Chelsey's cat.

He had given himself enough leeway to drop it off and still get to work on time.

The staff of the Green Fig usually arrived thirty minutes before they opened at noon for the take-out-only lunch crowd. The café had opened three years ago and was doing well. The soups were always tasty, and everyone employed by the Green Fig always provided good customer service. Sierra wouldn't have it any other way. People always came back and told others. They'd discovered word-of-mouth satisfaction was the best form of advertisement. Today a couple had driven all the way from New Orleans. They thought the take-out kegs of soup were cute and a novel idea.

He sipped his beer and his thoughts shifted to Margie. He had appreciated seeing her again. It had been dark Saturday night and the streetlights hadn't given her much justice. In the brightness of daylight, he saw just how attractive she was. He could remember her as a young girl who would often sit on her parents' porch and watch when he cut their yard.

Back then, he'd barely paid her any attention, but the grown-up Margarita, or Margie, had caught his attention—and held it tight. He recalled her saying that she was now retired and had moved back to the cove to take care of Mr. Chelsey. That was thoughtful of her to take on that responsibility.

He would want to believe if his and Lydia's only daughter had lived, she would have grown up to return to the cove on occasion to check on him. Heck, he would have hoped that Dasha, who'd died of an asthma attack before her second birthday, would have been a daddy's girl and never thought of moving away like all the other young people in the cove usually did once they finished high school.

He would admit it got lonely living here without Lydia.

They'd had a good marriage that had lasted over twenty years. He was glad they'd finally gone on that cruise out of New Orleans they'd always talked about. She had deserved it. After he was shot, he didn't know what he would have done if she had not stuck with him all through the rehabilitation period.

She had not given up on him and had refused to let him give up on himself. It was only with her love and support that he'd walked again. He had taken her death hard when she'd suddenly passed away of a heart attack close to twelve years ago.

As he took another sip of beer his thoughts shifted back to Margie. Saturday night she'd said her last name was Lawson. She wasn't wearing a ring so he figured she was no longer married. Was she divorced? A widow? He figured Emma, head cook at the Green Fig, would know, since she seemed to know about most people's business in the cove. However, he didn't want to put ideas in her head if he were to ask.

Levi had been alone for a long time and preferred things this way. He'd decided years ago after losing Lydia that he would never remarry. One woman in his lifetime had been enough for him, and he doubted he had the ability to love anyone else. His heart was one and done with Lydia. But then he would admit he had liked talking to Margie.

And she was pretty. Very pretty.

Smiling came easy for her and she had a friendly disposition. She wasn't pushy, either. He recalled that Lydia hadn't been buried a good week before the women began calling, offering to bake him pies and inviting him to dinner.

He declined all of it and told them he knew how to bake his own pies and cook his own dinner. Pretty soon they stopped calling and he was glad of it. He did things to keep busy and was satisfied with that. And when he began feeling lonely, he had Chip.

Hours later, after watching the news and several of those crime shows back to back, it was time for him to go to bed. Getting up from his chair, he headed for the bedroom. When he'd finally settled between the sheets and closed his eyes, for the first time it wasn't Lydia's face he saw that night.

It was that of Margie.

19

Saint jumped into the water thinking it had been years since he'd gone swimming at night, but here he was doing that very thing. After they'd made love, Zara had been determined to go swimming and he had no problem joining her.

"How does the water feel, Saint?"

Treading water, he turned around and admired her two-piece bathing suit. As cute as it looked on her, he didn't intend for it to stay on her for long. Besides, with as much skin as it was showing, she might as well swim without it anyway. It didn't matter that he'd seen her naked a lot tonight. He would never tire of seeing her exposed body.

"The water feels good. For some reason the bay always seems warmer than the ocean," he said.

The moon shone overhead, and stars lit up a velvety sky. Zara had dimmed the floodlights around the yard, providing the perfect ambience for a nighttime swim. The setting was ideal.

"Okay, then. Here I come."

He watched her dive into the water with the expertise of

an Olympic aquanaut and the gracefulness of a swan. He immediately knew she was one hell of a swimmer. She surfaced with ease and tilted her body to glide toward him. He welcomed her with open arms.

She smiled and pushed hair from her face. "You're right. The water feels good." She reached out and ran a hand along his chest and stomach. "You feel good."

He thought she felt good, too. When her hand explored below his waist he became amused when she realized he was completely naked. "Evans Toussaint! Where are your swimming trunks?"

"Over there," he said, tilting his head toward the porch where he'd draped them on one of the chairs. "I prefer swimming without them."

She grinned. "Don't you think that's a bit scandalous?"

"Sweetheart, didn't you know today is Temptation Tuesday?" he whispered, leaning close and licking the sensitive area below her ear.

"Temptation Tuesday?" she inquired with a breathless sigh.

"Yes. Some refer to it as Tantalizing Tuesday. Others think of it as Thrilling Tuesday."

She looked at him and held his gaze. He was still holding her at the waist, and her body felt good next to his. "What do you think of it as, Saint?"

He smiled. "I think of it as just what I intend to make it for you. Terrific Tuesday."

He lowered his head and captured her mouth with his as if he wanted to swallow her whole. They had made love earlier, several times. He kissed her with a hunger that was filled with a need he could only associate with her. Why was he so addicted to her kiss? To everything about her? Suddenly, he knew why. He was allowing her to do something he swore he wouldn't allow another woman to do. Get under his skin.

That realization had him breaking off the kiss. However, he still held her in his arms, unable for the time being to release her. According to their plans for the week, they would have lunch together on Friday. He needed to put distance between them until then. Somehow, over the next two days he had to pull himself together, collect his senses and remind himself that she didn't want anything serious and neither did he. They both had been there and done that and preferred not to go there again. All they wanted was to enjoy each other sexually. That kind of arrangement might not work for some, but it worked for them.

He had said he intended to make this a Terrific Tuesday and would keep his word. "Come on, it's getting late. Let's swim back and forth for a while," he whispered against her ear.

"Alright."

They did for a half hour and then he drew her into his arms and carried her to the bay's shore where he'd placed a huge towel earlier. He was already naked and it didn't take long to remove her skimpy and sexy bathing suit. When he joined her on the towel the need to make love to her again was so strong it nearly took his breath away.

Then he remembered. "I need to grab a condom."

"No, you don't, unless you truly want to. I'm safe and I believe you are, too. And I'm on birth control."

Saint truly didn't want to, although he knew he should. Being skin to skin inside her could make the situation between them worse. Hadn't he felt the need to take time to pull himself together over the next couple of days where she was concerned because she was getting under his skin? What she was suggesting would be like pouring kerosene on an already blazing fire. However, at that moment he was too weak to resist her offer.

"I'm all in, Zara, if you're sure."

"I'm sure, Saint. That's how I want you. All in. No pun intended."

His hand cupped the side of her face, and he leaned in and kissed her hungrily as a need consumed every inch of his flesh. She tasted hot, delicious and all woman, and at that moment he wanted as much of her as he could get. It didn't matter that they'd made love mere hours ago. He wanted her again. He needed her again.

This kiss was burning out of control, and he pressed her back onto the beach towel. Pulling his mouth away he began licking her throat, reveling in all the sensations he was feeling. He wanted more. Positioning his body between her open legs, his hands slid around her back and curved around her backside and lifted her as he thrust inside her. When he'd gone as deep as he could go, the thrusting began, and he couldn't hold back the guttural sound stemming from deep within his throat. Nor could he suppress the emotions that were unleashed by being inside her, skin to skin.

"Saint…"

She'd moaned his name and the sound made his hunger for her become ravenous. The feel of her inner muscles gripping him while in the most intimate part of her had him moaning her name as well. "Zara…"

She was always an equal participant in their lovemaking, refusing to let him make love to her without making love to him. Their eyes met and she lifted her arms to wrap around his neck and began licking around his mouth, chin and neck, while lifting her body to receive each one of his thrusts.

As he continued to rock against her, over and over, he knew

the exact moment an orgasm of extreme power slammed into each of them. The same degree of lust consuming his senses had taken over hers. More than just pushing him over the edge, Zara had taken him to another universe.

"Saint!"

She screamed his name when another orgasm hit her, and her tremors caused another to detonate inside him as well. When he finally got the quivers of his body under control, he pulled her into his arms. Even with wet hair and swollen lips from his kisses, he thought she looked breathtaking. It took a while before he was able to finally speak. "Did I make it terrific for you, Zara?" he whispered against her lips.

"Yes," she said, licking the side of his neck, chin and lips again. "It was tempting, tantalizing and terrific all rolled into one."

Smiling, he leaned forward to kiss her again.

Two days later Zara was walking into the arts-and-crafts store on the boardwalk. "Good morning, Ms. Fanny."

The older woman greeted her with a huge smile. "You've run out of paint already, Zara?"

Zara chuckled. "No, I'm starting something new and need additional colors." She had decided to paint a portrait of Saint without him posing for it. She would do it from memory. That shouldn't be hard to do since she had such vivid images of him in her nightly dreams.

Tuesday night had been as terrific as he'd set out to make it. However, he hadn't stayed overnight, like she assumed from the overnight bag he'd brought with him. Why he'd changed his mind she wasn't sure. She couldn't think of a single thing that would have made him leave after they'd made love on shore after their swim, showered together and then made love again.

Maybe she was overthinking things. It could have been that he had an early-morning meeting Wednesday that he'd forgotten about. When he'd left, he told her he would see her on Friday, which indicated he wouldn't be seeing her again before their scheduled lunch. He had told her to call him if she needed help moving boxes. She had spent yesterday packing for the second straight day and decided to take a break today and paint.

She had made her purchases and was walking back to where she'd parked her car when she heard her name being called. Shading her eyes from the brightness of the sun, she saw it was Samantha Groover. What on earth did the woman want with her?

They'd never been introduced. Zara only knew who she was because Sierra had pointed her out to her at the engagement party. She recalled that Samantha had been trying to get Saint's attention every chance she got, the same woman who apparently told other women she had an advantage over their interest in Saint because he'd once had a crush on her in the sixth grade. Like that truly mattered.

"Zara?" the woman asked when she came to a stop in front of her.

Zara pasted a smile to her lips, wondering why the woman looked upset. "Yes. And you are?" she asked, refusing to let the woman know she already knew who she was.

"I'm Samantha Groover."

She offered Samantha her hand, but the woman didn't take it. Instead, she said, "You know what I detest about rich women like you?"

She was about to tell Samantha that she didn't even know her, but curiosity made her say, "No, what?"

"They think money can buy them anything. Personally, I

think it's pretty selfish of you to waltz into town and decide Saint will be your flavor for the month. He's a swell guy and is only dating you because you threw yourself at him. Anybody who knows Saint can see that you're not his type."

Zara fought back rolling her eyes. "And I guess you know his type."

"Yes. Saint needs a woman who will have a permanent place in his life. Not someone who's in town one minute and out the next. You only want him because he's available."

Zara tilted her head. "You honestly believe that?"

"Why not? Rumor has it that your boyfriend recently dumped you and you're in town licking your wounds."

She wondered where this woman got such misinformation. Her breakup with Maurice was over two years ago. "Look, Samantha. If you have a problem with me spending time with Saint, then I suggest you talk to him about it. He's a grown man who makes his own decisions about who he wants to be with. Have a good day."

With that, Zara turned and walked off. Had it been so blatantly obvious to anyone who'd watched them dance just how much she'd wanted Saint that night? What had she expected when she'd kissed him in front of everyone the way she had? Jeez. No wonder Saint had suggested they pretend to be having an affair. Her behavior that night had dictated it.

Still, like she'd told the woman, if she had an issue with her and Saint dating, then that was something she needed to address with Saint. Just in case Samantha didn't, Zara had every intention of telling him herself.

Saint quickly walked across the pier toward the cottage. He'd been surprised to get the text message from Zara. All it said was, **We need to talk!!**

Those two exclamation points were a good indication that whatever they needed to discuss was serious. He'd tried calling her, but she hadn't picked up. What was that about? What in the hell was going on? Was she upset that he hadn't stayed the other night? He honestly didn't think so. One thing he knew about Zara was that she wasn't the clingy type. If that wasn't it, then what was?

Tuesday night he had been consumed with a need for her the likes of which he couldn't define. He'd long ago accepted this thing between them defied logic, but what he'd felt Tuesday night was playing with emotions he'd declared null and void after Mia. It had scared him.

He was an in-control kind of guy and, granted, he'd lost some of that control with Zara, but he was determined not to lose all of it. When he felt emotions clouding his senses, he knew he had to put some distance between them. He was glad it had worked because now he felt more in control of his senses again.

As he made his way across the pier, he figured she knew he was coming the minute he'd entered the access code. When he got halfway across the pier, he saw her. She'd stepped out onto the porch with her arms folded over her chest. She was wearing a blouse and jeans, standing with her legs braced apart. She didn't look happy. No. She appeared to be in a fighting mode, something he'd never seen her in before. *What the hell...*

Concern consumed him. She was upset. She looked angry. He walked up the steps and when he reached for her, she took a step back. That was something else she'd never done before. "What's wrong, Zara? You had me worried when you didn't answer my call."

She lifted her chin. "I needed time to calm down."

He lifted a brow. "Calm down? What happened?"

"Today I was confronted by Samantha."

"Samantha?"

"Yes, Samantha Groover. You know, the woman who kept getting all in your face at the engagement party. The woman who thinks since you had a crush on her in the sixth grade that it means something now. Well, she thinks I should back off from you."

"What!"

"You heard me."

Saint rubbed a hand down his face. "Let's go inside, and I want you to start from the beginning and tell me everything."

"So, there you have it, Saint. I don't need or want that kind of drama."

He crossed the room and pulled her into his arms. This time, she let him. "No, you don't, and I'm sorry for it. Samantha had no right to say that to you, and I'm glad you told me about it."

She pulled back and stared up at him. He could see anger still in her eyes. "Of course I was going to tell you about it. Samantha Groover thinks you need a woman who wants a permanent place in your life, and I'm in the way of that happening."

"You of all people know better than that."

"Yes, but it wasn't my place to tell her."

"No, it wasn't, and I will handle it."

He tugged her back into his arms and neither said anything for a long moment. Then she stepped back again. The anger he'd seen in her eyes earlier had dissipated some. "People like Samantha were the reason you wanted us to pretend we were having an affair, wasn't it?"

"Yes," Saint said.

Although he hadn't said anything to Zara, Samantha's words reminded him of what his mother had said to him on Monday. Not verbatim, but too close to suit him. Had Irene Toussaint shared those same thoughts with Samantha?

"The one thing that bothers me, Saint, is the fact when I do leave Catalina Cove it will be as if everything she accused me of will appear true. That while I'm here temporarily, I'm only with you because you're available."

"And we both know that isn't true. We have a history they don't know about."

"Yes, but what happens when I leave? They're going to think I'm just another woman who broke your heart."

"And we will know better. You're the woman who helped heal my broken heart."

A smile touched her lips. "And you're the man who helped to heal mine."

It was the first smile she'd given him since he'd arrived. It was a small smile, but he would take it. And he would take this, too, he thought as he lowered his mouth to hers.

Margie entered the Green Fig and saw how busy it was. However, she noted most of the customers were standing at the take-out line. She had tried persuading her father to join her here for dinner, but he hadn't wanted to miss reruns of *Oprah*, which he saw at four every day.

She offered to record it for him, but he said he preferred seeing it when it happened. She didn't bother reminding him those were old shows from twenty or so years ago, but figured he knew that and hadn't wanted to be bothered. He'd asked her to bring him back a bowl of whatever the special of the day was. He'd eaten here before and liked their soup.

"Hello, welcome to the Green Fig. Will someone else be joining you or will you be dining alone?" a waitress asked.

"I'll be dining alone."

"This way, please."

Margie followed the woman and glanced around. It was a nice restaurant. She loved the decor and liked how the booths were set up as well. She slid into the seat and found it quite comfortable. A menu was placed in front of her.

"What would you like to drink?"

She glanced up at the young woman who looked to be around college age. "I'll have a cup of herbal tea."

"I'll bring it right out." The young woman did in a timely manner and Margie thought that was good customer service.

She studied the menu and thought the soups listed sounded delicious. She decided to try the cabbage and bacon soup. She recalled it had been her favorite of all Ms. Ella Marie's soups. If her granddaughter could make soups as well as her grandmother, then Margie figured she was in for a treat. The picture of it on the menu looked scrumptious and it was served with hot garlic bread.

"Hello, Margie. Glad you've decided to pay us a visit."

She looked up into the smiling face of Levi Canady. "Yes, and from the menu everything looks delicious."

"It is. What have you decided?"

"I think I'll try the cabbage and bacon soup."

"Good choice. And how is Mr. Chelsey?"

"Dad is fine, and he loves that collar you bought for Butterball. I love it, too, and it's working fantastically. Now when Butterball gets out and wants to prowl, he doesn't get far because you can't miss him all lit up like a Christmas tree." She grinned.

Levi returned her smile. "I'm glad, and I'll let your server know of your choice of soup. Bread, hot from the oven, will be delivered to you shortly."

"Thank you, and Dad asked me to bring back your Thursday soup of the day."

"That's broccoli and cheese today. I'll let your waitress know."

When he turned to walk off, she called out to him. "Levi?"

He turned around. "Yes, Margie?"

"I'd like to invite you over for dinner on Sunday." And not wanting him to think she was being too forward, she added, "To thank you for getting that collar for Butterball."

He shoved his hands into his pockets. "Your dad thanked me and that was all the thanks I needed. To be quite honest, he really didn't have to. Like I said, he would help me out when he let me cut your parents' yard as a kid. He knew how much I needed the money."

That was something else her father had told her. Levi's father had been an alcoholic. His parents barely got by because of the money his father used to buy booze instead of taking care of his family. The man had died when Levi had been fourteen, and he and his mother had to move in with his paternal grandparents.

"Does that mean you won't be coming to dinner?" she asked, trying to keep the disappointment out of her voice.

"No, it doesn't mean that at all. I would love to come, and I appreciate the invite. I just don't want you to think you owe me a meal because of that cat collar."

She smiled. "Would it help matters if I said I'd like to invite you because I think you're a nice person?"

"Yes, and I'm looking forward to it. What time do you want me there?"

"What about around three? Dad likes to eat not long after he gets home from church."

"Three will be fine. Do you need me to bring anything?"

"No. Are you allergic to any foods?"

"None that I know of."

"Great! I'll see you Sunday at three."

Levi turned to walk off, then turned back to say, "Again, thanks for the dinner invitation, and I'm glad you decided to dine at the Green Fig today. I hope it's not your last time."

"It won't be," she replied.

Levi held her gaze for a long moment as if what she'd said had a double meaning for him. He gave her a smile that warmed her insides, before nodding and walking away.

20

Zara had slipped between the bedsheets when her cell phone rang. She recognized the ringtone. It was Saint. "Hello."

"Hello, Zara. You won't have to worry about Samantha confronting you about me again."

A part of her wondered what he'd said to Samantha. Then another part didn't want to know. He was a problem solver. It was his problem and he'd handled it. "Thanks."

"And just so you know, I also talked with my mom."

She raised a brow. "Your mom?"

"Yes. I figured Samantha had gotten some of her ideas and assumptions from her."

Zara released a deep sigh. "You did say on more than one occasion that your mother wanted grandkids, and she was sending single women your way. I can understand her wanting you to be involved with someone in a more serious way, Saint. Like everyone else, she knows I'm only in town temporarily."

"Like I told her again tonight. The choice of the woman I want to be involved with is not hers to make. It's mine." He paused a moment and then asked, "We're still on for lunch tomorrow, right?"

"Yes, we're still on."

"I have a meeting at ten, but it should be over around noon. You pick the place and I'll meet you there."

"Umm, what about Andrew's?" she suggested. "I heard it's getting good reviews."

Andrew's recently opened in the cove. Andrew Bertelli had been born and raised in Catalina Cove. Like others, he left for college and never returned. For the past ten years he'd received numerous awards and recognition as a top chef in New York. Thanks to a Reid Lacroix low-interest loan, Andrew had purchased an unoccupied warehouse near the shipping district and transformed it into an impressive two-story Italian restaurant. It opened last month and was getting a steady stream of satisfied customers.

"Then Andrew's it is," he said. "I ate there with Vaughn and Reid when it first opened. The food was excellent. You won't be disappointed."

"I know I won't be."

"I have another idea, too. How about dinner at my place on Sunday?" he asked.

"At your place?"

"Yes."

She'd never been to his home before. Had never assumed she would get an invitation. "Dinner at your place on Sunday sounds great."

"By the way, how did packing go today?"

"I didn't do any today. Since I'd packed two days straight, I decided to take a day off to paint. I was leaving Ms. Fanny's art supply store when I ran into Samantha."

There was no need to tell him that her encounter with

the woman had ruined her entire day, and she hadn't felt like painting after that. "Instead of painting, I relaxed in one of the chaise lounges and read a book. As usual, the view of the bay was spectacular, and it felt good to just relax and read."

"Did you read anything interesting?"

"Not unless you're into romance novels."

The sound of his chuckle made her breath catch. She wondered how long it would last, her total awareness of him whether he was near or far, seen or unseen, naked or clothed. Even the sound of his voice over the phone stirred desire within her.

"Unfortunately, I'm not," he said.

She was tempted to tell him regardless of whether he was into them, he could definitely be a romance hero in any novel that she'd ever read. "I can't wait to see your home on Sunday, Saint."

"Nothing fancy. I bought it for all the land that came with it. Five acres. The location works for me since it's halfway between town and my parents' home."

"It's on the bayou, right?" she asked.

"Not right on the bayou but close enough."

"So, what will we be having for dinner on Sunday, Saint?"

"I haven't decided. What would you like?"

"Umm, surprise me," she said in an amused tone.

"Okay, I can do that."

They talked a little while longer about various topics. She told him she'd gotten a call from Vaughn to say they'd arrived in the Maldives and that he and Sierra were having a wonderful time.

"I'm glad to hear that. He hasn't called into the office, which means he's giving his wife all of his attention."

"And that's the way it should be. I'm sure he knows he left the place in capable hands," Zara said.

"Thanks for the vote of confidence. I'd better let you turn in. It's almost midnight."

She couldn't believe they had talked on the phone that long. "It is, isn't it. I hadn't realized it had gotten so late."

"Good night, Zara. Pleasant dreams, and I'll see you for lunch tomorrow."

"Good night, Saint."

After ending the call, Zara realized that it was the first time she and Saint had engaged in a telephone conversation that lasted more than five minutes. And she had enjoyed it.

Saint peeked over the top of his menu and asked, "See anything you like?"

Zara smiled. "Yes, plenty. But I think I'm going to get the lasagna. I've heard from Donna Elloran how good it is. What about you?"

"I think I'll have the chicken and mushroom ravioli." He placed his menu on the table. "I heard it was good as well."

He took a sip of wine and looked at Zara. She had arrived at Andrew's before him, and the moment he'd walked in and scanned the restaurant, he'd seen her. As usual, she looked beautiful. The way she had styled her hair emphasized her high cheekbones, fine straight nose and what he thought were kissable, well-shaped lips.

Her beauty held a sensuality that drew him to her like a powerful magnet. Regardless of whether he wanted it to or not. Mia had been pretty as well, but there was something about Zara's beauty that he couldn't define. It was more than surface beauty. Since getting to know her he'd gotten to know her inner beauty, too.

He was glad she had been satisfied with his handling of the Samantha Groover issue and hadn't asked any questions about it. He wasn't sure what foolishness his mother had led Samantha to believe, but she had honestly assumed the only competition she would face in her pursuit of him was from Mia, whom his mother felt he was still carrying a torch for.

Samantha even admitted to confronting Kristen Hunt and Robin Dyer. Now he knew why those women had backed off. Not that he had a problem with that. However, he had a problem with Samantha assuming she had any dibs on him at all. He had told her in no uncertain terms that she didn't, and that she owed those women an apology for making them feel that she did. He told her that he wasn't interested in her, and the only woman he was interested in dating was Zara. At the end he felt she'd gotten the message loud and clear.

To be honest, he still wasn't sure his mother had gotten that same message. Although she'd been appalled that Samantha had confronted Zara and those other women about staying away from him, she was still concerned he would be deeply hurt when Zara left town. She had a feeling the relationship meant more to him than it did to her. Again, he had stressed to his mother that the woman he chose to share his life, no matter how long or short the period of time that would be, was his decision to make and not hers.

He blinked, noticing Zara's lips were moving. "Excuse me? What did you say?"

She smiled—that smile to him was bewitching, beguiling. Simply adorable.

"I said that I had company while packing today."

"You did?" he asked, reaching for one of the slices of fo-caccia from the basket the waitress had placed on the table.

"Yes. Donna dropped by. She was excited because they

found out their baby is going to be a girl. That's what they were hoping for, a little sister for Ike."

He smiled. "I'm happy for them."

"So am I, and I could have bottled her excitement. They already have a name picked out but won't be sharing it with anyone until the baby is born." She tilted her head and said, "And speaking of names, how did you become an Evans instead of just an Evan?"

She wasn't the first person to ask him that. "Evans was my mother's maiden name and she wanted me to have it."

"Makes sense, but I like you as Saint."

"I think most people do. My paternal grandmother began calling me that. She claimed I was such a good baby. Besides, it was the last five letters of my last name. The nickname stuck. Did you ever have a nickname?"

She shook her head. "Nope. I was named after my great-great-great-grandmother, Princess Zara. My parents took great honor in that and even called me Princess Zara at times."

After chewing his piece of focaccia and washing it down with another sip of wine, he said, "I recall studying about the kidnapped African princess in school. As you know, Catalina Cove's history was a required subject."

"Yes, I do recall that. Of course, I'd grown up hearing about Princess Zara long before I went to school. Trust me when I say my parents had convinced me I was special." She chuckled as she dipped a piece of focaccia in garlic oil before taking a bite.

Saint watched the tantalizing movement of her mouth. When she licked a drop of oil from her lips with the tip of her tongue, he felt a hardness press against his zipper and twisted in his seat. "According to the story," he said, "Princess Zara Musa was a beautiful African princess on a ship sailing to the

Caribbean. LaFitte captured the ship, decided he wanted the princess for himself, kidnapped her and brought her to his home here in Catalina Cove. He married her and built her one of the most magnificent houses in the cove, which he named Zara's Haven. Together they had six children, of which you and Vaughn are descendants."

A huge smile lit up her face. "Yes, but it was only proven last year that he'd married Princess Zara. For years, some claimed she was just one of his many mistresses. I'm glad Sierra and Vaughn found the authentic marriage license."

At that moment the waitress came to take their order. After she walked off, Saint leaned back in his chair and said, "Princess." He thought of saying Angel, the name she'd used when they'd first met, but now he thought she looked more like a princess than an angel. "I like that name for you."

"Why? Because of Princess Zara?"

"No, because I see you as a princess."

She tilted her head. "I don't think I act like a princess. At least all through my life I've tried not to. My parents were snobs, and I know and accept that. However, the one thing Vaughn and I agreed never to do was to think we were better than anyone else."

The last thing Saint wanted was for her to think calling her Princess was somehow negative. In his mind it was all positive. "To me, a princess is kind, and you are that, Zara. I watch how you interact with people. You're friendly and remember most by name when you see them again. The majority of those living in the cove are aware you were born a Miller. One of those wealthy Millers. However, you don't let that define who you are. Neither does Vaughn. That's why the two of you are so likable."

He took another sip of wine. He meant that. Even his

mother attested to that. Although she'd never spent time with Zara, Irene Toussaint knew others who had, like Juanita Beckett, the town seamstress, and Ms. Fanny, who owned the art supply store. They all thought the world of Zara. Still, he knew his mother's main concern was not wanting him to get hurt again by love.

"Also," he continued, "being a princess to me means you're passionate about a lot of things, your work with fashion as well as your charity work." When she lifted a brow, he said, "Before I met you as Vaughn's sister, he used to tell me that you regularly donate a large part of your profits to various charities. He was proud of you and although I didn't know you at the time, so was I."

She shrugged. "Vaughn can't talk because he does the same thing."

"Regardless, I think it's commendable." Then in a lowered voice he said, "Another thing I know you're passionate about is making love to me. Whenever we're together I feel your passion, Zara. All the way to my bones."

There was no way he could express that he more than felt it. Whether he'd wanted to or not, he'd become addicted. Even now as they were talking, heat was curling his insides, threatening his control. It made him want to lean over the table and kiss her.

He understood why she'd kissed him that night when they were dancing in front of everyone. Desire had consumed her to the point primal instincts had kicked in. It had for him, too. He'd been able to control it. She had not. They sat there staring at each other in silence. He could feel the heat building, stoking that passion he'd been talking about.

"Would the two of you like some more wine?"

The waitress's words snapped them out of their reverie.

Breaking eye contact with Zara, he looked at the waitress, smiled and said, "Not for me."

Zara said, "None for me, either. Thanks."

When she walked off, Zara asked, "How long do you think this will last, Saint?"

He knew what she was asking about. All that sexual chemistry between them that seemed to be growing stronger with every passing day. "What makes you think it will end?" he asked.

Saint could tell his response surprised her. "Of course it will end. Remember, you and I reached the conclusion that nothing lasts forever," was her response.

Yes, they had said that many times, especially when it came to love. Neither of them believed in happy endings. Nothing about that had changed. Or had it?

He pushed the thought from his mind. There were times when he was with Zara that he couldn't think straight. Like now. All he wanted to do was suggest they skip lunch and go somewhere, preferably to the cottage, and make love for the rest of the day, all night and all day tomorrow...and the next.

What was crazy about the idea was that if he were to suggest it, she'd probably be right there with him. This affair between them would end when she left, but the intense sexual chemistry that made it feel like they were the only two people in the universe would not.

"Do you need me to bring anything on Sunday?" she broke into his thoughts to ask.

He smiled. "Just yourself. I'll have everything else covered." He doubted she knew just how much he meant that. But then, from the way she was looking at him, maybe she did.

"You haven't given me your address."

"You don't need it. I'm picking you up and taking you back

home." But then maybe he could convince her to stay at his place the entire night. The thought of her sleeping in his bed had desire pulsing deep within him. After their lunch date he would return to work knowing he would not see her again until Sunday. For some reason that day seemed so far away.

That made him ask, "What are you plans for tomorrow?"

A dreamy smile spread across her face. "I plan to sleep late and start that new painting whenever I do wake up."

"What are you painting now?" he asked.

The waitress arrived with their food before she could give him an answer.

21

The beeping sound alerted Zara that Saint had arrived, and she was ready.

Like she'd told him she'd planned to do, she had slept in late yesterday and painted. Then she'd joined Vashti, Bryce and Donna for brunch at Shelby by the Sea to celebrate Donna's good news. They'd all been excited when Ashley had stopped by with the baby who they all thought was the spitting image of Ray.

Velvet, who'd left for Phoenix to help her best friend Ruthie with her upcoming wedding, had FaceTimed with the group to see the baby, hear about Donna's good news and to thank them for their friendship and support over the past two years while living in Catalina Cove. Everyone could hear the happiness in her voice and was looking forward to her wedding in August.

Of course, the ladies at brunch had brought up what they'd thought of as Zara's "hot" dance with Saint and "the Kiss." Because her friends knew more than most, she'd told them she and Saint had decided to pretend taking their romance to the next level, and that was all there was to it.

They hadn't been convinced. Donna warned her about the possibility of her and Saint falling victim to their own *pretend* game like she and Isaac had done when she'd come back to the cove for a class reunion a few years back.

In the cottage, Zara looked at the painting she'd told Saint she would be giving him. The one of that vacant building. There was no reason for her to keep it since there was no way she would consider opening a boutique here.

She placed the painting in a special wrapping. Then, like she usually did whenever she knew Saint had accessed her property, she went to the window to watch him walk over the pier that would bring him to the bay. When he had made it to the end of the pier, she grabbed her crossbody purse and the painting to stand on the porch.

It was a hot Sunday afternoon, and a cool breeze coming off the bay felt good as it caressed her skin. She had chosen to wear a pair of white Capri pants and a yellow top, telling herself it had nothing to do with the fact Saint had once told her that yellow was his favorite color.

A smile spread across his face when he saw her, and at that moment something pulled deep within her. Something she hadn't felt in a while. Emotions. By now, she should be accustomed to the strong sensations where Saint was concerned, but not emotions. Hadn't they agreed to keep emotions out of their affair? Keep them on their "can't do" list?

The one good thing about the situation was that when she returned to Boston, he would be out of sight and out of mind. Or would he? The last two times she'd left the cove to return to Boston, he hadn't been out of mind. In fact, he'd been lodged deep in her thoughts. However, she was determined that this time would be different. That phone call she'd received earlier in the day would be the kicker.

Maurice had called. It was the first time she'd heard from him in almost a year. He had finally given up trying to convince her that he loved her and only her. He wanted her to hear it from him that he would be getting married at the end of the year. She didn't ask who he was marrying. She'd known before he'd said the name. She wished him well and ended the call, and then proceeded to block his number.

Her ex-boyfriend had moved on and so had she. He was giving that other woman—the one from his past—something he'd never offered to her. Marriage. In a sense it proved he had never moved on, although he might have thought he had.

Now she was glad she hadn't let him wear down her defenses to give him another chance. More than anything, she owed it to Saint for motivating her to forge a pathway forward. Maurice's call today had proved it.

She then thought of the man walking toward her, who was smiling as if he was glad to see her. He'd offered the same woman his hand twice and she'd turned him down both times. What was wrong with some people? It was so understandable why neither she nor Saint wanted anything to do with love. They'd found out the hard way it wasn't all it was cracked up to be. And like they would remind themselves—nothing was forever.

"Hello, Zara."

Just hearing his voice comforted her. As if he detected something was wrong, he opened his arms to her. Setting the wrapped portrait aside, she moved into those strong arms, and he held her as she buried her face in his chest. To be held by him and to inhale his scent gave her strength.

"What's wrong, sweetheart?"

Zara pulled back and looked up at him. She was getting used to his terms of endearment that he used frequently and effortlessly. "Nothing is wrong. Now everything is final."

He lifted a brow. "Final?"

"Yes. Maurice called this morning to let me know he's getting married at the end of the year."

She could feel the intensity of Saint's gaze searching her face. "And how do you feel about that?"

Zara smiled at him, and it was a genuine smile. "That's just it, Saint. I don't feel anything. I always knew I was over him, but this showed me just how much I am. I wished him well and I meant it. Evidently, it wasn't meant for us to be together."

She paused a moment and then said, "He's marrying the woman he cheated on me with. A part of me regrets the two years we were together. The love and trust that I gave him that he didn't deserve. But then another part doesn't have any regrets because that period taught me a lesson. My heart won't get trampled again. I won't allow it. Do you understand that?"

Zara didn't have to ask him because deep down she knew he understood. Falling in love had rendered him a similar blow. Heartbreak. She admired people who could recover from it, meet someone and fall in love again. Vaughn had done it. So had Sierra. They had taken a chance on love again and she appreciated them for doing so. For her, it wouldn't be that way. The risk would be too much to bear.

"Yes, sweetheart, I understand." He lowered his mouth to hers and gave her the kiss she'd desperately needed.

"Your home is beautiful, Saint."

"Thanks. There are still things I need to do to it, but I'm satisfied for now. It had been vacant for years, and I got it at a good deal."

"Who used to own it?" She was standing in the middle of his living room, glancing around.

"The Conyers. They never had any kids and when they died it became what is considered abandoned. Out of habit, Reid Lacroix buys all abandoned property in Catalina Cove."

Zara raised a brow. "Why?"

"To prevent someone not living in the cove from moving in and doing whatever the hell they want. He will only resell the property to anyone living in the cove or who was born here."

Zara shook her head. "He really takes his self-appointed role as Catalina Cove's gatekeeper seriously, doesn't he?"

"Yes, and the townspeople love and appreciate him for doing so. Especially for this area of Catalina Cove."

"Why this area?"

"This is bayou country," he said. "Most people living in this part were born and raised here. Like them, Reid understands and appreciates the importance of preserving it."

"Can you see the bayou from here?" she asked.

"Only from my back porch through the trees." He crossed the room to stand in front of her. "Do you want to see it?"

"I'd love to."

Taking her hand, he led her through his dining room and kitchen to the back porch. Opening the door, he moved aside to let her step out before him. "All this land is yours?" she asked, looking around.

"Yes, all five acres." He handed her a pair of binoculars that he kept on his porch. "Use these to take a look past that huge cypress tree."

"That huge tree that seems to be touching the sky?"

He grinned at her observation. "Cypress trees can grow up to one hundred and twenty feet tall. That one has prob-ably reached its full height, and I figure it's about a hundred years old. If you look past its six-foot-wide trunk, you can see the bayou."

He watched her adjust the binoculars to her eyes. "Yes, I can see it," she said. She lowered the binoculars and handed them back to him. "Thanks for sharing that with me, Saint. Now that you're back, do you think you'll ever move away from the bayou again?"

"Yes, but no time soon." He decided to tell her something that only a few people knew. He hadn't even told his parents. "I've purchased some oceanfront property in Reid's new housing development."

Her eyes showed her surprise. "You have?"

"Yes, but I don't plan to build anytime soon. For now, I'm satisfied with living here."

"Purchasing that property in Reid's development was certainly a good investment," she said.

"Just like buying that vacant building in town would be for you."

When she didn't say anything, he said, "Thanks for the painting. You know what I plan to call it?"

"No. What do you plan to call it?"

"*Imagine.*"

"So, what are you feeding me today, Saint?"

It hadn't gone past him that she'd deliberately changed the subject. He had no problem letting her. In a way, he shouldn't have said anything. She'd made up her mind about that building, and he should respect her decision and let it go. He wondered why he was finding it hard to do so.

"For starters, grilled trout, red beans and rice, and bayou bread. I even cooked those crab cakes I told you about. And for dessert, I've prepared bayou beignets."

"What's the difference between a bayou beignet and a New Orleans beignet?"

A huge smile tugged at his lips. "I'll let you answer that question for yourself."

"Thanks for inviting me to dinner, Margie." Levi hoped it wouldn't go unnoticed that although the invitation had been from both her and Mr. Chelsey, he was thanking her personally.

Her father was taking his after-dinner nap and Levi had talked Margie into walking in the shipping district along the boardwalk. At first, she seemed hesitant but then she changed her mind and agreed.

"You're welcome, Levi. I'm glad you came."

"No reason for me not to. I figured you were a good cook, and I was looking forward to your company."

She looked over at him. "That was kind of you to say."

"I meant it. That's something you'll get to know about me. I mean what I say."

She nodded. "We've walked for a while. Shouldn't we go back now? I'd think your leg would be bothering you."

Before he could say anything, she quickly added, "Dad told me about your injury."

Levi figured as much, but then knowing Mr. Chelsey, he wouldn't have told her if she hadn't asked. Her doing so didn't bother him any, not when he was lucky to be alive. He could have died that night.

"Naw, it doesn't bother me now. Walking on it is good. When I sit still and it gets stiff, that's when it bothers me."

"Oh."

He wanted to spend this time with her, and definitely wanted to get to know her better. He should find that odd because since Lydia's death he hadn't been interested in any other woman. But he was attracted to Margie, that was for certain.

"Tell me about your husband, Margie."

She was quiet as they continued walking. Then she asked, "What do you want to know?"

"Anything you want to tell me."

"Okay," she said with a nod. "Ron and I met at a medical convention. He was a doctor, and I was a nurse. We hit it off, began long-distance dating and got married a year later. We were married for thirty-five years until he died of an aneurysm at his medical office." She paused and then continued, "There were no signs, no symptoms. It just happened while he was seeing a patient. I worked as his nurse at the office, but on that particular day I had a dentist appointment. By the time I made it to the hospital, he was gone."

She stopped walking and turned to lean against the railing and gaze at the ocean.

"I'm sorry. I shouldn't have brought up those unhappy memories for you," Levi said.

She looked at him. "I'm fine. It's been three years."

He shrugged as he stood beside her and looked out at the ocean as well. "Doesn't matter. It could be three, ten or twenty. You never get over losing someone you love."

She watched the water for a few beats, and then said, "Now tell me about your wife."

He met her gaze. "Lydia and her parents moved to the cove when I was sixteen and in the tenth grade. I'd heard about the new girl and how pretty she was, but when I saw her that day in our English class, I was immediately smitten."

Margie laughed. "Immediately?"

He laughed back. "Yes, immediately. Her parents were strict and wouldn't let her begin dating until she was seventeen. I patiently waited. They did allow me to walk her to school and back home. But I never got invited inside. Everything changed when she turned seventeen. I got invited to Sunday dinner."

"Wow."

"That's what I thought, too, and it lasted for every Sunday until we finished school. Then she left for college, and I left for the military. She remained my girl all through that time and then after college, she came home and planned our wedding. By then, my time in the military was up and I returned to Catalina Cove and tried out for the police force, and Lydia was a third-grade teacher here. We were happy during the twenty-four years of our marriage. Like your Ron was a special man, my Lydia was a special woman."

"Then we were blessed, weren't we?" she said softly.

"Yes, we were. But Lydia and I had our share of sorrows. Losing our only child, Dasha. She was a beautiful little girl who died before her second birthday from an asthma attack."

"I'm sorry, Levi. Ron and I lost our first child, too. He was born with a hole in his heart and only lived a week. That was hard on us, so I can imagine how difficult things were for you and your wife."

They started walking again and for a while they strolled in silence. Then he said, "I'm attracted to you, Margie. I believe you know that. What you might not know is that you're the first woman I've felt anything toward since Lydia."

When she didn't say anything, he continued, "I've been a widower for close to twelve years. You only lost your husband three years ago. You might not be ready to start seeing anyone, and if that's the case, I understand. However, I'm hoping we can be friends."

She smiled at him. "You're right. I'm not ready for anything other than friendship right now, Levi. Thanks for under-standing."

"Alright, Margie, then a friend-only relationship is what we'll have."

For now, he thought, hopeful that one day that would change.

22

Zara sealed up another box and looked around. She would never have thought she still had this much of her belongings at Zara's Haven. She'd even come across the pom-poms she'd used as head cheerleader. Seeing the crown her father had placed on her head as Miss Catalina Cove High had taken her down memory lane. She could honestly say she'd relished her high school years.

So far, she'd packed over twenty big boxes. Some of the items she would donate to the high school and some to Goodwill. The items she wanted to keep, she'd put in a storage facility here in the cove. Checking her watch, she knew her stomach was growling for a reason. It was past lunchtime. She had leftovers from dinner with Saint yesterday and couldn't wait to warm them up.

Dinner had been delicious, and he'd shown just what a good cook he was. And he'd been right about those crab cakes. Over the meal he'd told her more about the bayou and she'd let everything he said sink in. You could take the man out of the bayou, but you couldn't take the bayou out of the man. She liked that about him. He was true to who he was. Just like she embraced the French part of her, he did the same with the bayou part of him.

She headed downstairs, recalling how as a little girl she would use the banister of the staircase as a sliding board. No matter how many times her parents had scolded her for doing so. She hadn't cared one iota that the carvings on them were originally meant for a castle in Ireland, but thanks to LaFitte and his gang of pirates, they'd ended up here instead.

In fact, she'd been told that a number of pieces in the house had been smuggled in from other countries. That was one of the reasons this mansion didn't give a Southern feel, like the other ancestral homes in the cove. Everything in the house was fit for a queen...or rather a princess. LaFitte made sure of it when he'd presented this house and its contents to Princess Zara.

A part of her often wondered if Princess Zara ever fell in love with the man who had kidnapped her, or if she had been in love with her intended groom, the Caribbean prince she was promised to. She'd been on that ship to the Caribbean to get married. LaFitte had certainly put an end to that.

Moments later Zara was in the kitchen using the microwave and looking around at the double ovens, stainless-steel appliances and granite countertops. The one thing she loved about this house had been this kitchen. She remembered when her mother had asked that it be modernized, and her father had been quick to accommodate her. After that, the newly enlarged butler pantry had been Zara's favorite hiding place as a child.

As she went to sit out on the screened-in patio to eat her lunch, she saw it was another hot day. Yesterday had also been hot...in more ways than one. She had done something that definitely hadn't been planned. At least not by her. She'd known they would eventually make love in Saint's bed, but she certainly hadn't planned on spending the night.

After dinner they had walked around his property, and when they returned to the house, she was hesitant about making love, although that was what she'd wanted them to do. The last thing she wanted was for his parents to visit him unexpectedly. He assured her that wouldn't be happening because his parents had left for Memphis to visit friends for ten days. They would return in time to attend the Blueberry Festival. He had taken them to the New Orleans train station that morning for the eight-hour ride. They'd already texted him that they were safe and sound in Memphis.

Knowing there wouldn't be any interruptions, she was all in. By midnight, she'd been too exhausted to dress and leave, and he'd been too drained to get dressed and drive her home. So she'd spent the night. He'd been glad about it and even admitted that not only had he wanted to make love to her in his bed, he also wanted the experience of waking up and making love to her in his bed the next morning. Well, he'd certainly gotten both things.

They had awakened at daybreak and after making love, he took her home so he could go to work. She hadn't expected him to make love to her again when they'd reached the cottage on Pelican Bay, but he had. After spending the night in his bed, he still managed to leave her this morning in hers with a satisfied smile on her face. Evans "Saint" Toussaint was definitely something else. What a man.

She had settled into the chair on the patio when a boat carrying the Ellorans went by Zara's Haven. Donna, Isaac and their two-year-old son, Ike, were taking advantage of the coolness on the ocean to escape the summer heat. They seemed so happy together. One day over doughnuts and coffee Donna had shared their story of how they'd gotten a divorce only to remarry years later. It seemed second chances worked for some but not for others.

Her cell phone rang, and her body recognized the ringtone. It was Saint. She felt him in every pore, nerve and pulse, and nearly closed her eyes on a moan. "Hello."

"How is your day going, sweetheart?"

She'd gotten used to that term of endearment from him, but still smiled every time he said it. "It got off to a wonderful start, thanks to you this morning."

"Glad to hear it. You're the reason my day is going great as well. However, I just realized that we didn't plan out the week."

"No, we didn't, did we? What do you have in mind?" she asked.

A part of Saint wished she hadn't asked him that. What was always on his mind was making love to her. The memories of yesterday and this morning had him fighting back a groan of heated lust. "I'll let you plan things for this week, Zara."

"You might not want to do that," she warned.

"Why not?"

"With me leaving in three weeks, I might be tempted to cram a lot onto the agenda," she said.

"I wouldn't have a problem with that." The last thing he wanted was to be reminded of when she would be leaving. He would see her again at Jaye and Velvet's wedding in August, but that meant he would go about a month without being in her bed and her being in his. But then who was to say when he saw her at the wedding that she would want to resume their hookups? What if during that month apart she met someone?

Why did that thought bother him when it shouldn't? They were not in a committed relationship and never would be.

"I have an idea," Zara said, breaking into his thoughts.

"And what's your idea?"

"I suggest we not do a schedule. Like before, you're welcome to the cottage anytime. I had planned to do breakfast at the Witherspoon Café tomorrow morning. Do you want to join me?"

"I would love to. What about tonight?"

"What about tonight?" she asked.

"May I see you tonight?"

"Like I said, Saint. You're welcome to the cottage anytime."

After he ended the call, Saint stood up from his desk and walked to the window to look out. Shoving his hands into his pockets he thought about the time he'd spent with Zara since she'd returned to the cove. Had it been three weeks already? He appreciated all his time spent with her, especially when she'd come to his home. It felt good having her there. He liked their talks about various topics and their walk around his property. However, more than anything, he had appreciated her interest in the culture in which he'd been born. That was the one thing Mia hadn't wanted to hear about. Anything about his bayou ancestry. To her, it didn't matter where you came from, it was where you were going in life that was important.

Saint didn't believe that. His ancestors were Bayou Creoles. He had been born and raised in the bayou. He embraced his French, African and Spanish heritage. He was the man that he was today because of it. He would admit while living in Seattle it hadn't mattered. However, here in Catalina Cove it mattered because that was what made the cove so special. The richness of the various cultures.

Saint returned to his desk when his buzzer went off. "Yes, Mrs. Dorsett?"

"Jade Grisham and Kia Harris have arrived for their meeting with you."

He checked his watch. They were early. "Please send them in."

When the door opened, Mrs. Dorsett escorted in the identical twins who were all smiles. He'd heard they sometimes liked dressing alike to make up for the years they hadn't been together. Reid and Vaughn could tell them apart. Saint couldn't and wouldn't even try.

They would be entering their last year of college in the fall and had been hired as summer interns. That wasn't a bad deal when your grandfather owned the company. This week they would be shadowing each member of the Lacroix Industries executive team. Beginning next week, they would cross-train on every job in the building. Reid wanted them to know every single detail about the multimillion-dollar company that one day would become theirs.

Saint moved around the desk to welcome the two young women who would one day be his bosses.

"I think it's wonderful, Mom, that you've met a guy. It's about time."

Margie shook her head, wondering if her daughter had heard a word she'd said. For the past ten minutes, she had been telling Bellamy about Levi, how they met and what a nice and kind man he was. She had ended by telling her that Levi had admitted to being attracted to her, and that she was attracted to him, although she hadn't admitted that to Levi.

She wasn't ready for an involvement with a man and, with him, all she was looking for was friendship. Some might think that was too much information to be sharing with her daughter, but she and Bellamy always had a close relationship.

"And before you go off on me and accuse me of not listening to everything you've said, Mom, I was listening, but I picked up something in your voice."

Margie lifted a brow. "What?"

"Regret. You might have told this Levi guy that all you're ready for is friendship, but I think you want more and you're just afraid to go beyond that."

Margie thought about what her daughter said as she sat at the dining room table. She could see into the living room, where her father was sitting in his favorite chair watching the news with Butterball in his lap. Every so often she would see both her father and the cat doze, which meant the television was watching them more than they were watching it.

"It has nothing to do with being afraid, Bellamy. I just don't think I'm ready."

"And why not? Dad's been gone for three years, closer to four, actually. It's time to accept he's not coming back and move on, Mom. David and I want you to be happy. Dad would want you to be happy, too."

That, she knew to be true. "It takes time for your heart to shift gears and go in another direction, Bellamy."

"I know that's probably true, but the first step is shifting those gears. You're a beautiful woman who is a loving person and full of life. I saw some of that energy and vivacity leave you when Dad died. David and I were worried about you. For a while, David even thought of moving back to Dallas and working at a hospital there. He'd gotten Cheryl on board with the idea, but I talked them out of it."

Margie frowned. This was the first she'd heard of her son and daughter-in-law thinking about doing such a thing. She was glad Bellamy had talked them out of it. "For them to move from Wisconsin when they're doing so well at the hospital there would have been ludicrous."

"I agree, but they love you so much they were going to do it regardless. I convinced them you were okay, and that I had talked you into getting grief counseling and knew you'd be fine."

Margie would be the first to admit those counseling sessions had helped. But that didn't mean she was ready to throw herself back into a romantic relationship. "I'm fine. Moving back to Catalina Cove to be with Dad was the best thing I could have done."

"I think so, too, Mom. David and Cheryl do as well. And this Levi guy just might be the person you need in your life right now."

As Bellamy's words sank in, Margie dismissed the latter comment. Instead, her mind focused on the former. She had mentioned David, Cheryl and herself—she hadn't mentioned Sam. In fact, come to think of it, Bellamy hadn't mentioned her husband the last couple of times they'd spoken. Of course, Margie had asked about him because she liked her son-in-law a lot. Thought of him as a second son. Whenever she asked about him, Bellamy would say he was doing fine and kept the conversation moving.

"Bellamy?"

"Yes, Mom?"

"Are things alright with you and Sam? I've noticed you haven't mentioned him lately."

Bellamy paused, then said, "I didn't want to tell you until you'd gotten settled in with Granddad. I didn't want you to worry about me."

An uneasy feeling consumed Margie. "What's wrong, honey? What's going on?"

She heard the crackling in her daughter's voice when she said, "Sam asked me for a divorce, Mom."

23

Zara looked at her reflection in the full-length mirror. The Blueberry Festival had started two days ago, and she was excited about it. Not only would this be the first one she'd attended since leaving for college years ago, but also this time she would be attending with Saint.

It was hard to believe she'd been in the cove a month already. Vaughn and Sierra had returned from their second honeymoon with radiant smiles that seemed to be permanently engraved in their features. She was glad they'd savored their time in the Maldives, and undoubtedly savored each other.

Zara shifted her gaze out the window. It was a beautiful Saturday morning and numerous pelicans were out on the bay. She and Saint had decided to make a full day at the festival. Last week they'd spent a lot of time together, sharing breakfast, lunch and dinner practically every single day. Then they'd shared a bed each night at the cottage. While his parents had been out of town, he hadn't had to check on them each day. He would leave from her place to go to work and then return in the evenings.

The brightest spot of her day had been in the evening, when

she would look out over the pier and see him walking toward the cottage. Nothing looked sexier than Saint with his suit jacket slung over his shoulder and a swagger that would take any woman's breath away. With the fading sun as his backdrop, it was definitely a grab-your-camera moment.

Most days, she would stand on the porch, waiting for him to step off the pier and onto land. More than once, she'd waited at the end of the pier, and he would sweep her off her feet into his arms. She blushed thinking of that day when they'd made love right there on the pier.

People no longer stared when they saw them together in town, which meant their fake affair was working. The dance and kiss were no longer on anyone's minds. She would be the first to admit that it hadn't been easy keeping their relationship passionate but emotionless since they spent more time together now than before. It couldn't be helped when Saint was such a wonderful guy.

More than once she'd questioned his ex-girlfriend's decision to let a good man like him go. The woman had gotten two marriage proposals where some women never received one—like her. There was no way she would turn a marriage proposal from Saint down.

She blinked when she realized the significance of that thought, when there was no way she would accept a marriage proposal. She was through with men. As far as she was concerned, one heartbreak in a lifetime was enough to have to deal with. There wasn't one man who could be trusted with her heart ever again.

Her thoughts shifted back to Saint. He was a special person and one day a woman would enter his life who was deserving of everything there was about him. She appreciated every moment she spent with him, even those times when they would sit in the kitchen, over coffee or wine, and talk for hours about anything and everything. He knew more about her than Maurice ever had, and he'd told her a lot about himself and the life he'd lived in Seattle.

Then there was the wealth of business knowledge he generously shared with her, offering smart suggestions…but only when she asked for them. The one suggestion he'd given that she hadn't asked for was about that vacant building.

Whether he knew it or not, that idea had somehow taken root in her mind. Every time she passed by the building on her walk to the Witherspoon Café, she no longer saw it as it was now; she imagined it as she'd depicted it in her painting. That had to be the reason why when she'd passed by it yesterday morning, she had taken a picture of the For Sale sign. She was actually thinking about buying it. Would it be so bad if she did? Why had she thought it would when she knew, like Saint said, it would make good business sense?

She knew the reason without thinking hard about it. Buying that building meant more frequent trips to Catalina Cove. Deep down, she knew the real reason the prospect of a connection to the cove was something she didn't want to think about. Namely, Saint.

Whenever they were together, although she wished differently, she was consumed with a need only he could quench. She'd tried building an immunity against it, but so far, nothing had worked. An attachment to him or any man was the last thing she wanted or needed in her life. It didn't matter one iota that Saint was a man with a keen sense of intelligence, intense integrity and loving-kindness and tenderness most didn't possess or want to show. He was someone any woman could love and would want to love. She could not be that woman. No matter what.

Suddenly, her heart slammed against her ribs at the thought

that it might be too late to stop what she hadn't wanted to ever feel again. Deep emotions for a man.

"I meant to ask if your parents enjoyed their trip to Memphis?"

Saint smiled down at Zara. They were walking around the Blueberry Festival grounds with his arm draped around her shoulders as they moved from one booth to the other. "Yes, they always relish any time spent with the Givenses."

He thought she looked gorgeous in her shorts set. And that straw hat on her head gave her one hell of a sexy look. When she'd opened the cottage door his gaze had roamed from head to toe. Lust had instantly ignited within him. He had to fight the urge to sweep her into his arms, take her into the bedroom and make love to her instead of going to the festival.

"Givens? Are they related to Mia?"

Her question interrupted his thoughts. "Yes, they're her parents."

"Oh."

It wasn't what she'd said but how she said it. For some reason she sounded surprised. "I mentioned to you that night I took you dancing in New Orleans that the Givenses and my parents struck up a close relationship and began doing things together during the time Mia and I were together."

"I recall you saying that," she said, softly. "I guess I assumed with your and Mia's breakup, the close friendship between them had waned."

"That's an understandable assumption to make. Both sets of parents were upset with Mia each time she turned down my marriage proposals. The Givenses didn't stay mad at Mia long since she's their only child. I think our parents see it as a phase she's going through, and they're still holding out that she'll come to her senses one of these days."

"Are you holding out for that, too, Saint?"

He frowned and ceased walking. Turning to her, he said, "You of all people know better than that." He rubbed a hand down his face. "My parents, as well as Mia's parents, should know it as well since I've made it pretty clear there will never be a Saint and Mia again. That ship has sailed."

"Do you think they got it?"

"No," he said, honestly. "But it doesn't matter what they think since I know better. Mia and I haven't communicated since we broke up. As far as I'm concerned, she got on with her life and I've moved on with mine."

They began walking again. "I understand Vaughn and Sierra got back," he said, wanting to change the subject.

"Yes, and according to them they had a great time. Sierra's parents returned with Teryn, and of course they were glad to see her. They plan on resting up some and will attend the festival's closing activities tomorrow."

Saint drew Zara closer to him when a group of people passed by in the crowded aisle. He loved the feel of her beside him and was getting used to her being with him. Seen or unseen. He doubted that she knew that over the past month she'd become an integral part of his life, whether he wanted her to or not.

All he had to do was remember the weekend before when he'd taken her dancing again to that same nightclub in New Orleans. Like months before, they danced to several slow songs. More than once he maneuvered her to a darkened area of the dance floor to steal a kiss or two. Maybe three.

"You want to share a corn dog with me, Saint?"

He leaned slightly away to look at her, making sure she looked at him. "I'd share anything with you, Zara."

He thought the smile that lit up her face was priceless. Unable to help himself, he leaned forward and brushed a kiss across her lips. It had been quick, yet he'd felt her shiver. It always amazed him how deep and profound their responses were to each other. At that moment he wanted her with a fierce intensity that almost took his breath away.

"Saint?"

"Yes, sweetheart?"

"Just so you know, Mr. and Mrs. Ivanstall saw you kiss me."

He grinned. Everybody living in the cove, both young and old, knew what a busybody Mrs. Ivanstall was. "So, they saw me. Should I apologize for kissing you?"

"No, don't apologize for anything you ever do with me."

"In that case." He leaned in to kiss her again. It was short but longer than the last one. There was no doubt in his mind it left her knowing what he had in store for later.

When they began walking again, he said, "Oh, by the way, the folks invited you to their Fourth of July cookout. I know it's the day before you leave to return to Boston, so I understand if you can't make it."

"I can make it and I'd love to go."

Levi Canady was enjoying another walk home and inhaled the scent of the sea. Then there was the smell of blueberries, which always seemed more prevalent during the Blueberry Festival. Business at the café had been booming with lots of people in town for the past three days. Instead of staying open for half a day like usual on Saturdays, the Green Fig had been open all day to take advantage of the festival crowd. Although Vaughn and Sierra had returned, Sierra hadn't yet come to the café. That made him feel good knowing she knew he had everything under control.

He glanced up at the sky. As usual, the stars were shining brightly, and all was quiet. This was one of the few nights Chip wouldn't be there when he got home. Malcolm Leopold, who owned a female French bulldog named Bell, had asked months ago if Chip could mate with Bell. Hopefully, the union would produce enough puppies for each of Malcolm's four grandkids to have one.

Levi figured over the next two days Chip would be having the time of his life with Bell. In a way he was a wee bit jealous. That surprised him since he'd never given thought about mating with a woman since Lydia. It didn't take much to figure out the reason why such a thing had crossed his mind.

Margie.

He hadn't seen her since their stroll on the boardwalk and she'd stated she only wanted to be friends. He should have been happy with that, since friendship had been all he'd wanted… at first. But that Sunday when he'd been invited to dinner, he could feel himself wanting more. But there was nothing he could do when the lady of his thoughts wasn't interested.

He was about to cross the street, heading in the direction of his house, when a figure coming toward him stopped him. He immediately noted from the slight build it was a woman and not a man. As the person came closer, he saw who it was.

"Margie? What are you doing out so late? Don't tell me Butterball got out again."

When she came to a stop in front of him beneath the streetlight, he could see the worried lines beneath her eyes. "Levi, hello. Fancy running into you tonight. Dad and Butterball are fine. In fact, they called it an early night and are home asleep."

"So, what got you out walking alone after nine at night so far from home?"

She glanced over her shoulder. When she turned her head back, he saw her surprise at how far she'd walked. "I hadn't realized I walked so far. I had a lot on my mind. But it's just a couple of blocks. Besides, this is Catalina Cove."

"Yes, this is Catalina Cove, but you should never get the feeling of being too safe in any environment."

"I know you're right. But the same goes for you, too."

He grinned. "I might be a banged-up ex-cop but I'm an ex-cop nonetheless. I can still handle the bad guys. However, thanks to Sheriff Grisham, I would be the first to admit crime is almost nonexistent in this town."

She grinned as well. "See what I mean?"

"Yes, but we had a lot of visitors for the festival, although I noticed that Catalina Cove's policemen are out in full force."

He then remembered what she'd said about the reason she was out walking. "Is everything alright with you, Margie?"

She broke eye contact with him and looked down at the sidewalk. When she raised her head, he saw tears glistening in her eyes. In concern, he reached out and took hold of her arm. "Margie? What's wrong?"

She said, "It's my daughter."

"Your daughter? Is she okay?"

"Physically, Bellamy is fine, but I don't know how she's doing emotionally."

He could hear the pain in her voice. "Do you want to talk about it over coffee, Margie?"

She lifted a brow. "Over coffee?"

"Yes. We're a lot closer to my place than we are to yours. I make a pretty decent cup of coffee, and I'd love for you to have a cup with me."

She didn't answer at first. He knew she was thinking about his invitation to his home. When he thought she would refuse, she said, "I would love to have a cup of coffee with you, Levi."

24

Zara slipped out of the bed, trying not to awaken Saint. Their wants and desires had been in rare form after returning from the Blueberry Festival. Who would have thought that a one-night stand would come to this? They had been two travelers who'd wanted no more than a night of pleasure to help heal broken hearts. They'd gotten more than the healing they'd sought. But she'd never intended for their fake affair to lead to this, an affair that was, on her part, anything other than pretense.

What have you done, Zara? she silently asked herself, as she looked over her shoulder at the man sleeping soundly in her bed. A man she knew for certain she had fallen in love with. A man she knew would never love her back. She had known that. It was the plan from the very beginning.

No emotional attachment. No commitment. No expectation of anything other than the moment.

How could she have forgotten the very elements on which their hookups had been founded? Pretending an affair should not have changed anything, but for her it had. Spending more time with Saint over the past weeks had sealed the deal for her. She had seen what Mia Givens had failed to see. Evans Toussaint was a keeper. A man worthy of any woman's love.

Leaving the bedroom, she closed the door and went into the kitchen. Today had been perfect. The weather, the Blueberry Festival and the man she'd spent it all with. She'd even met Saint's parents when they ran into the older couple at one of the booths. Although they were friendly enough, she could pick up on his mother's guarded air. Regardless, Irene Toussaint had reiterated the invitation to join them on the Fourth of July. Zara had thanked her and said she would be there.

Zara thought about what Saint had told her earlier. Namely, the Toussaints and Givenses had a close relationship that had been built on the belief the two families would one day be united by marriage—Saint and Mia's. Why would his mother want her son to get back together with a woman who had caused him heartbreak?

A part of her wanted to think that Saint's mother believed another woman was worthy of her son. Otherwise, she wouldn't keep trying to fix him up with local single women. Yet, it was possible she was still hoping there would be a Saint and Mia one day. Why was the woman stuck on Mia as a future daughter-in-law, and why did it bother Zara that she was?

She had just poured a glass of wine and taken a sip when she heard a sound behind her. Turning, she saw Saint leaning against the kitchen door with a sleepy look on his face. If seeing him walking across the pier with his jacket slung over his shoulder was a sexy image, then this was another level. That barely woke look in his still drowsy eyes, which were filled with intense need, took her breath away. At least he'd pulled on his khaki shorts, although they weren't fastened, and the zipper was undone.

"You left me," he grumbled. His throaty voice washed over her body like a sensual caress.

"You were asleep, and I didn't want to wake you."

He strolled over to her in that sexy walk of his. "Sweetheart, you can wake me up anytime." When he reached her, he took the wineglass from her hand and placed it on the counter before pulling her into his arms and kissing her.

How was she to prepare for when she would leave him to return to Boston? Specifically, the night that would be their last one together. And deep down she knew it would be the last. She couldn't expect him to be willing to renew their hookups whenever she came back to town. He needed to get on with his life like she needed to get on with hers. But then, how would she manage to get on with hers when she loved him? Would that be the story of her life? Falling in love with men who couldn't or wouldn't love her back?

She forced the thought from her mind as Saint deepened the kiss to the point she began purring. When he finally released her mouth and pulled her closer to him, she knew what she should do was to suggest that after tonight they stop seeing each other. She should be spending more time with Vaughn, Sierra and Teryn since they were back in town. But she was spending her time here at the cottage where she and Saint had turned it into a lovers' hideaway. There was no way she could ever return here to Pelican Bay and not be swamped with all the memories they were making here together. In a way, she would need those memories to fight all the lonely days that lay ahead of her when they parted ways.

"Zara…"

"Hmm?" She pulled back to look at him when he didn't respond. She saw something in his eyes and when he blinked, it was gone. "What is it, Saint?"

He drew in a deep breath. "Nothing." He then pulled her back into his arms to kiss her again.

"Come on in and make yourself at home, Margie."

Margie looked around as she entered Levi's home. Because it was dark she hadn't seen much of the structure outside; however, she could tell it was a Victorian-style home, just like her parents' home. It wasn't sitting on a lot like all the other homes on the street but sat on what appeared to be several acres of land. He told her this parcel had been in the Canady family for generations and the first Levi Canady, according to Catalina Cove history, had been a faithful crew member who'd once saved Jean LaFitte's life. His family had been proud of that fact evidently, which was why there had been a Levi Canady named in every generation since. It would have ended with him, though, since his only child had been a daughter.

The moment Margie crossed the threshold and he turned on the lights she saw that like her parents' home, it had a welcoming feel. Another thing she noticed was how neat and clean it was. It definitely didn't look like a single man with a dog lived here. And speaking of a dog...

"Where's Chip?" she asked, recalling the dog's name.

Levi led her through the living room to the kitchen. "Chip is on loan as a stud for a few days."

"Excuse me?"

He looked over at her. "A friend of mine has a female version of Chip named Bell. He's ready for Bell to have puppies and asked if Chip could impregnate his Bell. He hopes it'll be successful and will result in enough puppies to give one to each of his four grandkids."

"Oh." She figured he'd seen the blush she hadn't been able to hide.

"Please have a seat at the table, Margie, and I'll get the coffee started."

"Thanks," she said, sitting down.

She watched him head for the coffeepot to start it going. Scanning the kitchen, she noticed that unlike her parents' home, his had all modern appliances and evidently, at some point, he had remodeled with granite countertops. She liked the spacious setup.

"I baked a sour cream pound cake on Sunday and there's some left. Would you like a slice to go with your coffee?"

"You bake?" she asked, surprised. Ron had been a great physician, but she would never have allowed him in her kitchen. She had a feeling Levi probably could do anything he put his mind to doing.

"I try to. It's one of my favorite pastimes," Levi said, intruding into her thoughts.

"Yes, I'd love a slice."

It wasn't long before he had poured them both cups of coffee and then, after placing slices of cake on the table, he sat across from her. After saying grace, he asked, "So, what's wrong with your daughter that has you all upset, Margie?"

She wondered if anyone ever told Levi that he had such a gentle, calming voice. She took a sip of coffee and then remembered her conversation with Bellamy and how what her daughter had said still pained her.

Taking a deep breath, she met Levi's gaze and said, "A few nights ago my daughter told me that her husband has asked her for a divorce."

Levi didn't say anything for a minute and Margie felt he was giving himself time to digest her words. Then he said, "I'm really sorry to hear that. Have they been married long?"

"Five years. They got married two years before Ron passed

away. It was a beautiful wedding and the two of them were so happy then."

Levi sipped his coffee. Then he asked, "And he asked her for a divorce?"

"Yes," Margie said, remembering everything Bellamy had told her. "It seems he's been having an affair for the past eight months with a woman at work. They are both married and decided they want to be together. She is divorcing her husband and..."

"He is divorcing your daughter," Levi finished for her when Margie found it difficult to get the words out.

"Yes," Margie said, fighting back tears. "I just don't understand it, Levi. Ron and I felt our son and daughter had struck gold when they selected the people they had fallen in love with. The people they wanted to spend their lives with."

Levi said, "Unfortunately, divorces are pretty common these days."

"So is infidelity, obviously," Margie said, trying not to sound bitter. She had tried to call Sam for the past two days and he wasn't taking her calls. According to Bellamy, he had moved out of their home two months ago.

"I am very upset with my daughter right now," she said.

Levi raised a brow. "Why?"

"Because all this was going on right before I moved back here. She was caught unawares, didn't have a clue. But she didn't tell me, Levi. She said she didn't because she knew her grandfather needed me, and if she'd told me, I would have changed my plans to move back to Catalina Cove."

"Would you have?"

Margie shrugged. "Probably, but that's beside the point. I had no idea what she was going through. My son and his wife knew but neither of them told me anything because Bellamy asked them not to. I'm upset with them as well." She paused a minute. "I know they're adults but still, they are my children, Levi. They are all I have left from Ron, and I want them happy."

"No one can assure happiness, Margie," he said in that calm voice. "We can want it, but things happen in life we have no control over. The way I see it, for him to disrespect her the way he did, and for the other woman to disrespect her husband the same way, is downright despicable and they deserve each other. Your daughter is better off without him."

"I know, and that's the same thing she said, but still. I know how hard this must be for her. How much she is hurting."

"Then be there for her when she needs you. But the one thing we can't do is fight their battles for them."

"I know. I just wish that we could." She swiped at her tears, hating that he was seeing her now, at this wretched moment. "I guess you think I'm going overboard with this."

"No, I don't think that at all." He paused. "Had she lived, my daughter, Dasha, would have been thirty-one this year. I'd want to think that had she come to me and told me what your daughter told you, my first instinct as a father would be to find the guy and beat the hell out of him for hurting my child. But I want to think the ex-cop in me would have given me more control of my temper. However, nothing can downplay a parent's love, care and concern for their offspring. No matter how old they are."

She released a deep sigh. "Thank you for saying that."

"You are welcome, but you really don't have to thank me."

A part of Margie felt like she did because he'd seen how upset she was and invited her to his home for cake and coffee to talk about it. It was nice having someone to talk to. This was the type of conversation she definitely couldn't have with her father because he'd be disappointed as well. He'd liked Sam, too.

"How could all of us have misjudged Sam's character? He betrayed Bellamy for eight months. Eight months, Levi. A woman he'd vowed to love, honor and protect. And hadn't that other woman vowed the same thing to her husband when they got married? Well, at least there weren't any children involved. And to think, it was just last year when Bellamy and Sam had talked about starting a family."

She appreciated Levi for not saying anything as she went on her angry tirade. She saw the understanding in his eyes and, for her, that was enough. She drew in a deep breath. Now that she had gotten all of it out, she felt better and honestly wanted to change the subject. So she then told him about the knitting group she had joined.

"You knit?" he asked.

"I used to years ago. Mom taught me. I wanted to start doing it again since I have a lot of time on my hands. I figure if I get back into it now, I can have a few items knit for my family by Christmas. I will definitely be marking Sam off my Christmas list," she said with a huff.

Levi grinned. "And I don't blame you one bit for doing so."

"Thank you." She checked her watch. "I need to go. I don't want to leave Dad and Butterball alone for too long. Thanks so much for the cake and coffee. The cake was delicious. So was the coffee."

When she stood and began gathering their plates and cups off the table, he said, "You don't have to do that."

"Yes, I do, Levi. It's the least I can do." She went to his kitchen sink. He followed and she felt something radiating off him. Strength.

Together, they washed up the cups and plates. Then he said, "Now I'll walk you home."

"You don't have to do that. I know my way."

"I'm sure you do but there's no way I'm not going to make sure you get home safely." He took her hand and led her toward the door.

It didn't take long for them to make the two-block walk. When they reached her door, she turned to him. "Thanks, Levi, for everything tonight."

"I'm glad I was there for you." Then he said, "Good night, Margie."

She opened the door and was about to go inside when she turned back around. "Levi?"

He'd made it down a couple of steps and stopped and turned. "Yes?"

"I recall you saying that you're off from the Green Fig on Wednesdays."

"That's right."

"It's prayer meeting night at church and one of Dad's church members always comes by to pick him up. They serve everyone dinner and usually Dad's gone for a couple of hours. I plan to cook anyway that night regardless. How would you like to come to dinner, and then afterward if you'd like, we can take a stroll along the boardwalk again?"

Margie knew that technically she was asking a man out, something she'd never done prior to now. Granted, she'd invited him to dinner before, but her father had been there with them.

He smiled. "I'd love to do that, Margie."

She returned his smile. "Okay and thanks."

25

Saint stood at his office window with his hands shoved into his pants pockets and his mind filled with thoughts of Zara. Lately, his thoughts were always on her. More so since his parents were back from Memphis.

Their return meant she shouldn't be the only thing that occupied his time and attention. He was back to checking in on his folks, seeing them most mornings and visiting in the evenings as well. That meant he didn't start his day waking up with Zara in his arms as often as he'd like. And more times than not, it was close to bedtime by the time he arrived at the cottage.

His mother had prepared dinner a few times, and her expectations were that he would join them. He noticed she never asked about Zara, but then she'd stopped bringing up Mia, too, and he was glad about that. In fact, he'd noticed she hadn't mentioned Mia since their return from Memphis. He'd hoped at some point Mia had had a heart-to-heart talk with her parents, similar to the one he'd had with his, and that both sets of parents now accepted that there was no longer a

Saint and Mia nor would there ever be one again. However, he was constantly thinking about a Saint and Zara.

She would be leaving the cove in less than ten days, and he wasn't sure how he felt about that. He wasn't fooling himself with that train of thought. He did know how he felt since he'd fallen in love with her.

He'd known the exact moment when he'd accepted that as fact. It had been one night last week when he'd shown up at the cottage and she was wearing his T-shirt. The same one he'd given her that first night they'd spent together. She'd worn it before a couple of times, but for some reason seeing her in it when she'd stepped out onto the porch to meet him had done something to him.

For the past month, he'd constantly told himself that although there was this special, unshakable, passionate bond between them, it would eventually get old or wear down. It never did. If anything, it got stronger each time they were together, made love or breathed the same air.

He could talk to her about anything and usually did. They'd gotten into the routine of him telling her how his day had gone, and she would tell him about hers. Being seen with her seemed right and normal. People had gotten used to it. More than once, some of the older people in town, even Selma Bivens of all people, had pulled him aside to say that he and Zara made a nice couple.

He knew that Zara had finished packing up everything for the Historical Society, and had started painting a new picture, although she hadn't told him much about it or shown it to him. However, she had shown him a few clothing design ideas she'd come up with while here. He liked the fact that she would seek his business advice about things and often used it. However, the one thing he wished she'd done—namely, to seriously consider purchasing that building—she hadn't. Too late now since he'd noticed the For Sale sign was no longer in the window.

One day she would realize it was a missed opportunity, although a part of him had an idea why she hadn't been interested. Zara didn't want anything of value that would tie her to Catalina Cove. Vaughn and his family were enough.

And then there was the cottage on Pelican Bay.

Zara loved that place, and he loved it, too. For him it was synonymous with her. He would never forget the first time she'd invited him there, that night after they'd gone dancing in New Orleans. The same night they'd seen each other, two and a half years after their anonymous encounter, and discovered the deep sexual chemistry they'd shared was still alive and kicking. Neither had a problem with picking up where they'd left off, since they both knew there would never be anything serious between them.

What he now felt for her was as serious as it could get. Although he'd tried telling himself time and time again what he'd felt for Zara was only physical, lust with a capital *L*, he soon realized what he felt was more emotional than physical.

He was convinced she was different from any woman he'd been involved with, which hadn't been many. Although he tried not to compare, when he was with Zara he realized how many concessions he'd made during his relationship with Mia. Concessions she felt entitled to but never reciprocated. She'd never asked what he'd wanted. It was always what *she* wanted.

Saint could now accept that Mia's turning down his marriage proposals had been a blessing. He hadn't seen it then, but he sure as hell saw it now. Mentally, he was doing a lot better without her. However, he couldn't say the same thing when it came to Zara. He wasn't sure how he would handle things when she left and they ended their affair.

He turned when he heard the knock on his office door. "Come in."

Vaughn walked in smiling, but evidently, there was a look on Saint's face that made his smile vanish and him ask, "Saint? Are you okay?"

Saint wished he could answer truthfully and admit that no, he wasn't okay. The woman he loved more than life itself, who happened to be Vaughn's sister, would be walking out of his life in a little more than a week and there wasn't a damn thing he could do about it. Not a damn thing.

So instead, he said, "Yes, I'm okay."

"Are you sure you're okay, Zara?"

Zara glanced across the booth at Sierra. Her sister-in-law had called and invited her to lunch at the Green Fig. Although she tried being herself, undoubtedly Sierra had picked up on something. She could say that yes, she was fine, but that wouldn't be true. She wasn't fine and just the thought that she would be leaving Catalina Cove next week had her rethinking things.

She was certain Sierra had heard that she and Saint had been spending a lot of time together while she and Vaughn had been away. However, Sierra hadn't asked her anything about it.

"No, I'm not okay," she said, honestly.

"What's wrong?"

It took Zara about twenty minutes to cover everything. Since Sierra had seen the dance and kiss, she thought the idea of a faked affair had been a good one. And she wasn't surprised of the outcome. She'd detected Zara was falling for Saint a while ago. She also thought Saint was falling for Zara as well. Zara didn't agree with Sierra on the latter.

"Will you tell Saint how you feel?"

Zara was surprised Sierra would even think that she would. "No, of course not."

"So, you plan to give him up?"

Zara drew in a deep breath. "I don't have him in the first place. Falling in love wasn't part of the agreement." She looked away, not wanting Sierra to see the tears glistening in her eyes.

Sierra reached out and touched her hand. "Things change, Zara. People change and so do the paths they establish for themselves. It most certainly did for me." She paused a moment and said, "When I returned to Catalina Cove, I'd pretty much determined in my mind and heart what my pathway would be and what it would not be. After being betrayed the way I had, no man was in my future. Then in walked your brother. I fought Vaughn on every turn. Even after I'd realized he had captured my heart, I fought him. In the end love won. Maybe it will for you, too."

Sierra let go of her hand, leaned back in her seat and gave Zara a conspiratorial smile. "You know what I'd do if I were you?"

Zara lifted a brow. "No, what?"

"Do the same thing Vaughn did to me. Change how a person thinks about love being a part of their future. You and Saint have established a close relationship, and I can see it's not just based on sex. I've watched the two of you together since Vaughn and I returned. Especially that night the four of us went to dinner. He was so attentive to you. So caring. I don't believe it was an act. He was sincere."

Zara refused to get her hopes up about anything. "Saint

was just being Saint. You've even said everyone knows what a nice person he is."

"I think it was more. I believe it and Vaughn believes it as well."

"Vaughn?" Zara asked, surprised.

"Yes. He saw that very public display between you and Saint at the engagement party. Granted, he knows you can handle your business and won't interfere, but he's still your brother and would be concerned about your reputation. And before you ask, the answer is no. Vaughn hasn't said anything about it to me. But I know my husband. He's probably glad everyone assumes there's more going on between you and Saint, and Vaughn might assume that as well."

"Well, there's not more going on. Like I said, it's all an act." Zara could tell that Sierra wasn't all that convinced but figured it would be obvious when she left to return to Boston.

"Dinner was wonderful, Margie. I hope you let me invite you to dinner the next time," Levi said as they strolled along the boardwalk.

"You don't have to do that, Levi. Besides, you invited me over for cake and coffee that night I poured all my troubles out to you. I needed someone to talk to and I'm glad you listened."

"I appreciated your company."

Levi meant what he said and was glad he'd been there for her that night. "Have you talked to your daughter again? How is she doing?"

"Bellamy is tough, and I think she will survive this. Of course, it's somewhat embarrassing for her because now she's discovering who her real friends were. It seems a few of them knew about Sam's affair but didn't tell her about it. She feels betrayed. But then…"

He looked at Margie and prompted her. "But then what?"

"I'm not sure Bellamy would have believed them had they told her. She trusted Sam implicitly. I think that's what's hurting her so much. Finding out that trust was not warranted, and he was undeserving."

They stopped walking when a nice boat passed by and Levi waved at the occupants.

"Friends of yours?" Margie asked.

He smiled down at her. "Yes, that's Ray Sullivan and his family. It's a nice evening to be out on the water."

"Ray Sullivan? I recall hearing that name somewhere."

"You probably have. Ray owns the water-taxi service in Catalina Cove," Levi said.

"That sounds nice for the cove."

"It is. He's had to purchase two more boats," he said. "Would you want to take one with me over to New Orleans? I got two tickets."

She paused, considering, and then said, "I would love to do that. It sounds like fun. Let me know when so I can make sure Dad will be okay." She chuckled. "He'd probably be glad to see me gone for a while. He thinks I hover over him too much. I honestly don't want to do that."

Levi had a feeling that she did, but he didn't see it as a bad thing. He thought someone wanting to take good care of a loved one as a good thing. "I'll let you know the specifics when I get home and look at the ticket. Do you want me to call Mr. Chelsey's landline at the house or would you feel comfortable giving me your cell number?"

"I have no problem giving you my cell number, Levi." She pulled her phone out of her jacket pocket. "What's your number so I can call you?"

He rattled off his number and when his phone rang in his

pocket, she smiled and said, "There. Now we have each other's number. You can call me anytime."

He appreciated the invitation but knew that nothing had changed, and their relationship was still limited to friendship. "Thanks, Margie."

"Good evening, Mr. Levi."

Levi turned to the couple standing in front of them. He smiled when he recognized them. "Brody and Freda. How are you two?"

"We're fine. Thanks for asking," Freda said.

"I see we all had the same idea about taking a stroll along the boardwalk tonight," Brody added.

"Yes, it's a nice evening," Levi said. He then introduced Margie. "This is my friend Margie Lawson. She's Mr. Chelsey's daughter. Margie this is Brody Dorsett and Freda McEnroe. Freda's bakery supplies desserts to the Green Fig."

Margie extended her hand and smiled. "I went to school with a Harold Dorsett, and I also recall a Fredrick McEnroe."

"Our fathers," Freda said, grinning.

Margie then turned sad eyes to Brody. "I was sorry to hear about Harold. He was a fine man. Dad used to tell me what a great job he was doing as fire marshal."

"And it's a job Brody is now doing," Levi said, proudly. "I don't think Catalina Cove would know what to do without a Dorsett as a fire marshal."

"I can believe that," Margie said, grinning. "And how is your mom, Brody? I went to school with Kate as well."

"Thanks for your condolences, and Mom is doing fine. She's finally retiring in September after working for Lacroix Industries for over thirty years."

"That's wonderful." Margie glanced over at Freda. "If I recall, your father used to own a bakery. Right on this board-walk. Sold the best beignets."

Freda's smile widened. "You have a good memory. Dad ran the bakery until his death nearly ten years ago. I had finished college and was living in Ohio. Mom closed the bakery and moved out there with me."

"How is she?" Margie asked.

"Mom's doing great, and once she got used to the Ohio weather she managed quite nicely and loves it there. I moved back to the cove and opened my own bakery. I'm hoping that one day she'll move back here, but I won't hold my breath for that to happen. She has her friends in Cleveland and says her life is there now."

"I understand," Margie said. "Moving back to the cove was certainly a big decision for me. But now I'm glad I did. There's no place like home, especially when home is Catalina Cove."

"I think a lot of us found that out and are glad to be back," Brody said. "Well, I hope the two of you enjoy your walk. We're taking the water-taxi service to New Orleans to see a play."

"I hope the same for you two," Levi said, and watched as the couple walked away, thinking they looked good together. From what he'd overheard Freda tell Sierra, she and Brody were nothing more than friends. Just like him and Margie. "I'm glad you feel returning to Catalina Cove was a good move for you, Margie."

"I do, Levi, and if that invitation to dinner is still out there, I'll take it."

With a huge smile, he said, "It's still out there, and I look forward to you joining me."

26

Zara's eyes flew open when she heard footsteps walking on the pier. Since she was outside on the porch, she wouldn't have heard the buzzer alerting her that someone had gained access to Pelican Bay. After going for a swim, she'd stretched out in one of the chaise lounges to take a nap. The way the cottage was built, you had a good view of the bay and the pier regardless of whether you were on the front porch or the back.

Trying to focus with her sleepy eyes, her heart rate kicked up a notch when she saw the man walking across the pier was Saint. They had talked that morning and he'd mentioned he would see her later. However, later for him usually meant after eight since he was helping his father repair a boat dock after work.

She checked her watch. It wasn't even two o'clock yet. Was he taking a late lunch? Pulling herself up to a sitting position she couldn't help but smile as he got closer. As usual, she saw just how handsome he was.

When he reached the porch, he took the steps and came over to her, leaned down and gave her what she thought was a kiss that could fill a woman's mind with all kinds of salacious thoughts. He might be called Saint but when it came to kissing and lovemaking, there wasn't a single saintlike thing about him. Some of the things he'd introduced her to in the bedroom bordered on sinful, but so dang pleasurable.

She had barely released a purr when he broke off the kiss. She couldn't help licking her lips, wanting more of his taste. "You've been swimming?" he asked.

"Yes, I decided to take a swim and then I fell asleep." No need to tell him he had occupied her dreams during that time. To wake up and see him crossing the pier had been like a dream come true. "Your visit this time of day is a surprise."

"I couldn't get much work done for thinking about you. So here I am," he said.

His words made her feel good inside. "You came here for lunch? You should have called me. I would have whipped you up a mean sandwich."

He was amused. "How mean?"

"Peanut butter and jelly mean."

He leaned in and swiped a kiss across her lips. "Thanks, but I had something to eat already. We had a two-hour meeting and Vaughn ordered in lunch."

"That was kind of him."

"We all thought so. Since I finished with all my appointments for today, I decided to leave work early. So here I am."

The thought that he came to Pelican Bay after leaving work swelled her heart. "And I'm glad to see you."

He sat in the chaise lounge across from her. "How did the surprise bridal brunch go?"

She'd mentioned to him yesterday that Donna Elloran was hosting the event for Velvet. "Velvet was surprised, and the brunch was only attended by her closest friends here in the cove. It was nice. She had pictures of her wedding dress. It's beautiful and I can't wait to see her in it."

"I bet Jaye can't wait to see her in it, too."

Zara smiled, knowing that was true. "So, Mr. Toussaint. Why were you thinking of me today?"

"I always think about you, Zara."

Her heart pounded in her chest, while thinking he was definitely laying on the kindness rather thick. But then, that was Saint for you. Another thing she was noticing was how he kept looking at the bathing suit she was wearing. It was a little more daring than the ones she'd worn before when they'd gone swimming together. It was a two-piece, but it was one of those barely there thong styles. Definitely not something she'd wear out in public, but she had no problem wearing it privately for Saint. And from the way he was looking at her, he obviously liked what he saw.

"Have I ever told you how much I like your tattoo?"

She grinned. "You've told me a number of times." No need to remind him of the times he'd kissed and licked it. That pelican above her navel had gotten a lot of attention from Saint.

"I've been thinking about you a lot, too," she admitted truthfully.

"You have?"

Zara thought he actually sounded surprised. "Yes, I have. In fact, I have something to tell you."

"What?"

She pulled up into a sitting position. "I took your advice, Saint."

He tilted his head. "My advice about what?"

"That vacant building in town. I bought it."

Zara's words had Saint inhaling deeply. It wasn't just the thought that she'd taken his advice that was affecting him, but the implications of her doing so. However, he might be assuming those implications. The last thing he needed was to get his hopes up about anything.

She was staring at him expectantly, and he suddenly realized he hadn't commented on what she'd said. She had to be wondering why. "I didn't think you would do it, Zara. Congratulations."

She shrugged those sexy shoulders he loved touching and licking all over. "Thanks. I wasn't going to but the more I thought about it, the more I knew that you were right. Buying it would be a great opportunity."

"Will it be modeled as the shop in your painting?"

He saw the excitement in her eyes when she said, "Yes. Eventually."

Now for the real question he needed her to answer. "That means you'll be coming back to Catalina Cove more often, right?"

Instead of answering she tilted her head and held his gaze for a moment. She asked, "Does the thought of that bother you, Saint?"

"Why would it?" he asked, knowing, however, it probably would. She would be yet another woman he'd fallen in love with who would never want to settle down into marriage.

"I would think you'd have gotten on with your life, and my appearance might throw our affair and subsequent breakup back into the spotlight. You know how some people like to stir things up anew," she said.

Yes, he did know. Wasn't it just a few days ago that he'd appreciated his mother for not bringing Mia's name up? He'd reacted too soon. She had mentioned her that very morning. Letting him know that job Mia had taken in Florida three years ago had recently been the casualty of bankruptcy...as if he cared one iota.

Again, he noted Zara was waiting for him to respond, so he said, "Let them stir things up all they want. I can handle it."

He would leave it at that. There was no way he would say what he normally would say regarding his thoughts about jumping back into a serious relationship with a woman. That it wouldn't be happening because he wasn't interested. He now knew he would be interested if the woman was Zara. He would entertain a serious relationship with her at any time. He loved her.

He knew he couldn't tell her that. She'd told him how she'd felt about commitment countless times. She wasn't interested. If nothing else, Mia had taught him to take a woman at her word about what she would and would not do.

Deciding this topic of conversation was over, he let his gaze roam all over her. "I like your swimsuit. It's a good thing you're on a private island and not at the beach."

She glanced down at herself. "You think this is a little too much for the beach?"

"No. I think it's a lot too less for the beach. However, it looks great on you." He thought that was an understatement. She looked gorgeous in all the bathing suits he'd seen her in.

"Thanks. You want to go swimming?"

Since he spent a lot of time at the cottage, he kept a pair of swim trunks here. "Swimming sounds nice, but I'd rather do something else."

He knew she had an idea just what that something else was. "So, what do you think about that, Zara Miller?"

Getting up from the chaise lounge, she walked over to him. He stood as well and snaked his arms around her waist. She tilted her head back to look up at him, and at that moment he knew letting her leave would be the hardest thing he ever had to do.

Leaning down he captured her lips with his. There was nothing gentle about this kiss, deliberately so. He wanted her to feel the same degree of heat that was simmering through him. He wanted her heart to pound and accelerate like his was doing. He wanted desire to take control of her mind and senses like it was with his. But more than anything, he hoped like hell she felt something other than passion in this kiss. He wanted her to feel all the love he was trying to keep under wraps because he knew to unleash it would mean nothing but another heartbreak. He wasn't ready for another woman to tell him she wasn't ready to accept the love he had to offer her.

By the time he finally broke off the kiss, her arms were wrapped around his neck and her body was plastered to his. "Saint…"

"Hmm?" he asked, using the tip of his tongue to lick around her mouth.

"I… I…"

He lifted his head to gaze deep into the captivating hazel color of her eyes. "Yes, sweetheart? You what?"

"I want you."

He smiled at her. "And I want you, too." Then he swept her into his arms and carried her into the house.

The moment Zara's back touched the bed Saint kissed her again. Instinctively, her mouth began mating greedily with his. His kiss was unapologetic and provocative, with a wildness in his taste that made her head reel. He deepened the pressure with those strong, hard, sexy lips, exploring her mouth for all it was worth. Not only did she groan, she also began shuddering from head to toe. He didn't merely kiss her, he made love to her mouth with toe-curling determination and deep possessiveness.

He released her mouth and slid out of bed to begin undressing. She couldn't help but give him an appreciative smile because she loved it when he stripped for her. He removed each garment slowly and seductively, and she licked her lips and watched him.

Zara knew he got turned on knowing she was getting an eyeful of everything. While watching her watch him, he removed his shirt and his chest expanded as his breathing grew just as erratic as hers.

It still mystified her just how strong the sexual chemistry between them continued to be. Everything about him could turn her on. His look, his touch and even the sound of his voice. Whenever she was with him, she felt pure raw desire that both aroused her body sexually and stirred her mind. And now it mesmerized her heart. She'd even come close to confessing her love for him a short while ago on the porch. That slipup meant she needed to have more control of her emotions.

Which was easier said than done. When he stood before her completely naked, she felt a hypnotic pull to him and stood up from the bed. Now it was his time to watch her undress. It wouldn't take long since she was in her two-piece swimsuit. However, she felt naughty and decided to make it worth his while.

She knew how much he liked her breasts, so she took her time undoing the top. The deep look of desire in his eyes was beginning to affect her nerve endings. Especially those connected to her nipples. It didn't take much to remember the way he would lick them, like they were the tastiest treat he'd ever had. From the way he was looking at her exposed breasts, she had a feeling he was thinking the same thing now.

Tossing the top aside, she adjusted her body to slide the bottom portion of the swimsuit down her legs. There was nothing to it and she tossed it aside to join the top. Saint barely gave her time to readjust her body on the bed when he swooped his mouth down on hers like a starving man. Like all his kisses, she felt his wants and desires. More than anything, she wished, oh, how she wished, she could feel his love. But he'd told her more than once that love no longer had a place in his heart. She had felt the same way, but he had changed her mind. What was the chance of her changing his? Could she?

All thoughts were vanquished from her mind when he broke off the kiss to trace a path of kisses from her neck and down her chest toward her breasts. Her nipples hardened in response and the second he slid one between his lips, she heard him emit a deep guttural sound from his throat.

She figured that he intended to drive her over the edge when his hand lowered between her legs and a finger eased inside her. She groaned from the stroking and massaging that finger was doing to her, filling her with wants and needs that matched his own. He suddenly lifted his head to stare at her and the intensity in the depths of his gaze immobilized her. She saw passion in his eyes, but there was something else there, too. A look she'd never seen before.

Before she could figure out if she was actually seeing something or imagining it, he lifted her legs to wrap them around his neck and buried his head between her thighs.

"Saint…"

It flashed across her mind that maybe she should start calling him Sinner. What he was doing to her, and the way he was making her feel, had to be bad. But then she decided it felt too good to be bad. His tongue, she decided, should be outlawed.

A jolt of something sensual shot through her when the tip of his tongue began making wiggly motions with incredible intensity that made her scream out her pleasure. He ignored her scream and continued his assault.

"Saint!"

She screamed again when another orgasm struck. Only from this man could she receive maximum pleasure and be consumed with so much desire. When he finished, he moved up her body and latched his mouth to hers. She could taste herself on his tongue. That made her come again.

"Saint...please." And she was still moaning for more.

"I intend to give you everything you want, baby," he whispered as he spread her legs apart and positioned himself between them.

Before she could draw her next breath, he slid inside her and began thrusting deeply. Gripping his shoulders, she held on tight, knowing he intended to give her the ride of her life. They mated with an intensity that had her groaning and him growling. It was as if this connection was meant to last forever, and neither could get enough.

He pumped harder and she grinded against him, refusing to miss a beat. She needed this. She wanted it and she loved him. When she left Catalina Cove, the memories were all she would have, and she intended to store up as many of them as she could.

As her body continued to experience the most potent and powerful ecstasy imaginable, she knew giving him up when she returned to Boston would be the hardest thing she'd ever have to do.

27

Saint slowly became awake and the first thing he noticed was that he was in bed alone. He shifted positions and when he did, he drew in the scent of his and Zara's lovemaking. The potency of it was still in the air, all in the bedcovers and absorbed into his skin. He looked out the window and saw dusk was just settling. Although he was certain they'd spent the last five hours in bed, it had been early when he'd arrived.

Pulling himself up to sit, he rubbed a hand down his face. He doubted Zara knew just how attached he was to her and that was a good thing. Could he convince her to love again?

His thoughts shifted to what she'd told him about buying that vacant building. He had named that painting *Imagine* for a reason. She had even acknowledged that meant she would be visiting Catalina Cove on a more frequent basis. However, at no time did she hint it had anything to do with him. He was certain when she left for Boston next week their affair would end, and she had no intentions of restarting it whenever she returned to town.

Frankly, he wouldn't want her to do so anyway. It would

be just like his relationship with Mia had been. One that ultimately didn't lead anywhere. He wasn't sure he could handle that sort of involvement with a woman again. Did that mean he would have to settle? Give up passion, desire and the strongest sexual chemistry for a woman that he'd ever known, to settle for someone who didn't stir those things in him, but wanted marriage and a family? Why couldn't he be like some men and have it all?

He heard Zara moving about in the other room and wondered what she was up to. It was past dinnertime. Did she want to go out to eat, or would she prefer him to grab takeout? There was only one way to find out. Stepping from the bed he slid into his trousers. The moment he opened the bedroom door he picked up the scent of food.

Zara was cooking. On occasion she would surprise him with a cooked meal or two. It didn't take long for him to realize she was a pretty good cook, although she admitted it wasn't something she liked doing all the time. While in college she befriended someone from Atlanta who loved cooking and had shown Zara how to prepare several dishes, mostly of Southern cuisine. But then there was no way you could be born and raised in Catalina Cove without knowing how to prepare a few seafood dishes. Even if your parents were wealthy enough to have a personal cook that prepared all the meals. Zara had once told him how their cook had no problem letting her assist her in the kitchen whenever Zara's parents were away traveling.

He entered the kitchen and found her, bent over and looking into the oven. He wasn't sure what she was cooking but whatever it was, it smelled delicious. But then *she* looked delicious. She was wearing a short robe and he had a feeling she didn't have a stitch of clothing on underneath it.

Deciding not to torture himself by standing there lusting after her, he said, "Something smells good."

She closed the oven door and quickly turned to him and smiled. "I hope so. I'm preparing a seafood potpie."

He lifted a brow. "You know how to make one of those?"

"Of course." She held out her hands in front of her. "Don't let these hands fool you, Mr. Toussaint. They are good for a number of things."

He suddenly got hard thinking of what some of those things were. She certainly knew how to use them on him. "I believe you. Need help with anything?"

"No. In fact, it's almost ready. You've been sleeping awhile."

"Your fault, Zara. You wore me out."

And she had, he thought. It was easy to recall how she rode him hard several times. Where she had definitely worn him out, she looked pretty damn refreshed herself. And beautiful. She looked so captivating standing there smiling at him, he was almost weak in the knees just looking at her.

"Hmm, there is something you can do. Saint?"

"What?"

"Select the wine for dinner."

Yes, he could do that instead of standing there, rubbing his chin and staring at her like a besotted fool. "Okay."

When he headed for the wine cabinet, she asked, "Will you be able to stay long?"

He turned and smiled. "I plan to stay the entire night, if that's okay with you." He knew why she'd asked. Since his parents had returned, he'd been helping his father work on the boat dock. And because his mother had decided she wanted to try out several breakfast menus that she'd collected while in Memphis, he'd joined them for breakfast a few times this week. He would be the first to admit that it was reducing the amount of time he'd been spending with Zara. Once she returned to Boston he would welcome any opportunity to stay busy. But now he wanted to spend every moment with her that he could.

"That's definitely fine with me. Like I've always told you. You're welcome to my cottage on Pelican Bay at any time."

He wanted to cross the room and swoop her into his arms and carry her back to bed. Instead, he walked over to her and wrapped his arms around her. He was tempted, damn was he tempted, to tell her how he felt about her, but he couldn't risk another woman rejecting his love. He rested his face against the softness of her neck and inhaled the unique scent of her skin.

"That's good to know, sweetheart," he whispered, and wondered if that invitation extended to whenever she returned to town. He drew in a deep breath knowing he couldn't go there. He wanted more than she would be willing to give.

Zara opened her eyes, not sure what had brought her awake. She shifted her gaze to Saint, who was lying beside her asleep. At least with his eyes closed, and the deep, even breathing from his nostrils denoted that he was. She looked over at the clock on the nightstand. It was way past midnight. After eating dinner, they cleaned up the kitchen together before returning to bed.

He had promised over dinner to pleasure her through the night, and he'd delivered. She had barely recovered from one orgasm when he was plying her with another. Saint had the ability to arouse her over and over again then satisfy her to her body's content.

Because she had taken a nap earlier, she wasn't all that sleepy and decided to pick out a book and read awhile until she was sleepy again. Because their legs were entwined and he had his arms wrapped around her spoon-style, there was no way she could get out of bed without him knowing it. The last thing she wanted to do was wake him up since she figured he needed his sleep, but it couldn't be helped. She needed a potty break anyway.

The moment she began easing out of his arms, his eyes flew open and the most gorgeous pair of dark, sleepy eyes looked at her. "Where are you going, sweetheart?"

His deep, husky voice was tempting her to say, "Nowhere," and snuggle close again. Instead, she said, "To the potty," since that would be her first stop.

He let her move, and then closed his eyes again. Getting out of bed, she headed for the door but paused to look back at Saint. She enjoyed the times she spent with him, morning, noon or night. Then there was the joy she felt waking up next to him.

After using the bathroom, she went upstairs. She settled in a chair, determined to finish reading the romance novel she'd started a few weeks ago. Whenever she purchased a book that she liked, she'd buy three versions, a print copy for those times like now when she wanted to hold a book in her hands. She'd also buy it for her e-reader for when she preferred reading in bed, and she would buy the audio version for when she wanted the book read to her.

She didn't have many chapters left. Although she knew there would be a happy ending, the fun part was watching the couple maneuver their way there. She wasn't sure how long she'd been sitting there reading when she sensed a presence. Glancing up she saw Saint standing across the room. His feet were braced apart, his trousers hung low on his hips and he was bare chested.

"I missed you in bed with me."

She figured in a week's time her place beside him in bed would end anyway. She didn't want to think about that. "I couldn't get back to sleep so decided to read awhile."

He came into the loft. She was glad her painting on the easel was covered. She wasn't ready for him to see her latest project. It would be her final gift to him. Looking at the bookcase he said, "I never paid any attention to all these books before. There's quite a collection."

Zara followed his gaze. "Mom loved reading, and some of those books were handed down to her through generations. Just like that copy of *The Three Musketeers*. That one was her favorite. The author, a Frenchman by the name of Alexandre Dumas, was a friend of my maternal great-great-grandfather. That copy was part of its first printing in 1844. I promised my mother that I would always keep the collection of books she has here."

He walked over to the bookcase and pulled out the book. The moment he opened it, an envelope fell to the floor. She watched as he bent to pick it up, glanced at it and then said, "It's addressed to you."

She lifted a brow. "Me?"

"Yes," he said, crossing the room to hand the envelope to her.

She recognized the script. It was her mother's and, like Saint had said, the letter was addressed to her.

28

With nervous fingers Zara opened the envelope. She took a deep breath and began reading the letter inside...

To my very own Princess Zara,
I am no longer with you but hope you are truly happy. My hope is that you have found someone to love and who truly loves you in return. Never give up on love. If you find it, then fight for it like your life depends on it.

One day while painting my beautiful pelicans outside, I stumbled across a whiskey bottle that had been unearthed by a recent storm. Inside was a map. I wasn't sure if it was authentic or not, and I decided not to share details of it with anyone. Especially not your father. I could see him destroying Pelican Bay in search of buried treasure that probably didn't really exist.

Instead of destroying the map I've left it for you to decide what you want to do with it, since the cottage on Pelican Bay now belongs to you. I figured sooner or later you would find my letter. If I'm still alive, then we can decide together. Otherwise, the decision is yours.

Love always,
Mom

PS As for the whiskey bottle the map was found in, I hid it
behind the bookcase.

Zara exhaled and unfolded the map that was attached to study it. All her life she'd honestly thought pirates' treasure maps were a myth. Obviously not. But then this could very well be a fake.

"Zara. You okay?"

She looked over at Saint, who was watching her with a worried expression. "Yes, I'm fine. The letter is from my mother, and it contains a pirate's treasure map."

"A treasure map?"

"Yes." She handed the letter and map to him. "If it's authentic I can only assume it's from LaFitte."

It didn't take Saint long to read the letter and study the map. He then looked at her. "Do you think it's authentic, Saint?" she asked.

He shrugged those broad shoulders she liked clutching whenever they made love. "Not sure, Zara. I guess the X mark denotes where the treasure is supposedly buried. But…"

"But you don't believe it?"

"I'll admit it's pretty far-fetched. But the paper it's drawn on looks old. Like it could have come from that time period," he said.

"But if the map is real, then the exact location can be established, right?" she asked.

"Yes. With modern technology, scientists have the ability to pinpoint the exact locale and position of just about anything without digging the first hole." He studied the map and then added, "The way it was drawn I'd think this *X* here is a location on Pelican Bay. However, there are two other markings in other locations. Not sure if that means anything."

Zara studied the paper with him, not sure about anything either. She had a good mind to find the whiskey bottle the map came in, put it back inside and rebury it somewhere or throw it into the ocean. But what if it was authentic?

"I know the final decision of what you want to do is yours, but I suggest you talk it over with Vaughn."

She had a feeling Saint would suggest that. Of course she didn't have a problem telling Vaughn about the map, but she felt the decision of what to do about the map was a journey that she and Saint should take together. She wasn't sure why she felt that way, but she did.

"Fine. We'll talk it over with Vaughn, but only after we determine if the map is authentic."

He lifted a brow. "We?"

"Yes. You and I are in this map thing together, Saint. If you hadn't pulled out that book and opened it, I might not ever have seen that letter."

"Eventually, you would have."

"Maybe, but when? I've been in this section of the room a lot of times but never thought of reading that book. In fact, I've avoided doing so because it was my mother's favorite. She would often read it to me while I was growing up, and the memories were too much to bear."

He shook his head. "I don't know, Zara. I consider that map as yours."

She lifted a defiant chin. "And I consider it ours. We found it together and it's a mystery that we should solve together."

"Need I remind you that you're leaving next week?"

No, he didn't have to remind her of that, but she also wanted to believe that nothing happened by chance. Not even their meeting nearly three years ago. What were the odds that just months after her breakup with Maurice such a man as Saint would enter her life the way he had? They'd both acted out of the norm that night by hooking up, thinking they would never see each other again.

Then they had. Two and a half years later when neither had resumed their relationships with their exes or someone else, and when the sexual chemistry between them was just as powerful as before. Now, one month shy of their night in his hotel room hitting the three-year mark, they were in an affair, although that hadn't been their original plan.

Zara couldn't help but latch on to her mother's words in that letter...

"My hope is that you have found someone to love and who truly loves you in return. Never give up on love. If you find it, then fight for it like your life depends on it."

But how could you fight for love if the person whom you loved didn't love you in return? She wondered if her mother regretted settling for a loveless marriage. Had there been someone out there she would have preferred marrying other than her father?

Meeting Saint's gaze, she said, "I have no problem extending my time here if I need to. However, the first thing we should do is to see if the map is authentic and then go from there. In the meantime, we need to agree that the map will be our secret, and we won't tell anyone else about it."

He hesitated a moment before saying, "Okay, it will be our secret."

Levi gazed across the table at Margie. She had called him that morning saying she had good news to tell him, so he had invited her to breakfast. Over the past weeks they had been spending time together, either by inviting each other to dinner or lunch. She liked Chip. His dog, who usually wasn't all that friendly to strangers, immediately liked her. Levi knew why. Margie was a likable person.

She had arrived early that morning to help him cook breakfast. It wasn't the first time she'd been in his kitchen, but it was the first time she'd felt comfortable enough to move around in it like it was hers. He had talked to his best friend, Preston Crane, about his budding romance with Margie, and Preston was happy for him and encouraging.

Preston had said what Levi had always known. Lydia would not have wanted him to live his life alone. She would have wanted him to meet someone and share a good life with that person. Could Margie be the one? He liked her a lot, and he appreciated her company. If he was honest with himself, he would admit to feeling more for Margie than just friendship. However, he was patiently waiting for her to want the same thing.

"So, what is this good news you want to tell me, Margie?"

She was beaming and he thought now what he always did. She was beautiful. "It's about Bellamy."

"What about your daughter?"

"She's decided to move to Catalina Cove."

Levi couldn't help but smile. He knew how worried Margie had been about her daughter since her cheating husband had asked for a divorce. "That's good news."

"I think so, too. She's discovering it's too uncomfortable for her to remain living in Syracuse. She and Sam have the same friends and those mutual friends are beginning to bicker among themselves over who their allegiance should be with. Of course, the women are siding with Bellamy because of what Sam did. However, the husbands, who are mostly Sam's frat brothers, feel their wives shouldn't take sides and should accept the new woman in Sam's life since she's his choice."

Margie paused. "I know it's disheartening for Bellamy because when she married Sam his frat brothers considered her as their sister. I know she is hurting in knowing they would easily accept Sam's treatment of her for the sake of brotherhood."

After taking a sip of coffee, Margie added, "Bellamy feels she needs a fresh start, and Catalina Cove would be ideal. She's contacted the hospital here and has an interview next week. It just so happens they have an opening in their cardiology department."

"Well, I am happy for her and looking forward to meeting her."

Margie smiled over at him. "And I'm looking forward to you meeting her as well."

Saint leaned back in the chair at his office desk, thinking of everything that had transpired after he and Zara had found that map and then retrieved the whiskey bottle. However, from the markings it had, it was actually a rum bottle. Over coffee they had used her laptop to research who they could seek out for authentication. Luckily, he had recalled the name of the person Vaughn had used at the Historical Society to verify the authenticity of their great-great-great-grandmother's marriage license that had been found last year. He recalled Vaughn saying that Stuart Bauer had been the epitome of discreetness. Nothing would be revealed until he and Zara wanted it to.

He still found it hard to believe that Zara thought the map belonged to the both of them, when it was rightfully hers. Whether she knew it or not, to include him showed the degree of trust she had in him. If that map proved to be authentic, she knew he would not take advantage of her in any way. He doubted she knew just how much he appreciated that trust.

He glanced at his watch. He would be meeting Zara for lunch to give her an update about the meeting he'd had with Bauer first thing that morning. The man couldn't be definite, but he suspected the map was authentic due to the paper it was written on. Of course, he would have to do a thorough investigation to verify the handwriting to see if it was indeed LaFitte's. Another reason Bauer was excited about the finding was due to the rum bottle, one known to have been produced in the early eighteen hundreds, in and around the coastal region near Galveston Island and the Caribbean. If authentic, that find alone was worth millions.

Saint's thoughts were interrupted by the buzzer on his desk. Clicking on, he said, "Yes, Mrs. Dorsett?"

"Jade and Kia have arrived for their meeting with you."

"Please send them in."

He had met with the Lacroix twins a few weeks ago. At least that was who he thought of them as, although their last names weren't Lacroix. However, there was no doubt they were Reid's granddaughters. They favored their father, Julius, who'd been Reid's son, and since Julius favored Reid, you could see a strong family resemblance. But then, he would admit on some days he thought they looked a lot like their biological mother, Vashti Alcindor Grisham, as well.

Since his last meeting with them they'd made the rounds, cross-training on various positions within the company. From the feedback he'd received, both young ladies had great personalities and were eager to learn and had caught on quickly. The meeting today would be a recap of what they thought of the company that one day would be theirs.

He stood when the door opened and they entered.

★ ★ ★

An hour later Saint was entering the Oyster Shell Fish Camp. The restaurant had opened its doors a few weeks ago and already it was giving LaFitte's Seafood House some strong competition. Carter Purcelli had been another one who'd taken up Reid's offer of a low-interest loan.

After graduating from college, instead of returning to the cove to live after his mother passed away, Carter had moved to Toronto and worked for years in that city's management. Now he was back home and, like Sierra was doing with her soup café, Carter was using recipes that had been in his family for generations.

Saint scanned the room and saw Zara. She was having a conversation with one of the waitresses as if they were the best of friends. Her friendliness was just one of the things that drew him to her and had captured his heart. And damn, she was holding it tight.

He was glad she was extending her time in the cove to discover the outcome of the map. He would take any reason to delay the inevitable. When the waitress walked off, as if Zara felt his presence, she looked his way and smiled. It was so radiant that he almost missed a step as he walked toward her.

Today she looked stunning in a pretty yellow sundress. His favorite color. No matter what color she wore, she would wear it well. However, while holding her gaze he couldn't help recalling how she'd looked this morning when they'd awakened beside each other wearing nothing at all.

When he reached her table, he brushed a kiss across her lips, not caring that the restaurant was pretty busy with the lunchtime crowd. "Hello, beautiful," he said. Then he took his seat.

"Hello to you, too, handsome."

He grinned. He didn't think he was handsome, but if she

thought so, he would take the compliment in stride. "Have you looked at the menu yet?" he asked.

"Yes, and I've already placed our orders with instructions to not start cooking anything until you get here."

"I appreciate that."

That was another thing that amazed him about her. She had a penchant for detail and the memory of an elephant. They'd eaten here twice before, attending the grand opening and again one evening for dinner. The first time, he'd ordered the fried red snapper that was cooked with Carter's grandfather's special seasonings. The second time they'd dined there, she suggested he try something else on the menu. He replied that he didn't have to—he was stuck on the fried red snapper and that was that.

"What did Stuart Bauer say?" Zara asked anxiously.

It didn't take long to cover everything with her since they hadn't been interrupted by their waitress. Nor had Zara cut in to ask any questions. When he'd finished his spiel, she said, "Over a million dollars for that old bottle?"

"Yes," he said. "I guess it's good to know it's worth all that, considering the time and effort it took for us to get it from behind that bookcase."

"You mean the time and effort it took for *you* to get it from behind that bookcase," she said with a mischievous grin. "I was savoring the view of your tush every time you got on your knees to try another way to retrieve it."

He couldn't help throwing his head back and laughing. He hadn't been aware she'd been watching him recover the rum bottle. All he knew was that when he'd finally gotten it and stood up in triumph, he'd found her naked and ready to tumble him back to the floor. "Have you told Vaughn you might be extending your time in Catalina Cove?"

"Yes, I told him when we talked this morning."

"Did he ask you why?"

"Vaughn doesn't ask anything about any plans I make or change. I think he's just glad I'll be hanging around awhile longer. That's why I haven't told him that I've purchased that building yet. I don't want him to get any ideas. If it were up to him, I would be moving to Catalina Cove permanently."

Knowing that would never happen, he was glad when the waitress returned with their food. Over lunch, she told him about her new designs that would be coming out next spring. She also told him that her attorney had made offers to the landlords of each of her boutiques to buy them like he'd suggested. He admired her skills and savvy as a businesswoman and her willingness to take sound advice. He could see why her shops were so successful.

Saint no longer counted the days he had left with her. He'd been given a reprieve for now and appreciated it. As far as he was concerned, she might be anxious to hear from Bauer but he wasn't. He would take each day, one at a time, and look forward to spending them with her.

"My parents are looking forward to you joining them for the cookout on the Fourth."

She tilted her head and smiled at him. "And I'm looking forward to joining them as well."

29

"I'm glad you've extended your time in Catalina Cove."

Zara glanced across the table at Sierra. They had met for lunch at a pizza shop in town. "I bet Vaughn couldn't wait to tell you."

Sierra chuckled. "You certainly made your brother's day. Of course, he thinks that building you bought in town is why you're extending your visit another week or two."

Zara took a sip of wine. She'd had breakfast with Vaughn that morning and had told him about her purchasing that building. He was both surprised and elated. Like Saint, he thought it was a great business move.

"And you don't think that's the reason?" she asked Sierra.

"Heck no, although I think it helped your cause."

Zara lifted a brow. "My cause?"

"Yes, your cause. The closer it was getting to the day you were leaving, the sadder you were becoming."

"Sad?"

"Yes. Like you were about to lose your very best friend."

Great analogy, Zara thought, returning her attention to her

meal. That was exactly how she'd felt. Her best friend who'd become the man she loved. She looked at Sierra. "I've fallen in love with Saint, Sierra."

Her sister-in-law gave her an understanding smile. "I know. I've known for a while, probably before you even realized it yourself. Mainly because that's how it was with me and Vaughn. Velvet knew it long before I could. She said she saw it in my eyes whenever I talked about him, or whenever she was with me and he would appear, or whenever his name would come up. I had it bad and so do you."

Sierra sipped her wine, then added, "What I don't think you realize is that Saint is doing the same thing."

Zara tilted her head. "What?"

"Exposing his emotions. His love for you shows in his eyes whenever your name comes up or whenever the two of you are together."

"How do you know?"

"I've noticed it and Vaughn has, too. I think your brother deliberately mentions you to Saint just to see it happen."

Zara's jaw dropped in surprise. "You're kidding, right?"

"No. Vaughn might stay out of your business and give you the space you deserve and are entitled to, but that doesn't mean he's not observant to things where you're concerned. You're his sister. He's convinced Saint loves you, but he's not sure how you feel about Saint. He believes Maurice ruined any other man's chances of capturing your heart."

Zara had believed that for so long, but Saint had proved her wrong because she knew she did love him. When she'd remained silent, probably for too long, Sierra said, "Unlike Vaughn, I've made my own observations about some things."

"What things?"

"Like the relationship you and Saint shared was more than

that hookup-partners thing. The strong sexual chemistry between the two of you told the real story. It's special."

"Special? It's lust, Sierra. I might love Saint, but contrary to
what you and Vaughn might think, he doesn't love me back."

"Why do you think he doesn't?"

Zara shrugged. "He hasn't told me that he does."

"Have you told him how you feel about him?"

"No. But Saint has said numerous times that he would never
give his heart to another woman."

"And I've heard you say that you'd never give your heart
to another man. If those emotions can change for you, why
can't they change for him, Zara? I think you owe it to yourself to find out if they have before you leave Catalina Cove."

What if Saint did love her and she didn't have a clue, just
like he didn't have any knowledge about her feelings for him?
Would it be such a bad thing to confess her feelings and let
the chips fall where they may? She wondered…

He would either tell her the feelings were mutual or they
weren't. Sierra was right. One way or the other, she needed
to know before leaving town, and more than anything, she
hoped that they were mutual.

"Levi, I'd like you to meet my daughter, Bellamy. Bellamy,
this is my good friend Levi Canady."

Levi extended his hand to the young woman who he
thought probably looked like a younger version of Margie.
She had the same dark eyes, high cheekbones and rounded
chin. She was definitely a very attractive woman, and he knew
if she were to move to Catalina Cove, she would capture the
attention of several young men.

"I'm happy to meet you, Bellamy."

"I'm happy to meet you, too, Mr. Canady."

"You can call me Levi."

"Okay, Levi."

Margie and Bellamy had arrived at the Green Fig for dinner and had just been seated when Levi had noticed them. He'd known from Margie that Bellamy had arrived in town late last night for her interview that morning. "How did your interview go?" he decided to ask her. He thought the smile that spread across her face was similar to the one he often saw on Margie's.

"I think it went well. They will be interviewing other applicants and will let me know something in a week. They gave me a tour of the facility and told me that due to Catalina Cove's growing population, a new hospital is planned to be built on land being donated to them."

"Yes, that was announced at a recent town hall meeting," Levi said. "The wealthiest man in town, Reid Lacroix, has donated land for that purpose. That way people living in the cove won't have to travel to New Orleans or Baton Rouge for more extensive and advanced medical services."

"I think that's a wonderful idea and it was very generous of Mr. Lacroix."

"Yes, it was. Well, I'll get back to work," Levi said. "I'm glad I got a chance to meet you, Bellamy. How long will you be in town?"

"I'm flying out first thing in the morning since I'm needed back at work. Hopefully, on my next trip I'll be able to stay longer. It's been a while since I've visited the cove. Growing up, my brother and I used to visit my grandparents every summer. The town has certainly grown."

Levi laughed. "And it's still growing, but even with the growth it will always retain that small-town feel. As a cove native I can appreciate that."

"I can, too," Margie spoke up. "After living in a big city

like Dallas for so long, I'd forgotten just how wonderful a small town could be. I'm glad I made the decision to move back home."

"And I'm glad you made the decision to move back as well," Levi said, smiling at Margie. He then glanced at Bellamy. "Enjoy the rest of your stay in the cove." To Margie, he said, "I hope the two of you like the meal."

"And I'll see you Saturday evening, Levi."

He smiled. "I'm looking forward to it." He then walked off.

Margie couldn't help watching Levi until he'd disappeared into the restaurant's kitchen and was no longer in sight. For some reason, she continued looking as if waiting for him to come back out.

The clearing of her daughter's throat made her turn to Bellamy, and when she saw the way her daughter was grinning, she said, "Sorry about that."

"No need to apologize. I must say Levi Canady is a handsome man. I can see why you're so taken with him."

Margie waved off her daughter's words. "Nonsense. I'm not taken with him."

"If you aren't, then you should be. I understand what you said about it taking time for your heart to shift gears and go in another direction. I found out that's true with my situation with Sam, so I can certainly understand how things were for you with Dad. The two of you had a good marriage and there was plenty of love.

"David and I always felt it with you and Dad. But just like I want to believe there is life for me after Sam, I hope you know there's life for you after Dad. You're still young, Mom, and I know Dad would want you to continue living. To be happy. I hope you'll take my advice and move beyond the friendship stage with Levi. I can tell the way he looks at you that he wants the same thing."

Margie didn't say anything for a moment. What she hadn't told Bellamy was that she'd finally made the decision to move beyond friendship, but she hadn't told Levi yet. Smiling, she confessed, "I agree with everything you've said, and I am ready for things to move forward for me and Levi. I plan to tell him Saturday. He's taking me to the movies. An early matinee."

A huge smile covered Bellamy's features. "Mom, I think that's great. David and I are rooting for you and Levi."

"David knows?"

"Yes. I told him about Levi and he agrees. We both want you to be happy again."

"Thanks." Reaching across the table, she took Bellamy's hand in hers. "And I want you to be happy, too. I know you're having a time of it after Sam's betrayal, but I want you to believe there is happiness in your future as well. I don't want you to give up on love."

"It will be hard for me to trust another man in my life, Mom. Sam ruined it for me."

"Promise me you won't give him that much power over you, Bellamy."

Sam was in such a rush to marry the other woman that Bellamy's attorney had advised her that Sam had given in to all Bellamy's demands without a fight. Not only had he signed the house over to her free and clear, but he'd agreed to all the other concessions she'd asked for as well.

Bellamy was quiet. When Margie tightened her hold on her hand, she said, "Okay, Mom. I will try."

"Wake up, sleepyhead, it's Saturday morning. Did you forget what we had planned for today?"

Zara slowly opened her eyes and smiled at the man looming over her. They had made love practically all through the night before finally drifting to sleep, snug, naked and their legs entwined. "After last night I need another hour."

"Last night you said you wanted us to get up early and go boating on the bayou."

"Umm, that was before you wore me out."

He leaned down to place a kiss across her lips. "I gave you everything you asked for."

Her smile spread, thinking he certainly had. "I wanted to wear you out, Saint."

"I know, and I was more than happy to let you try."

She sighed deeply, thinking just how much she loved this man. This had definitely been a busy week for them. On the Fourth of July, they had split their time between the cookout at his parents' home and the one Kaegan and Bryce Chambray had given, where it was announced Bryce was expecting again. Then they'd left the Chambrays to drive into town to watch the fireworks from the boardwalk.

Zara would have to say Saint's parents were welcoming and friendly. However, she had noticed the news that she would not be leaving the next day to return to Boston as originally planned had surprised them. When his mother had asked her why, like she had every right to know, Zara had merely told the older woman that she wasn't ready to leave yet. Saint had pulled her to him and brushed a kiss across her lips then said he was glad because he wasn't ready for her to leave, either. His open display of affection in front of his parents had made her feel special, even if she knew it shouldn't have.

Last night they'd driven into New Orleans to go dancing but had returned to the cottage before midnight with plans to go boating this morning. She'd been to Saint's house a couple of other times since he'd invited her to dinner that Sunday. However, she'd never gone boating with him on the bayou. Today was to be her day.

She wanted the day to start off with truth and admissions. Afterward, he might decide since she'd added emotions in the mix—feelings they'd originally decided had no place in their affair—it would be best if they cooled things between them. How would she handle it if he suggested that? Now was a good time to find out.

"Saint?"

"Yes, sweetheart?"

She loved it when he called her that, and he was doing it even more lately. "I need to tell you something."

Evidently, he saw the seriousness in her eyes and asked, "What do you want to tell me?"

She drew in a deep breath. "I…"

Before she could finish, his cell phone rang. He said, "It's Mom. She usually doesn't call me on Saturday mornings unless it's important. I wonder what gives."

Shifting positions, he reached out and grabbed his phone off the nightstand. Before clicking it on he smiled over at her and said, "Hold that thought, sweetheart."

Saint clicked on his phone. "Mom, what's up?"

"I'm at your house and you're not at home," his mother said, matter-of-factly.

"No, I'm not at home."

"It's seven in the morning."

"Yes, Mom, I know what time it is. So, what's up? Why are you at my house this early? Is everything okay with you and Dad?"

"Yes. I have good news for you."

He heard the excitement in his mother's voice. Reaching out, he pulled Zara closer into his arms before asking, "You have good news for me? And what's this good news, Mom?"

"Mia is here."

30

"What do you mean Mia's here?" he asked, quickly pulling himself up to a sitting position. He felt Zara, who heard his question, tense up in his arms. He wondered if, like him, she was remembering how when his mother, upon discovering that Zara had extended her stay in the cove, had looked like the cat that had eaten the canary. He would bet any amount of money Irene Toussaint had known Mia was coming to town. Hell, she'd probably planned it with the help of the Givenses.

"She came all the way to Catalina Cove to see you and to talk to you," his mother was saying.

"I'm sure she came to see you and Dad. There's no reason Mia wants to meet with me."

"Well, she does. What time will you be home?"

Saint rubbed his hand down his face, feeling more annoyed by the second. "I've made plans for today. *All day*. Besides, it doesn't matter, Mom. Mia made her decision about us over three years ago, and I accepted it and moved on. I'll talk to you later."

"Saint, wait! Mia came all the way from Florida to see you. Doesn't that mean anything to you?"

"Honestly, no. I'm not sure why she would do such a thing when we haven't been in touch for over three years."

"She's the person who needs to tell you that."

"Mia doesn't need to tell me anything. I hope she enjoys her time visiting with you and Dad. Goodbye, Mom." Out of respect, he waited for her to hang up before disconnecting the call.

"Your ex-girlfriend is in town?"

He looked at Zara. "Yes."

"Why is she here?"

"Hell if I know. Mom claims she wants to meet with me. Mia is the last person I want to see. You should know that better than anyone." And she should. He'd told her a lot about his relationship with Mia.

"Maybe you should talk to her to see what she wants," Zara suggested.

He frowned. "Why? If your ex-boyfriend showed up after having no contact with you for three years and asked to meet with you, would you grant him any of your time?"

"No, but then the situation surrounding my breakup with Maurice was different than yours with Mia. He betrayed me with another woman. Mia didn't betray you with another man."

"No, but double rejection of a marriage proposal is just as hard a pill to swallow, Zara."

She thought about what he'd said. But still… "If for no other reason, I think you should meet with her for closure, Saint."

He stepped out of bed and stared at Zara, feeling somewhat annoyed at her suggestion. "Closure? What makes you think there's not already closure between us?"

"The two of you were together for four years. That's a long time."

"Doesn't matter. I've moved on."

"Have you, Saint? Have you truly moved on?"

He placed his hands on his hips, his annoyance increasing. "What kind of question is that, Zara? Of course I've moved on."

It was bad enough he had to deal with Mia's unexpected appearance. Now on top of that, Zara was talking pure, unadulterated nonsense. It was as if she was intentionally trying to push him back to his ex-girlfriend. Why? Was there an ulterior motive for her doing so? Was she trying to find an excuse to end things between them? He didn't want to think that, but what other reason would there be for her to come up with this closure bull crap?

"Have you truly done so, Saint? You and Mia broke up over three years ago and I'm the only woman you've spent any real time with since then."

He frowned, holding her gaze. "And?"

"Nothing," she said, looking away.

He had a gut feeling there was something. He then remembered that before he'd received that call from his mother, Zara had been about to tell him something. And he could tell from her expression whatever she was going to say had been serious.

Rubbing his hand down his face again, he didn't want to think what that could mean. Hopefully nothing. Things had been going so well between them over the past weeks. Last night, on the day that would have been her last one in Catalina Cove had she not extended her stay, they'd gone dancing. Then later, they'd returned to the cottage and made love practically all through the night.

He had noticed a difference, an intensity that hadn't been there before. It was in the way she'd returned his kiss and in the way her body had taken his into it. It was as if she was determined to capture every moment—desperate almost.

That made him wonder...

He could understand her being that way if it had been their last night together and she was leaving. However, she had extended her time, so what was going on here? "What were you going to tell me before I got Mom's call, Zara?"

She looked away, out the window. "Nothing."

Nothing? That was the second time she'd answered him that way. He knew there had been something, and he had a feeling it was something he would not have liked. "Are you sure?"

She looked back at him. "Yes, I'm sure."

"Alright. Let's get ready to go boating."

Zara lifted a brow. "We're still going?"

She sounded surprised. "Is there a reason why we shouldn't?"

"No, I guess not," she said, slipping out of bed.

It wasn't what she'd said but how she'd said it that rattled him, set him on edge and, frankly, pissed him off. He'd promised himself after Mia that he would never become vulnerable to any woman again. "You know, you're right. Maybe I need to go see what Mia wants to talk to me about," he said, angrily grabbing his clothes from the chair and quickly putting them on. "We can do a rain check on boating since you'll be here for another week."

"Yes. Sure." She looked out the window again.

He started to say something and then thought better of it. Turning, he walked out of the bedroom.

Tears began streaming down Zara's face the moment she heard the door close behind Saint. Instead of telling him how much she loved him, she'd sent him to another woman. Namely, his ex. How could she do such a thing? Deep down she knew it wasn't Saint who needed closure from Mia; *she* was the one who needed the closure from the woman.

Nothing between her and Saint had changed. If anything, things were good. Better than ever. Over the past weeks, not only were they connected on a physical level, but they'd connected on an emotional level as well. Then why was it that, since she'd acknowledged her love for him, her mind was conjuring up all these worst-case scenarios?

She wiped away her tears but more continued to fall. She loved him so much but her knee-jerk reaction upon hearing his ex-girlfriend was in town wanting to meet with him had probably pushed him away. Why was there this need, before she put her heart on the line with him, to make sure he wasn't still carrying a torch for Mia? A torch Saint had assured her so many times was out? Why did she feel threatened by the woman's appearance in town?

Zara knew the answer. A woman from Maurice's past had taken him from her and the thought of that same scenario happening with Saint was a heartbreak she couldn't take. It would be more devastating than the first time.

She knew how she felt about Saint, but she had no idea how he felt about her. Although Sierra and Vaughn thought he cared for her, she wasn't sure of that and refused to assume anything. She couldn't and her heart, which had taken such a beating before, refused to let her.

She thought of what he'd said moments before leaving...

"Mia is the last person I want to see. You should know that better than anyone."

He was right, she should. They had shared so much over the past months. Their prior heartaches and pains, and the reasons why they didn't want to risk their hearts again. However, they'd never talked about a future with each other. She

wasn't even sure what to expect when she visited Catalina
Cove again. Would he want to continue their hookups? Or
was he ready to walk away from her to see what could be in
his future? A future without her.

Sitting down on the bed she couldn't hold back her tears.
She'd fallen so desperately in love with Saint that even now
her heart ached. What if he saw Mia and decided even after
all she had done that he still had feelings for her and would
give her another chance? What if...?

She closed her eyes against a fresh wave of tears, refusing
to think any longer. Thinking too much had gotten her into
this mess. She should have told Saint how she felt before he
left. He wasn't like Maurice. She knew that. Saint was a man
of honor and respect, thoughtful and kind. One who could
be trusted and admired.

Wiping the tears from her eyes, she stood, hoping and pray-
ing after he met with Mia that he would come back to her.
And when he did, she would tell him how she felt. Every single thing in her heart. Looking out the window, she saw the
day would be a nice one. Too bad she wouldn't be boating on
the bayou with Saint after all. She'd ruined her plans for that.

But she would have faith that whatever happened was meant
to be. She would prepare breakfast, do her yoga and then go
swimming. Today would be another relaxing, do-nothing day
while hoping the man she loved returned to her.

Saint went straight to his parents' home and walked in. He
found them seated around the kitchen table eating breakfast.
"Good morning, everyone," he said, getting their attention.

His mother beamed. "Saint. I knew you would come."

Had she? He switched his gaze from his mother to Mia,
who was sitting there looking at him. She looked the same.

Pretty as ever. But at that moment while staring at her, he felt what he'd known he would feel. Nothing. Whatever love he'd once had for her was gone. He hadn't needed to see her to know that Zara was the woman who now had his heart.

"Mia, you look well," he said.

"So do you, Evans."

Although his family and close friends called him Saint, she'd never done so. It hadn't bothered him before but for some reason it did so now. "Thanks. I understand you want to talk to me."

"Yes, I do."

"For Pete's sake, Saint. Let her finish her breakfast. There's no rush when you have all day," his mother said, all smiles.

He switched his gaze from Mia to his mother. If that was what she thought, she was wrong. "No, I don't have all day. Like I told you on the phone earlier, I've made plans for today." Although Zara wouldn't be joining him, he planned to go boating on the bayou by himself.

"What kind of plans?"

He released a sigh. Only his mother felt she had the right to ask. "I'm going boating on the bayou."

"That sounds wonderful. Maybe Mia can join you," his mother said.

When hell freezes over, he thought. There was no way Mia would join him doing anything. Zara was the only woman he wanted with him on his boat. "Sorry, but someone else will be joining me." What he'd said was a bald-faced lie, but his mother had no right to deliberately put him on the spot in front of Mia.

He looked back at Mia. "Please finish your breakfast, Mia. I'll be out back near the dock when you're ready to talk."

He then left the kitchen.

31

Saint had been standing, facing the bayou, when he heard the sound of movement behind him. He turned to see Mia approaching. She smiled upon meeting his gaze. "It's a beautiful day, isn't it, Evans?"

"Yes, it is," he agreed, wondering what nonsense his mother and hers had conjured up to persuade her to come here to see him. He figured he would find out soon enough.

"I'm sorry your mother tried pushing you into taking me boating, Evans."

"No problem. I know how to handle Mom when she tries getting into my business." He paused a moment and then when she came to a stop in front of him, he asked, "What do you want to talk to me about, Mia?"

She nervously glanced over her shoulder and then back at him and said, "Can we take a walk?"

He figured she'd asked that because she, like him, was aware his mother was watching them through the curtains. "Sure."

She moved in step beside him when he began walking. "I love your home. Your mom dropped by there after picking me up from the airport this morning. I didn't see the insides, but from the outside it's impressive. There's so much land."

"Yes, there is, but I'm sure my home and property aren't what you came all the way from Florida to talk to me about, Mia," he said, cutting to the chase.

"No, it isn't." She seemed nervous and Mia had always been a self-assured and confident woman.

She met his gaze and stopped walking and he did, too. "I made a mistake about you, Evans. It might have taken me three years to face that fact, but I have. The thought of marriage scared me because it was something I thought I would fail at."

He lifted a brow. "Why would you have thought that? Your parents have a successful marriage, and so did your grandparents on both sides. Why would you think you'd fail?"

"Mainly because I wanted to accomplish a number of things before settling down, and I wasn't sure I'd be able to do that while married. If you recall my mom and grandmothers were stay-at-home moms and they were satisfied with that. I'm different. I wanted a career and my career meant everything to me."

He'd known that and had never tried standing in the way of her having one. "I don't recall giving you grief about your work, Mia. I was always supportive."

"Yes, but you wanted to get married and start a family. I honestly wasn't ready for either. My boss had promised me a promotion so I knew it was only a matter of time before I would get it. I also knew that meant relocating to Florida. I had decisions to make. I figured you wouldn't want to relocate unless I agreed to marriage, and I didn't want to do that."

"Why are you rehashing everything, Mia?"

She shrugged. "Because I now know that I made a mistake. My career no longer means anything to me."

"Is the reason it no longer means anything to you because you no longer have one? At least not with Monroe, Hills and Luster since they went out of business?"

He knew her well and the blush that appeared on her cheeks told him he was right. If her career was still flying high, she would not be here. In a way he'd always known he came second in her life. She'd only considered him her safety net and nothing more.

"Okay, Evans, I admit losing my job was my wake-up call. But you knew that eventually I'd get my priorities straight and come to my senses."

"What makes you think that?" he asked.

She gave him a tentative smile. "Because according to our folks, you haven't been seriously involved with anyone since we broke up over three years ago. That means you've been waiting for me to get myself together."

She was dead wrong and so were their parents if that was what they thought. Granted, it took him a year after she had left to move on. But he knew, deep down, that he began truly living again that night he met Zara. Something about her had reached out to him. Of course, he'd assumed it was only physical. But when their paths had crossed again two and a half years later, a part of him had known differently.

He'd never been one to believe in predetermined destination until now. There was a reason Zara had appeared and then reappeared in his life. He hadn't been waiting for Mia to return. And she was wrong about him not being seriously involved with anyone. As far as he was concerned, Zara was an integral part of his life.

He met Mia's gaze and held it. She honestly believed what she'd said, and that in itself was sad. For him, it showed how selfish she was if she thought she could place him second in her life during the four years they'd been together, and then over three years after their breakup, when her life appeared to be falling apart, and after not having had any contact with him whatsoever, she could waltz back into his life and think he would be happy to take her back.

"You're wrong, Mia, and so are my folks and yours if anyone thought I've been waiting for you to come back. And contrary to what you've been told, I have been seeing someone seriously."

She waved her hand as if to dismiss what he'd said. "I hope you don't mean that woman you've been involved with over the past month. According to your mom the two of you are having an affair that will end when she leaves town."

Even if his mother was right, that didn't mean he would pick back up with Mia. She was a part of his past and he wanted her to stay there. Whereas he saw Zara as a part of his future. She might not know it now, but he was willing to do whatever was needed to break down her defenses…just like she had unknowingly broken down his.

"I will give you the babies you want, Saint. At least two."

He drew in a deep breath, attempting to hold his anger in check. She wanted him to take her back and dictate her terms? He had news for her. Zara was the only woman he wanted to have babies with. "Don't do me any favors, Mia."

"I don't understand why you're being difficult when I'm giving you what you want. Marriage and babies."

"And like I said, don't do me any favors." He knew at that moment what he wanted more than those two things was a woman he loved and who loved him. He loved Zara and maybe it was time to let her know it. Even if she didn't love him back now, he believed that one day she could and would.

What they had between them now—both in and out of

bed—was good. It was a start, and he honestly could see it going somewhere. He would have hope. She had bought that building in town and, for him, that meant he would see more of her. He just had to make sure she was willing to see more of him.

He gave Mia a smile that didn't quite reach his eyes when he said, "My affair might end and then it might not. If I have anything to do with it, it won't. I love her."

She lifted a brow. "You love her? You'll hang on to a woman who might not love you back?"

"It won't be the first time I've done so, will it?" he asked scoffingly. Before she could respond he said, "I'm glad we had this conversation, Mia." He truly meant that. Not for closure but to reaffirm what he already knew.

Saint met her gaze and then added, "I hope now you'll be able to convince our parents of something that I seemed to have failed at doing, which is to finally accept that I have not been waiting for you to return to my life. We are finished and there's no getting back together." He paused and added, "I wish you the best in all your future endeavors. Take care of yourself."

When he walked off Mia called out to him. "Evans?"

He stopped walking and turned around. "Yes?"

"I did love you."

Saint stared hard at her. "If that's true then your kind of love is something I can do without."

He turned and continued walking.

"Did you like the movie, Margie?"

"I did. I'm glad there's a movie theater here in the cove. I recall we used to have to drive all the way into New Orleans to see a movie."

He chuckled. "You remember those days, do you?"

"I doubt that I'd forget them. Granted, the movie theater here only has three screens. That's better than nothing."

"Tell that to the young folks. There's a petition going around to bring in one of those twelve-screen theaters."

Margie shook her head. "What are the chances of that happening?"

"Slim." He opened the car door for her.

She smiled as she slid across the leather. "I thought so."

When he started driving, he asked, "Do you want to stop somewhere before we get to your house? How about to get some french fries?"

She grinned at him. "You like french fries, don't you?"

"I love them."

"Umm... Do you have some fresh white potatoes at your house?"

"Yes, I grow my own. Why?"

"I want to make you french fries prepared my way."

When he stopped at a traffic light, he looked at her. "And what way is that?"

"Baked in the oven. I promise you'll love them."

He looked at his watch. "We've been gone for almost two hours. Don't you have to check on Mr. Chelsey?"

"No. Pastor Dawkins comes over on Saturday evenings to discuss tomorrow's Sunday school lesson with him. Then he usually stays awhile and the two of them watch the sports channel."

Levi smiled. "In that case, I'd love to try your baked fries."

Margie nearly held her breath when Levi bit into one of the baked french fries. When they had reached his house, they had gone into his garden together and she'd selected two of the biggest white potatoes that she could find. She peeled them and then diced them the size of regular french fries. Because Levi had a kitchen that was stocked with all kinds of seasonings, she had been able to create her mother's special seasoning that would give them a golden-brown appearance while baked.

When he finished the first one and reached for another, she slid the plate away from him. "I want to know what you think, Levi."

He grinned at her. "I think that was the best cooked fry I've ever eaten. It was delicious."

She smiled, pleased with his comment. "It's also healthier for you."

"And I loved the way they were seasoned."

"I thought you would. That was the seasoning Mom used on her fries. Dad and I weren't allowed to eat french fries, so she came up with her own, and for years because the seasoning helps bake them a golden brown, we thought we were eating fries cooked in oil, not baked."

"Well, you should get that seasoning patented. It's really good."

"I might just do that." She slid the plate back and took a fry for herself. After sampling, she agreed with him; it was really good.

"What other kind of recipes of your mom's do you have?" he asked.

"Several. All for a healthier version of foods without sacrificing taste. I know how to bake chicken that tastes almost fried. However, Dad puts his foot down on that one. When he wanted fried chicken, Mom had no choice but to pull out the skillet. I guess she knew what battles to pick."

They finished off the fries with beer. He'd been surprised to discover she preferred beer to wine like he did. After they tidied up the kitchen, she called to check on her dad. "Dad said he wished I would stop calling because he, the pastor and Butterball are watching the game."

She went to sit beside Levi on the sofa. "I guess that means you'll have me for company for a little longer. That's good because there's something I want to talk to you about."

He looked at her. "Okay, what?" he asked, shifting his position on the sofa to face her.

She nibbled on her bottom lip a moment before saying, "Weeks ago, we talked about our relationship, and I told you that I wasn't ready for anything more than friendship."

"Yes, I remember."

"Well, I'm ready for more now, Levi. That is, if you're still interested."

A huge grin appeared on his face. "Yes, I'm definitely still interested. Like I told you that day, you're the first woman I've felt anything for since Lydia. That hasn't changed, Margie, and I doubt that it will."

She smiled as she drew in a deep breath. "I hope that it won't. I want to continue to get to know you. I relish your company and doing things with you. What Bellamy told me before leaving was right."

"And what was that?"

She paused, then said, "That her dad wasn't coming back, and it was time for me to accept that and move on. Ron would want me to be happy and to live my life to the fullest. My children want me to be happy. Bellamy has met you and likes you. I talked to David and he's looking forward to meeting you."

"And I'm looking forward to meeting him."

"And I told Dad, and of course he likes you and knows Butterball likes you, too."

Levi laughed. "That's good to hear. So where do we go from here?"

"I still want to take things slow, Levi. One day at a time and spend as much time as I can with you."

"I want to spend as much time as I can with you, too. I understand there will be limitations due to Mr. Chelsey. Hopefully, we can include him in some of our outings."

"Yes, we can do that, but the older Dad gets the more he wants to hang around home," she said.

"We can do that, too."

"Thank you, Levi."

He took her hand in his. "For you, anything and anytime, Margie."

She gazed into the darkness of his eyes and studied the rest of his facial features. Bellamy was right. He was such a handsome man, and he was kind and thoughtful. She'd come to see that over the past weeks as she got to know him.

When he leaned toward her, she leaned in as well, knowing where this would lead. This would be their first kiss and she was ready. When his mouth touched hers, she wrapped her arms around his neck and leaned into him closer.

The contact of their tongues immediately sent a degree of passion stirring within her that she thought she would never feel again. She was wrong. Not only did she feel it, but she was being consumed by it. Instantly, automatically, a ball of need burst to life inside her, triggering a sexual hunger she hadn't felt in years.

At that moment she was aware of everything about Levi. The way he was holding her in his arms and the rock hardness of his chest. Unable to help it, her hands began caressing the sides of his neck as his mouth continued to claim hers. He was making her nerves dance, her brain race and heart skip. Levi Canady was quite successfully reminding her that she was a woman. A woman who at the age of fifty-five was alive and had a lot of love to give.

When he finally broke off the kiss, he pressed his forehead against hers as they both breathed in deeply, their breaths ragged. She had been introduced to his taste and he had been introduced to hers. When he leaned back and stared into her eyes, she felt her skin tingle.

Finding her voice, she asked, "So what do you think?"

He leaned in to brush his lips over hers, which made her shiver. Then, pulling back, he smiled and said, "I think the two of us will be good together, Margie. I will go as slow as you want us to but just so you know something."

Swallowing deeply, she asked, "What?"

"I intend to work really hard to become an important part of your life."

When he leaned in and captured her mouth again, she couldn't help but believe him.

It was close to nine that night when Saint returned home from spending all day boating on the bayou. Normally, he wouldn't hang out in the marshy inlet this long, but today he had needed that time alone. To think.

Everything he'd told Mia had been the truth and it was time she'd heard it. Just the nerve that she'd assume that even after over three years of non-contact she could reenter his life like she'd never left still had his insides boiling. But then he had loved her just that much and she'd known it. As far as he was concerned, they had been four wasted years, and she honestly wanted him to believe that she had loved him?

Just to think that he once thought she was everything he would ever want and need in a woman. In a wife. He now knew he'd been wrong. The reason things hadn't worked out between them was because it hadn't been meant to. He had deserved better. Just like Zara—her asshole of an ex hadn't deserved her, either. In the midst of heartache and heartbreak, one stormy night in New Orleans they had found each other, consoled one another and somehow given each other a pathway forward, not knowing that path would lead to one another.

As he began undressing to take a shower, he recalled each and every time he'd told Zara that he would never give his heart to another woman. Had she noticed he'd stopped saying that over the past weeks? Once he had accepted that he had given his heart to her?

No, she probably didn't have a clue, but she would soon since he'd decided to tell her how he felt. In other words, he intended to ask Zara to make their fake relationship a real one. He was willing to be patient and give her time to see that he was nothing like that asshole who had betrayed her. He was someone she could trust. Someone she could believe in, count on and build a future with.

Nothing between them had to change. When she returned to Boston he wouldn't be opposed to a long-distance romance if she wasn't. He'd checked and there were direct flights from New Orleans to Boston daily. He had no problem with the idea of traveling to spend time with her. But first, he needed to know how she felt. From their conversation this morning she might be ready to end things between them.

He refused to walk away from her without giving it his best shot. Looking at his watch he saw it was now close to ten. He could call her but what he had to say needed to be said in person. By the time he showered and put on more clothes it would be close to eleven.

He would wait until tomorrow and pay Zara a visit. He had no idea of what the outcome would be, but what he did know was that he loved her and intended to tell her.

32

Zara rolled out of bed and glanced at the clock on the night-stand. It was barely five in the morning, an hour before sunrise. She looked out the window and saw a thick fog covering the island. She wondered how long it would last. Shaking her head, she figured it would be that kind of day.

In the bathroom, she looked at herself in the mirror. Not surprising, she was a mess with her red swollen eyes and puffy cheeks after spending most of yesterday crying her eyes out. Saint hadn't called and he hadn't returned, so she could only assume he had spent the day with Mia.

For all she knew, he might have taken Mia boating instead of her. She hadn't called or texted him for fear that assumption might have been true. If so, she only had herself to blame.

Washing her face with cold water, she swore she would never cry over a man again. But wasn't that what she'd vowed after her breakup with Maurice? That was different. Maurice had found his way into the arms of another woman without Zara sending him there. If Saint was with another woman, it was all her fault for not trusting him.

She should have taken him at his word when he'd said he had closed the chapter on Mia years ago. That hadn't been good enough for Zara. Her heart had been on the line, and she'd had to make sure. Why hadn't she trusted him and believed that he knew his true feelings?

But then, what if once he saw Mia, all the anger, disappointment and hurt she'd caused evaporated, and he'd been willing to give her another chance? What if Mia, along with her parents and his, had broken down his defenses and...?

Zara shook her head. The one thing she did know was that Saint was his own man who made his own decisions. If he said things were over between him and Mia, then they were over, and she should have believed him. Still, she couldn't help wondering why he hadn't contacted her. She released a deep breath thinking it could very well be that he was upset with her for not believing that he knew his own mind. If that was the case, then his anger was warranted.

Not wanting to go back to bed, she decided to make a cup of coffee and go out on the porch, sit in her patio chair and await the sunrise. Hopefully, today would be better than yesterday.

After changing into a pair of shorts and a midriff top, she headed to the kitchen. The fog was at ground level. She just hoped she would be able to see the sunrise through it.

With her coffee cup in hand, she stepped out on the porch and settled in the patio chair. All around her, she could hear the pelicans, hissing and squawking. She figured they were probably angry at the thickness of the fog that prevented them from hunting for their morning meal.

Her thoughts shifted to Saint yet again. If she didn't hear from him by ten o'clock, she decided she'd drive over to his place. She wanted to believe he was there alone and the only reason she hadn't heard from him was because he was mad at her.

She had taken a few sips of her coffee when she heard footsteps on the pier. From the way her heart began pounding and the gush of feminine need that stirred to life in her midsection, she knew there was only one man who could elicit such a reaction from her. Saint. She couldn't make out anyone through the thick fog, but she stared intently in the direction of the pier, barely able to make it out.

Suddenly, a figure emerged from the fog. Although she still couldn't make out his face, every pore of her body recognized him. Goose bumps of awareness formed on her skin. She placed her coffee cup on the table next to her chair as her breath caught in a surge of yearning and need.

She stood, so sure it was him that she moved toward the steps. Before she reached the first step, he appeared out of the fog. The moment he stepped onto the porch she threw herself into his arms.

Saint tightened his arms around Zara as he held her. He inhaled her scent, the aroma of the woman he loved. "I'm sorry, sweetheart. I didn't mean to scare you. I didn't realize you were out here on the porch. You can barely see anything through this fog."

"You didn't scare me," she said, her gaze fixed on his face. "I knew it was you. I felt your presence. The fog is so thick I'm surprised you drove over here in it."

"I had to because there's something I have to tell you. It's something that I should have told you weeks ago."

"What?"

"I love you, Zara. I love you so damn much."

Zara burst into tears, and he drew her back into his arms.

He figured his declaration of love might elicit some reaction, but he honestly hadn't expected this. "Oh, baby, I didn't tell you that to make you cry. I know that you don't love me, and I understand and accept that. And I—"

She pushed herself from his arms and stared into his face as more tears shone in her eyes. "That's not why I'm crying, Saint."

Using the tips of his fingers to gently wipe away her tears, he asked, "Then why are you crying?"

"Because I love you, too."

Saint went still as hope rose up in his chest. He stared back at her. "What did you say?"

After swiping at more tears, she repeated her words. "I said the reason I'm crying is because I love you, and I wasn't sure you could love me back."

He drew her close, wrapping his arms tightly around her waist. "Of course I could love you back. I've known that I've loved you for a while. The reason I didn't tell you was because I didn't think you could love me back after what Maurice had done to you."

"And that's what I thought about with you. After Mia's double rejection that you couldn't love me."

"Then why did you suggest I go meet up with her yesterday? You of all people knew how I felt about ever getting back together with her."

"Yes, but hearing she was in town sent my mind into a tailspin. I figured the only reason she would come to Catalina Cove after all this time is because she realized she'd made a mistake and wanted you back. I knew I loved you. That's what I had to tell you yesterday. But once I heard she was here, I panicked. If you recall, Maurice betrayed me with a woman from his past."

Saint had forgotten about that. "I could never betray you with Mia or any woman, Zara. I don't want Mia back and told her that very thing. There's no doubt in my mind that I made my feelings very clear."

She slid her gaze from his to look at the bay. "You didn't contact me at all yesterday. So I thought…"

"That she and I were somewhere together?"

She turned her eyes back to him. "I did at first, but then a part of me—the one that trusts you—refused to believe that. After I thought things over, I woke up this morning and figured the only reason you hadn't called or come back yesterday was because you were upset with me."

"Yes, I was. After talking to Mia, I went boating on the bayou alone. I needed time to think. That's when I decided to come here and tell you in person that I love you and to plead my case for why we should stay together, and how we can retain our relationship after you return to Boston. The reason I didn't come here last night was because I didn't get home from the bayou until late."

She nodded. "Had I not heard from you by ten this morning, I would have shown up at your house to tell you that I love you and plead my case that we continue what we have."

He gently brushed the back of his hand against her cheek. "Really?"

She smiled up at him. "Yes. Really. It's too good to give up."

Saint smiled back at her. "Then I think we need to go inside to talk about these pleas of ours some more."

Draping his arm over her shoulder, he led her into the cottage.

"Now about those pleas," Saint said, placing Zara on the bed after stripping off her clothes and she had removed his.

It hadn't been much for him to take off hers. However,

since he'd worn a pair of jeans and buttoned shirt, it had taken her a little longer to undress him. A rush of desire clawed at her insides with every button she'd undone. Then, when his shirt was off, she had taken the time to reacquaint her hands with his broad chest and sculpted abdomen in between his potent kisses.

When she'd removed his jeans and boxers, they'd dropped to his ankles in a *whoosh*. But he'd refused to let her toy with his libido any longer. She hadn't protested when he had swooped her into his arms to carry her over to the bed.

The expression in the depths of his eyes sent a throb of desire rushing through her veins. When he moved into place above her, knowing what she was about to get, her body arched up to meet the downward thrust she knew he was about to make. Sexual need curled inside her stomach and then an intense mating between them began.

She moaned as her body was bombarded with sensation after sensation. The feel and smell of him sent her body into a daze of pleasure that only he could deliver. When he leaned in and captured her mouth, she dug her heels into his back and continued to arch in to meet his thrusts. His tongue stroked the inside of her mouth with the same intensity and rhythm that his manhood stroked between her legs.

When he threw back his head to groan out her name, simultaneously she screamed out his. She felt the spasmodic tightening of both their bodies, and she clung to him. Now that she knew he loved her, she didn't intend to ever let him go.

A smiling Margie opened the door to Levi. After their decision to become a couple last night, she had invited him to Sunday morning breakfast. Afterward, they would take the river taxi to New Orleans, where they would spend the entire day.

"Good morning, Levi," she said, moving aside for him to enter the house.

"Good morning, Margie," he said, returning her smile. "You look pretty this morning."

"Thanks." She closed the door behind him.

"And these are for you," he said, handing her a bouquet of fresh-cut flowers in a clear vase. "They came from my garden."

Her smile widened. "And you picked them this morning just for me?"

"Of course I did."

She placed the flowers on the table in the foyer and leaned in to brush a kiss across his lips. "Thank you."

"You're welcome." He looked around. Although he saw Butterball, he didn't see Mr. Chelsey. "Your dad has left for church already?"

"Yes. They serve breakfast to those who attend Sunday school." She grinned. "He says he likes my breakfast, but the ladies at church were serving shrimp and grits today and he refused to miss out on that. Pastor Dawkins picked him up moments ago."

"We're here alone?"

She grinned. "Not really. There's Butterball."

Levi glanced over at the feline and said, "Close your eyes, cat." He took Margie in his arms.

She had enjoyed his kisses last night and was definitely loving the one he was giving her now. They had agreed to take things slow, but each time he kissed her she wanted to tell him to speed things up a little. To speed things up a lot.

When he released her mouth, she dropped her head to his chest to draw in a deep breath. When she raised her head, she looked into dark eyes that had the ability to stir a degree of passion in her she hadn't thought she would ever feel again. She said, "I probably shouldn't tell you this, but I like your kisses. Maybe too much."

He grinned. "And I love giving you my kisses, and for me there will never be too much."

She laughed, loving the feel of his hands at her waist. "I might as well tell you that I told Dad about our decision this morning."

Levi raised a brow. "You did?"

"Yes. He said it's about time because he could tell we liked each other. Dad thinks you're a fine young man."

"Young man?" Levi shook his head. "My young days are over, trust me."

"Then I will bring them back because I refuse to feel old, Levi. At least, not too old."

"That sounds good to me."

"Dad also said he expects us to go to church with him sometime." She paused a moment and then said, "He told me why he thought you stopped going. After your wife died some of the single ladies in church became overeager and wouldn't give you a moment's rest."

He shook his head. "They became plum ridiculous."

"Well, you won't have that problem anymore because I'm your girl."

His hands tightened at her waist. "Yes, you are definitely my girl, and I would love for us to attend church services with your dad sometime."

"Good. He'll like that. Oh, I almost forgot," Margie said in an excited voice. "Bellamy called this morning. Catalina Cove Hospital made her an offer and she accepted it."

Levi's face lit up. "That's great news. That means she'll be moving here."

"Yes, in September. Dad invited her to stay here but she wants her own place. She'll be coming back in a few weeks to check out places. She wants to rent for a while before she buys anything."

"That's a smart idea." Then he said, "I have something to ask you."

"What?"

"I'm invited to a wedding in a few weeks in Phoenix. Will you attend with me as my plus-one?"

"I would love to. Thanks for inviting me."

"Thanks for agreeing to go with me."

"Come on," she said, taking his hand and leading him toward the kitchen. "You can tell me more about it over breakfast."

After making love a few more times, Saint and Zara had gone swimming. The fog had lifted and after an hour or so of frolicking in the bay, they pulled the chaise lounges together and were wrapped in each other's arms, kissing while intermittently sharing words of love.

"I love you, Zara."

"And I love you, Saint."

Saint doubted he would ever tire of hearing Zara say those words. In between their lovemaking they had agreed that when she returned to Boston, whatever it took, they would remain together. She would come here to visit more frequently, and he would go see her in Boston. They had no problem engaging in a long-distance relationship.

She'd told him about her plans for the building she'd bought and asked for his suggestions on a few things. They figured it would be another week or so before they heard anything about the legitimacy of the treasure map. He had a two-day business trip to New York and would be leaving on Tuesday. He invited her to come with him and she accepted. She would use that time to check on the boutique she had there. He in turn would go with her to Boston for a few days when she left next week. It had been years since he'd visited the city and he wanted to see the place she considered as home.

He'd given her more details of his conversation with Mia and how he honestly couldn't believe she thought he had been pining for her, just waiting for her to return to him. What was even more disheartening was that their parents had undoubtedly assumed the same thing, even after he'd told them countless times that he had moved on. Like he'd told Zara, in a way he was glad she'd suggested he go see her. Not for closure but for affirmation.

"Sierra called while you were out here inflating the beach ball. She and Vaughn invited us to dinner. You want to go? I think they miss Teryn already."

Saint knew from a conversation he'd had with Vaughn a couple of days ago that Teryn had left for a two-week camping trip with their church. "I'd rather stay and make love to you, but I guess we have to eat sometime."

"Yes, food is important," she said, smiling over at him. "We need to keep our strength."

"And replenish our energy," he said, leaning in and capturing her mouth again.

"This is for you, Saint."

He turned away from the refrigerator where he'd just grabbed a beer. Zara was standing in the middle of the kitchen with the painting she'd been working on in front of her. It was the one he'd yet to see. For some reason, she'd kept it covered whenever he was there. It was covered now.

Placing the beer bottle on the kitchen counter, he moved toward her. "Did you paint another vacant building, sweetheart?" The painting she'd given him weeks ago was hanging on the wall in his bedroom. Whenever he saw it, he was reminded of her and all the talented gifts she possessed.

She grinned. "Not quite."

"Then what did you paint this time?"

"It's not what but *who*," she said, uncovering the painting and holding it up for him to see.

Saint stared at it. Zara had painted him standing on the pier with his business jacket slung over his shoulder and an intense look on his face. His features were clearly defined, down to his eye color. The blue ocean water surrounding the pier was a perfect backdrop. Even the sky ahead was a captivating blue with a pelican flying about.

"Well," she hedged. "What do you think?"

He shifted his gaze from the painting to her. "You were able to paint this without me posing for it?" he asked, amazed.

"Yes. I painted it from memory of my sexiest image of you. I doubt that you know what it would do to me each time I saw you walking across the pier with your jacket slung over your shoulder. I got hot and bothered each and every time, because I knew you were coming here for me and what I would get when you got here."

Her words spiraled inside him, touching places only she had access to. "I think it is beautiful, Zara. I am deeply touched you took the time to do this." He took the painting from her to study it in more detail.

"You were on my mind most of the day anyway. I couldn't think of a better way of spending my time. I love you, Saint."

"And I love you, sweetheart."

He placed the painting aside and pulled her into his arms

to hold her and appreciate everything they had. All the love he felt in his heart was seeping through his veins. This was how love was supposed to be, how it was supposed to feel and how it was to be shared.

When she lifted her head to stare up at him, he stared back at her. Their love was meant to be. With that belief firmly planted in every part of him, he lowered his mouth to hers.

33

Saint opened the door to the cottage and then stood back to let Zara enter. "Did you enjoy our trip to New York, sweetheart?" he asked, while rolling in their luggage.

Zara swirled around the middle of the room. "Yes! It was wonderful. I love New York and being there with you was special."

She truly meant it. After checking in to their hotel room, they had bought tickets to a Broadway play for the following night. They'd eaten dinner at an Italian restaurant and afterward, they walked around Times Square.

He had a meeting the next morning and that gave her time to visit her boutique in Lower Manhattan. Then she had met with college friends for lunch at a café in Harlem. Later she and Saint had dinner before attending the play. Afterward, they met up with one of his NFL pals and his wife, who lived in the city.

Saint's business meeting had ended at noon the next day, so they caught the train to Philly to attend a jazz concert. He had booked them in first class, which came with their own little private compartment, a delicious meal and drinks. She thought it was so romantic. The trip to New York was what they had needed to further bond the love they shared.

"It's still early. Do you want to go out to grab dinner?" She walked over to him and wrapped her arms around his neck.

"There's no need. I talked to Vaughn before leaving New York. He told me the soup of the day at the Green Fig was black bean soup with crab meat and andouille sausage. He knows that's your favorite and offered to deliver some when we got back."

"That was kind of him, and he's right. That's my favorite as well as his. I'm surprised he'd willingly part with any."

"Vaughn's a good guy," Saint said, laughing.

"I know. That's why I plan to keep him as a brother." Turning, she said, "I need to go into the kitchen and—"

Zara didn't finish what she was about to say. Saint grabbed her hand and turned her back around. He whispered her name before leaning down to capture her mouth with his. She loved the taste of him and how his tongue took possession of hers with a hunger and greed that made her groan. More importantly, she loved him. All of him. Every single thing about him.

After the kiss, he stared down at her as they tried to bring their breathing under control. Then he reached up and gently caressed her cheek with the back of his hand. "You are amazing, Zara Miller, and I love you so much."

His words touched her. "I think you're amazing and I love you, too."

Then she watched as he took a little white box out of the pocket of his jacket before lowering to one knee. Her breath caught in her throat upon realizing what he was about to do.

Staring up at her with an intensity she felt in every part of her body, he asked, "Zara, will you marry me?"

Tears sprang into her eyes. She knew what asking her to marry him meant. He was taking a chance and putting his heart on the line. The last woman he'd asked that question, on two occasions, had turned him down. But Zara wouldn't. The man kneeling before her was her Saint, and she would be honored to spend the rest of her life by his side as his wife.

"Yes! Yes! Yes! I will marry you," she said, swiping at her tears. "I will be honored to become Zara Toussaint and have your babies. I know you will be a wonderful husband and father, and I promise to be a good wife and mother." And she meant every word.

A huge smile covered his face as he slid the diamond ring on her finger. She blinked twice when she looked at it. "Saint, this ring is beautiful. Simply breathtaking. I love it."

He kissed her hand that wore his ring before getting to his feet. "I'm glad you like it. I bought it while we were in New York but wanted to wait and propose here on Pelican Bay. This cottage will always be special to us."

"Yes, it will," she said, still swiping away her tears. She wondered when her mother had bequeathed Pelican Bay to her, if she had known the extent of happiness this cottage would bring her.

She stared down at her ring again. It was absolutely dazzling. Holding her hand out in front of her, she thought it looked amazing on her finger. "I love it, Saint," she said again.

"I'm glad you do. And just so you know, I called Vaughn from New York and told him what I planned to do. Your brother gave us his blessings. He and Sierra will be arriving shortly with our dinner and to help us celebrate our engagement. Before they arrive, I need to do this again." He pulled her into his arms for another kiss.

There was no telling how long the kiss would have lasted if they hadn't heard a knock at the door. Knowing the only other people with access to the bay were Vaughn and Sierra, she moaned in protest when Saint ended their kiss.

"Maybe we could pretend we aren't here," she whispered.

Saint laughed. "I'm sure they saw our car, so that won't work. Besides, they have our dinner." He brushed a kiss across her lips. "Just remember, from this day forward we have the rest of our lives."

She smiled at him. "Yes, we'll have the rest of our lives."

Vaughn and Sierra joined them for dinner. After they finished eating, champagne glasses were filled. Holding up his, Vaughn said, "Congratulations to Zara and Saint. I am truly happy for you two. Saint, you did something that I was beginning to worry was impossible. You captured my sister's heart."

"Yes, he did," Zara said, wrapping her arms around Saint and leaning into him.

"And she captured mine," he said, smiling down at her.

"I knew the two of you were meant to be together," Sierra said, grinning. "I knew you would not be leaving Catalina Cove without a ring on your finger, Zara. And, Saint, you did not disappoint. Wow. It is radiantly dazzling."

More champagne was poured, and additional toasts were made to the engaged couple. Saint would tell his parents their good news tomorrow. Once they got over their shock, he knew they would be happy for them.

Before leaving for New York, he'd visited them for what he hoped was his final talk concerning Mia. They told him not to bother. It seemed when Mia returned to the house, she had thrown a temper tantrum the likes of which they'd never seen. From her rants, they gathered that when the company she'd worked for had gone bankrupt, she'd lost a lot of money and was broke. She had been depending on Saint to take her back not because she loved him but because she needed him.

His parents had said that in all the years they'd known Mia they had never seen her act so unladylike and selfishly. The nerve of her only wanting to get back with him because she was down on her luck. His father said they hadn't gotten her to the airport quick enough to suit them. Saint thought it was sad they had to see another side of Mia, but in a way he was glad they had.

They had promised that from now on they would stay out of his business and just hoped one day he would meet a nice girl and marry and get her pregnant so they could enjoy grand-babies while they could. He smiled thinking they would be happy to know Zara loved children and would be eager to give them those grandbabies they wanted. Plenty of them.

Saint's cell phone rang and when he saw who the caller was, he excused himself and clicked it on. Moments later he caught everyone's attention when he let out a loud cheer. "Saint, what are you cheering about?" Zara asked when he'd ended the call.

He rushed over to Zara and pulled her into his arms. "That was Stuart Bauer. The treasure map is authentic."

Vaughn lifted a brow. "What treasure map?"

Saint and Zara then told Vaughn and Sierra about her mother's letter and the map. "I didn't want to tell you about it until I knew it was real."

Vaughn nodded in understanding. "And it's actually real?"

"Yes, it is real," Saint said. "We used the same guy you used to authenticate that marriage license you found. Stuart Bauer also said that the empty rum bottle the map was found in is worth millions on its own. According to the map, the treasure is buried somewhere on this property. It's up to Zara what she plans to do with the map."

Zara shook her head. "No, it's up to us what we want to do with it. We found it together."

"This calls for another celebration," Vaughn said, laughing. He proceeded to refill everyone's glasses. "To Saint and Zara on their upcoming marriage and their finding an authentic treasure map."

34

"One…two…three…here it comes!" Velvet Spencer Colfax said to the twenty or more single women, before tossing her bridal bouquet over her shoulder. The young woman who caught it and let out a happy scream was one of Velvet's college friends.

Zara stood on the sidelines next to her future husband. This was the first time she'd attended a wedding and didn't have to compete in the bridal bouquet toss. There was no need, she thought, as she gazed at the ring Saint had placed on her finger a few weeks ago.

She thought Velvet and Jaye's wedding had been beautiful. Velvet had looked absolutely gorgeous as she walked down the aisle on Reid Lacroix's arm. Zara saw Jaye's misty eyes as he watched Velvet come to him looking so breathtaking and radiant in an exquisite white Chantilly lace wedding gown. Zara couldn't help dabbing tears from her own eyes as she and five hundred-plus wedding guests watched Velvet and Jaye pledge their love and lives to each other. That made Zara look forward to her own wedding.

She and Saint had decided on a Valentine's Day wedding, which was only six months from now. The wedding and reception would be held at Zara's Haven. Saint was keeping it a secret where they would be going on their honeymoon and said he would tell her in plenty of time to pack the proper clothing.

To say Saint's parents had been elated about their engagement would be an understatement. They had made the announcement to the older couple together. His parents had apologized for not supporting their relationship. They'd honestly thought it was nothing more than a summer fling. They were happy it had been more than that and were glad that she would be joining their family. They thanked her for making their son the happiest they'd seen him in years.

Last week she and Saint had held a press conference to announce their finding of the treasure map. That was all the talk in Catalina Cove these days, and it had even made national news. From the map it was determined that treasure was buried on the property of two other homeowners in the cove, as well as Zara's. One belonging to Levi Canady and the other on bayou land belonging to the Dorsett family. Sheriff Sawyer Grisham had his hands full keeping the media, who'd descended on the cove, as well as treasure hunters, under control.

Outsiders had been disappointed to discover a Catalina Cove ordinance that had been on the books for years that forbade hunters to dig at will in search of pirate treasure. Unless there was an authentic map, verified and approved by the Louisiana Historical Society, and permission given by the property's owner, no digging was allowed anywhere in the cove.

The location of the treasure on Pelican Bay had been accurately pinpointed. It was a good one hundred feet from where the cottage sat. Zara and Saint decided to have the treasure dug up since it was far enough away from the cottage. The excavation team would be arriving in a couple of weeks.

Zara looked across the room and saw Levi Canady and the woman he'd brought to the wedding with him. The couple was often seen together around town. Zara had met Margie Lawson. It was obvious from how Levi looked at her, and she looked at him, that what they had together was solid. Zara could see forever in their future.

Jaye swept Velvet into his arms, carrying his bride out of the ballroom to clapping and cheers. They would return in a short while, dressed in traveling clothes, before leaving on their honeymoon. Everybody who knew of Jaye's determination to win back Velvet's love was filled with happiness that his mission had been accomplished.

Saint leaned down and asked Zara, "What are you thinking about, sweetheart?"

She looked up at him, her heart filled with happiness. "Several things. I was thinking how happy Jaye and Velvet are, and how overjoyed I am for them. I was also thinking that I can't wait for our own wedding day."

"I can't wait, either. February won't get here fast enough to suit me."

Zara smiled. "In the meantime, we'll have enough to keep us busy with all that's going on with that treasure map."

After making the rounds among bidders, the rum bottle had come in close to two million dollars, most of which Saint and Zara would donate toward building a wing that would be named after her parents in the new hospital.

They also decided to renovate the cottage in anticipation of the huge family they planned to have one day. They wanted at least four kids. She would be moving to Catalina Cove permanently and would manage the new store she planned to open there, as well as the one in New York. Sherri would continue to help manage the stores in the New England area. To Zara's surprise and delight, her landlords had accepted her offers to buy her boutiques.

She looked forward to living with Saint at his home on the bayou. The cottage on Pelican Bay would be their romantic getaway, and once they had kids it would become their family retreat.

"I was also thinking about Levi and Margie. I don't think I've ever seen him so happy," Zara said. "Sierra told me that her parents are elated that he's found love again. I understand things are really serious between him and Margie and would not be surprised if there's a wedding sometime next year."

"When it comes to love, nothing surprises me, sweetheart," Saint replied. Then in a serious tone, he added, "I'm happy for Levi, too. He's been alone for a while. And if there is buried treasure in his backyard, he will need someone by his side who he can trust and will have his back. I believe Margie will be that person."

Zara decided to ask him the same question he'd asked her. "What are you thinking about, Saint?"

He gazed at her with an intensity that made her heart swell. "I am thinking about the fact that on this very day three years ago we met, and how that night we spent together in my hotel room changed our lives. A stormy August night. It set into motion our pathway forward. Thank you for making me believe in love again, sweetheart." He leaned over and brushed a kiss across her lips.

"And thank you for making me believe in love again, too, Saint."

After he tucked her arm in his, she and Saint walked across the room to join Vaughn and Sierra. The happy couple had announced yesterday that they were expecting. All Zara had to say was the Maldives obviously had been one fiery hot honeymoon. She was elated at the thought of becoming an auntie.

She looked at the man by her side. They had a number of events to look forward to. The main one being their own special day in six months.

EPILOGUE

Valentine's Day

Everyone who'd been invited to attend Zara and Saint's wedding knew they would be witnessing one of the biggest and fanciest weddings ever held in Catalina Cove. The great-great-great-granddaughter of the cove's founder, Jean LaFitte, and his wife, the original Princess Zara, was getting married on the grounds of Zara's Haven.

Zara, dressed in a white off-the-shoulder lace-up-back wedding gown that she had designed, looked absolutely radiant as she walked down the aisle on her brother's arm. The handsome groom was all smiles and had held her gaze from the moment she had appeared until she stood by his side.

With a multitude of wedding guests looking on, most dabbing at their eyes, the couple recited vows they had written to each other, pledging their lives together forever. When Saint slid the wedding ring onto Zara's finger, he recited the words, "One and done. Forever."

A short while later, the pastor announced they were husband and wife. Before he could tell Saint that he could kiss the bride, he was already pulling Zara into his arms and giving her a kiss that seemed to go on forever...until the minister felt it was time to clear his throat. The couple would be honeymooning in the Canary Islands and then spending time in Paris.

The treasure dig on Pelican Bay had been successful when the excavators had uncovered a chest filled not only with gold coins but all kinds of jewelry and artifacts as well. The same findings resulted in the digs on Levi Canady's and the Dorsetts' properties. For that reason, the value of the treasures was still being tallied, and it was suspected to be far more than anyone originally assumed.

Those closest to Saint and Zara knew that as far as the couple was concerned, their true treasure was the love they'd found for each other at the cottage on Pelican Bay.

★ ★ ★ ★ ★